# *A*
# Promise
## *Between*
# Friends

Carol Rivers, whose family comes from the Isle of Dogs, East London, now lives in Dorset. Visit www.carolrivers.com and follow her on Facebook and Twitter @carol_rivers

*Also by Carol Rivers*

Lizzie of Langley Street
Bella of Bow Street
Lily of Love Lane
Eve of the Isle
East End Angel
In the Bleak Midwinter
East End Jubilee (*previously* Rose of Ruby Street)
A Sister's Shame
Cockney Orphan (*previously* Connie of Kettle Street)
A Wartime Christmas
Together for Christmas
The Fight for Lizzie Flowers

# A
# Promise
## Between
# Friends

# CAROL RIVERS

**SIMON &
SCHUSTER**

London · New York · Sydney · Toronto · New Delhi

A CBS COMPANY

First published in Great Britain by Simon & Schuster UK Ltd, 2016
**A CBS company**

1 3 5 7 9 10 8 6 4 2

Simon & Schuster UK Ltd
1st Floor
222 Gray's Inn Road
London WC1X 8HB

www.simonandschuster.co.uk

Simon & Schuster Australia, Sydney
Simon & Schuster India, New Delhi

A CIP catalogue record for this book is available from the British Library

Hardback ISBN: 978-1-4711-5316-7
Paperback ISBN: 978-1-4711-7677-7
eBook ISBN: 978-1-4711-5318-1

Typeset in the UK by Hewer Text UK Ltd, Edinburgh
Printed and bound in Great Britain by CPI Group (UK) Ltd, Croydon, CR0 4YY

Simon & Schuster UK Ltd are committed to sourcing paper that is made
from wood grown in sustainable forests and support the Forest Stewardship
Council, the leading international forest certification organisation. Our
books displaying the FSC logo are printed on FSC certified paper.

'Even if I'd known that love hurt like this, I'd never have settled for friendship' – Ruby Bright

# Acknowledgements

My thanks as always to the talented team at Simon & Schuster who turn my stories into beautifully bound books. To my agent Judith Murdoch, and to the many bookshops and retailers online and on the high street who make the Rivers novels available to the general public. Thanks especially to all those people who have shared with me their personal and often intimate accounts of the immediate post-war years. This was an era full of new life, love and excitement. But also of heartache for those who were unable to express themselves freely and publicly. I felt privileged to be able to set this book in such times. A special thank you to Janine Pulford, writer and editor of the eclectic mags4dorset and *Viewpoint* magazine, who has so kindly supported my books over the years. And last but not least, a thank you to our family for just being you, and hoping that each one of you will have the love and success in your lives that you all so richly deserve. Without you I wouldn't be writing.

The final word goes to all those amazing people who reach me by letter, Facebook, Twitter, Google+, Pinterest, Amazon and my website www.carolrivers.com.

With every book publication, I've made more friends; the East End of London during the early part of the twentieth century is a fascinating part of our social history, but without your support for my novels, I would never have had the chance to record it in fiction.

Love as always,
Carol Rivers

# Chapter One

*1953*

Ruby Payne was partying at the local dance hall with her friends, Kath Rigler and Kath's older brother, Bernie. They had all grown up together on the Isle of Dogs, the heart of London's East End, and had come through some tough times during the war. Ruby liked to think that she and Kath were more like sisters. While she had turned nineteen already this year, Kath's birthday was in just a week's time. They had spent the best part of the evening dancing and talking excitedly about their planned celebration at a pub in Hoxton.

'I'll drive us in style,' Bernie had assured them with a wink. 'You girls put on your finery and we'll paint the town.' Bernie, who was twenty-two, was tall and dark-haired like his sister and had been best friends with Ruby's late brother, Pete. Ruby had a soft spot for him, but she and Kath often took the mickey when he tried to chat up the birds. Bernie fancied himself as a charmer and with his exceptional good looks was never short of a date.

Ruby smiled when she saw Bernie with his arms around a girl, trying to smooch on the dance floor. This time, he wasn't having it all his own way. The blonde looked uninterestedly in the other direction.

'Your brother's wasting his time,' Ruby said to Kath, who, finding no partner, was dancing beside her. 'That girl only has eyes for the big guy on the door. I saw them outside as we came in. He was all over her and she was lapping it up.'

'Trust Bernie to try his luck on Mr Universe's bit of stuff,' Kath giggled from under her long dark curtain of straight hair. Ruby knew how conscious Kath was of her gangling figure. Tonight she was wearing flat pumps with her dark blue trouser suit, which brought her down to six inches above Ruby's petite five five, extended only by her slender high heels. 'My brother will get his nose rearranged one day.'

'Wouldn't do him any harm,' Ruby acknowledged with a grin. 'He might keep his hands to himself after that.' Ruby tossed back her shining blonde shoulder-length hair and felt it bounce lightly on her shoulders as she swayed her hips to the music. Her large hazel eyes were confident and had a mature expression for her young age. Wearing the new red-and-black polka-dot circle-skirt and white halter-neck blouse she knew she looked her best; but even though Fortuno's was crowded, she hadn't really seen anyone she fancied. Not that she'd been short of partners. She had enjoyed every dance, from the old-type swing to the new craze from America, rock 'n' roll. Fortuno's dance hall in Aldgate was no great shakes with its worn and tired decor. But there was plenty of floor space. And after all, it was the dancing she and Kath came for; switching off their humdrum, everyday lives.

'Enjoying yourselves, girls?' Bernie's deep voice broke into her thoughts as, now abandoned, he pushed his way through the crowd towards her and Kath. He put on his cheeky white smile, running a hand through his thick black hair.

'More than you, it seems,' Ruby chuckled, nodding at the girl who was making her way up the steps to the busy entrance and the burly package of muscles standing by the door.

'Not my type,' Bernie shouted above the music. 'She don't know what she's missing though.' He shrugged indifferently, but both she and Kath looked at each other in amusement. Bernie's ego was never dented, at least not for long.

'Fancy a dance, doll?' Bernie said as Kath was approached by a young man who pulled her into his arms and set off with her through the crowd at a rate of knots.

Ruby shrugged. 'Suppose so.' She didn't really like dancing with Bernie who seemed unable to stop trying out his charm offensive even on her. But since she was now alone, she gave in. 'Just one, Bernie.'

'One's enough, doll.' Bernie took her in his arms and, as usual, it always surprised her just how tall he'd grown – well over six feet – from the skinny kid he used to be. Ruby had to admit that as a crane operator in the docks he'd built up plenty of muscle, though he drove her insane always combing his boot-polish black hair into that floppy quiff across his forehead. 'Put one hand on me broad shoulders.' Bernie continued to tease, knowing full well his bravado would irritate her. 'And let Tarzan do the rest.' He pulled her against him, swamping her in a throat-choking cloud of hairdressing.

'Phew!' Ruby objected, trying to wriggle free from the clinch. 'What's that smell?'

'Come on, doll, don't be like that.'

'Not so close, Bernie. You're crushing me to death.'

'You're spoiling all me fun, as usual.'

'Just keep your hands to yourself,' Ruby chided gently.

Ruby was relieved to find that he took heed of her warning and they danced companionably for a while to Al Martino's 'Here In My Heart'. It was at times like this she really missed Pete, the brother she had adored and who had died unexpectedly two years ago.

At twenty-one, Pete had all his life before him. He was a happy-go-lucky East Ender who had got himself a great new job in the West End. He worked for a wealthy employer, who he chauffeured around the country in a very smart limousine. Like her, Pete had been a blond, as tall as Bernie, and had kept himself in perfect shape.

Ruby would never forget the scene. She'd found Pete in his room early one morning, lying, fully dressed in his suit, across his bed. A bottle of pills spilled across the cover. The smell of drink hung heavily in the air. She had shaken his cold body and knew instantly her Pete was gone. It was a shock her family was still recovering from two years later. The verdict of misadventure hadn't found them any closure.

The tragedy still haunted them all, especially her mum Babs.

Bernie snuggled in close. 'You're a lovely mover, Ruby, do you know that? You've got the best figure of any girl in here tonight.'

'Behave yourself, Bernie.'

'It's no fun being a saint,' he replied, ignoring her warning as his hands slipped slowly over her hips. 'And anyway, I'm paying you a compliment.'

'Well, you can keep your hands and compliments to yourself,' Ruby retaliated, tired of fending him off. 'I'm off to find your sister, so you'd better find someone else to dance with.'

She was on the edge of the dance floor when Bernie caught up with her. 'What is it with you lately?' he demanded, his dark eyes puzzled. 'Ever since I came home from me National Service, you've given me the cold-shoulder.' He stood blocking her path as the other couples turned to stare. 'All I'm trying to do is watch out for you as Pete would have wanted.'

Ruby stuck her hands on her hips. 'Don't use Pete as an excuse to get what you want, because it won't work.'

For the first time that evening she saw she'd hit home. 'Christ, Ruby, that's bloody rubbish,' he said huskily. 'I think too much of you to try it on.'

'You didn't when I was fifteen!' The words were out before she could stop them.

Bernie's face paled. 'Listen, I'll always regret that, you know I will. And I've paid the price of that particular quick cuddle.'

'So that's what it was to you?'

Bernie reached out to her. 'Course not. Don't twist my words. You know how I felt about you then.'

Just then, Jo Stafford's hit of last year, 'You Belong To Me', began to play. It was her most favourite ballad of all time. Her mood mellowed as she thought of her dead brother's fondness for the American singer whose records he collected.

Bernie, whom she knew so well, was probably thinking the same. Pete and Bernie had been close buddies and his intense black eyes were softening as though he too was remembering Pete and the past that united them all.

'Come on, let's make up,' he coaxed. 'Finish this number with me. It is Jo Stafford, after all.'

Ruby rolled her eyes, feeling the anger drain away. She and Bernie had shared a few reckless minutes together when they were teenagers and had lived to regret it. She had been as curious about sex as he had and one night after the cinema they had lost their heads. There had been no consequences, but they had taken an awful risk.

Bernie stepped forward and drew her gently into his arms. As they slowly and silently resumed their dance, Jo Stafford's sultry tones washed over the room. Although Bernie tried his best to make her laugh and keep their friendship on an even keel, Ruby wished that somehow she could find real romance. Someone who could really turn her on. She'd definitely never been in love, not even close. But what was love anyway? If Debbie Wilson at work was to be believed, it was the ring on a girl's finger that mattered. Debbie's every waking moment was devoted to her fiancé, Roger Stacey, who, in Ruby's book, was a crushing bore. No, it wasn't a ring she craved like Debbie did. Ruby was curious about life – and about men. All the boys she'd been out with had left her cold. Like Bernie, they all thought they were the bee's knees, with their leather jackets and corny chat-up lines.

Suddenly she was aware of a couple dancing close by. The boy was wearing a mohair suit and the girl, a tall brunette, was openly eyeing Bernie, giving it all she had. Bernie, who never missed a trick, began to put on his cheesy Dean Martin act, crooning loudly along to the tune. Ruby found herself laughing.

'What's so funny?' he demanded.

'You are.'

'You're just jealous of me charm, that's all.'

'You wish!'

As they continued to dance, Ruby thought about their shared childhood growing up in the slums of the East End. The four of them, Bernie and Kath, her and Pete, had been inseparable; they'd had to be to survive the poverty. No one had any money: they'd learned how to look after themselves at a very young age. Then, in '39, war broke out and a year later there were nine solid months of the Blitz. God, what a nightmare evacuation had been! The kids had been promised the sunny seaside, fresh salty air and good food. Instead they'd got damp and foggy Devon, living with strangers who resented the intrusion.

She and Pete had been billeted at a vicarage. Bernie and Kath, a farm. Five years away from the Smoke and Pete and

Bernie became a force to be reckoned with. They'd hated the village school. And the school hated them. No one had championed the lice-ridden cockney mongrels, with mouths as foul as drains. She still cringed at the old saying, 'Cleanliness is next to godliness.' It reminded her of delousing baths, forced prayers and endless Bible readings!

A whiff of Bernie's hairdressing snapped Ruby back to the present. 'Fancy a drink on the way home?' Bernie suggested breezily. 'If we leave early enough we can nip in the Bricklayer's.'

'Don't think so,' Ruby declined. 'I'm not in the mood.'

'Blimey, you are a right madam tonight.'

'And you're like a bloody octopus.'

'Thanks. Dunno why I bother.'

'Nor do I!'

But it didn't take long before he took to fooling around again and this time she pushed him hard. Much harder than she intended. With a look of astonishment on his face, Bernie went sprawling.

'You silly mare!' he exclaimed as, almost tripping over, he was made to look a fool in front of the brunette. 'What did you do that for?'

As she stood there trying to smother her amusement, she became aware of a man pushing his way through the crowd towards them. 'Now you've gone and done it,' she hissed, trying to warn Bernie. 'Look! They're sending management over.'

'It wasn't me that did the pushing,' Bernie argued, pulling his jacket firmly back on his shoulders. 'It was you.'

For a guilty moment they stared at the stranger who said nothing, but locked disapproving eyes with Bernie.

An older guy, in his mid-thirties, Ruby guessed. A few inches shorter than Bernie. He was broad and upright, with short brown hair styled carefully away from his face. Square jaw, unflinching brown eyes and wearing a dark, tailored suit and black roll-neck sweater to die for.

'Who are you staring at, mush?' Bernie demanded, his temper now short.

'Ease up on the lady, pal.'

'What?' Bernie's tone was incredulous.

'You heard.'

'Who the hell are you?' Bernie demanded, poking a finger in the air.

'Just offering some friendly advice.'

Bernie laughed. 'Well, in that case, you know where you can stuff it.'

Ruby hadn't ever seen Bernie so angry. If this got out of hand, there would be a price to pay. Namely them all getting banned from Fortuno's. And no way was she having that.

'Come on, Bernie, let's go,' she pleaded.

'This geezer doesn't work here,' Bernie decided loudly. 'What right has he got to stick his nose in our business?'

Shaking her head, Ruby swallowed. 'Bernie, give over. We don't want any trouble.'

The man inclined his head and smiled at her.

Ruby was transfixed; she couldn't drag her eyes away from his intense gaze. But she knew she had to do something to defuse the situation as Bernie puffed out his chest aggressively.

'Bernie, forget it. We can go to the Bricklayer's if you want,' she cajoled, pulling hard on his arm and managing to move him a few feet. 'Wait for me by the coffee bar. I'll meet you and Kath after I've powdered my nose.'

Ruby took a chance and left, hurriedly pushing a path towards the foyer. Glancing over her shoulder, she was relieved to see Bernie slinking off towards Kath who was sitting on a tall stool at the coffee bar.

She had almost arrived at the Ladies, when a hand came down on her shoulder. She turned, heart in mouth.

'The name's Nick Brandon,' the stranger said softly. 'I'm sorry, I didn't intend to butt in back there.'

Ruby's jaw dropped. 'Who are you?'

'Just an interested party,' he said, lifting an eyebrow. 'I thought that guy was pestering you.'

'What's it got to do with you if he was?' Ruby spluttered defensively. 'And anyway, he's a friend.'

'Then I guess you're in need of better friends,' he responded with a slight smile. 'You're a beautiful, classy girl. You could make something of yourself, do you know that? Don't waste your time in places like this.' His words were like a caress. Staring into his eyes she felt her body responding, trapped by some mysterious force connecting them. He said she was beautiful and classy. When had anyone ever told her that?

'Perhaps I can help you,' he said without hesitation. 'Take my card. Ring me tomorrow. Okay?'

Ruby looked down at the card he had pushed into her hand. *NICK BRANDON* was printed in large, bold capitals. Underneath was a telephone number.

When she looked up again, he was gone.

# Chapter Two

It was Monday morning and the least favourite day of Ruby's week. She was almost broke, too. Her 25s wage barely covered necessities. After paying her share of the rent, food and bills there wasn't much left over. Yet Kath was always going on about how lucky they were to rent such a cheap room from Bernie who had sub-let it from the landlord.

Cheap, yes, decent, no, Ruby thought dismally. One shabby bedsit in Poplar, fitted with a single bed and bed-settee, wasn't the luxury she craved. She tried to save on the bus fares by walking to work each day. But Larry's Poodle Parlour was at least thirty minutes up the Commercial Road and Ruby liked her beauty sleep. It was always a struggle to arrive by eight.

Still, she'd had an amazing Saturday night. As she paused her scissors over the poodle's floppy white fringe, she was back again at Fortuno's. Nick Brandon's card was in her hand. He had invited her to call him. My God, had it really happened?

Well, yes! Because Bernie had gone on about him all the way home. Was she sure she didn't know him? Why had he approached her and not some other chick? Finally Kath had told her brother to put a sock in it.

Ruby had examined the card at least a hundred times. A name and telephone number, that was all. Did she have the courage to phone? Would Nick Brandon even answer? And what would she say if he did?

'You going to trim that dog or eat it?'

Ruby jumped, realizing her friend Debbie Wilson, the poodle parlour's only other employee, was addressing her.

Ruby looked down at the poodle. Its frightened eyes were popping out of its sockets. 'I was miles away,' she said vaguely, nipping carefully at the fringe and scattering a shower of pure white fluff across the floor. 'I can't seem to get going this morning. Even though I slept most of yesterday.'

'What!' Debbie exclaimed. 'My mum would have a fit if I wasn't up to help her cook Sunday dinner. Rog gets me in at a decent hour, though. What time did you stumble in?'

'We went dancing then had a drink,' Ruby admitted cautiously, well aware of Debbie's disapproval.

'Don't know what you see in Fortuno's,' Debbie countered. 'It's a dive.'

'Yes, but I like it.'

'I suppose you went with Kath and that idiot brother of hers?' Debbie said accusingly as she dusted down her clean white overall. 'You could do so much better.'

Ruby thought it best to ignore this. Debbie could be really bitchy at times. She turned the poodle's head, attempting to complete the pom-pom trim. 'Stay still,

Delilah. I don't want to graze you.' She shook the talcum powder over the curly white fur. 'There, now, you'll smell nice for your owner.'

'So it's a given you didn't meet anyone?' Debbie said, resuming their conversation.

Ruby thought it safer not to mention her encounter with the mystery man. Not yet. After all, Saturday might turn out to be just a sweet memory.

'As I said,' Debbie harked on, 'Kath Rigler won't win you any friends, nor her brother.'

Debbie had only met Kath and Bernie a few times but had taken an instant dislike. Ruby knew Debbie and her boyfriend moved in what they thought were classier circles. And perhaps that was true in a way. Debbie came from a good family, a dad with a nine-to-five job, a mum who only had to look after Debbie and her two younger twin brothers. The Wilsons had lived all their lives over Victoria Park way in a nice house. A world away from the slums that she and Pete and the Riglers had grown up in.

Ruby distractedly brushed the dog hair from her over-all. If only Kath were to find herself a boyfriend. She could be pretty if she did something with her lank black hair and beanpole figure. But Kath was nervous of men. With a father like Alf Rigler, no wonder! A violent drunk, he had knocked seven bells out of his two kids and timid wife. And God knew what else, Ruby reflected, that poor Kath was too ashamed to disclose.

If only Kath could make new friends, Ruby thought wistfully. After twelve months of their living together like sardines in a can, Ruby had come to the conclusion they both needed to get out and about more.

Suddenly there was a yelp and Ruby stared down at the trembling poodle. A red patch of blood had formed in the dog's white fur.

'You cut too close,' Debbie accused as the little dog leaped from Ruby's arms. 'Mrs Freeman will kill you!'

Heart in mouth, Ruby gave chase. How had she managed to injure it so badly? At the desk, movement came from a muddle of woolly blankets on the floor. Just as she was about to investigate, a black car pulled up outside the parlour. It was a flash, foreign-looking motor, but Ruby couldn't see who was driving. Was it Laurence Dickens, the parlour's owner? Perhaps he had bought himself a new car.

'Perfect time to show up, Larry,' she muttered, wondering why he'd called at this time of day. He never usually collected the takings till six.

Then, to her relief, the car moved off again.

Ruby looked down for the poodle, but the little dog was gone.

'I've got her,' she heard Debbie wailing. 'Come and see.'

Ruby hurried out to the back. Debbie was holding the poodle against her chest.

'How bad is she hurt?' Ruby dared not look.

Debbie threw back her head and hooted. 'It's make-up, not blood! You must have spilled rouge on her. You was half asleep this morning when you did your face in the mirror.'

Ruby sighed with relief. 'Thank goodness. I had visions of old Mrs Freeman chewing my ear off.'

'She would have, an' all,' Debbie agreed, hurriedly checking the time by the clock on the wall. 'Look, we'd better get cracking. If you want to clear the mess in here, I'll take Delilah outside and hose her. She'll soon dry in the sun.'

Ruby nodded gratefully. 'Thanks, Debs.'

Ruby began to clean up, wondering if the parlour would ever make it big and fulfil Larry's dreams of matching the successes of the West End dog boutiques. When they first opened in the Commercial Road a year ago, Larry had promised they'd soon pull in the rich owners and make them a small fortune as it didn't take much nous to trim the hair from a dog. But so far, his prediction had fallen short of its mark.

Not that Ruby really minded. Laurence Dickens was a great boss. He'd chosen her from a long list of hopefuls. The wage was disappointing, but he let her and Debbie run the parlour as they liked. He was all right, was Larry. As employers went, he was one in a million.

Glancing out of the parlour's window she saw the black car again. It drove slowly past and Ruby hurried to take a closer look.

By the time she opened the front door and stood on the pavement, the vehicle had disappeared.

'Any sign of Mrs Freeman?' Debbie asked an hour later, now minus her heels and plodding about the back yard in wellingtons. Sliding a spade under the excrement, she shovelled the muck into the battered dustbin.

'Not yet.'

'Good. Delilah's still damp.'

The sharp September breeze blew across the yard and Ruby pulled a face. 'What a stink!'

'The bin's full. Didn't have a chance to clear up on Saturday before we left. One sniff of this and Larry would faint.'

'For someone who owns a poodle parlour, it's weird,' Ruby mused curiously. 'Larry don't like dogs. Or cats. Or anything with feathers.'

Debbie chuckled. 'Bonkers, eh? You'd think after his mum passed away, he'd sell up. But no. He simply got rid of all the livestock she kept, decorated through – and then hired us to run it as a poodle parlour.'

Ruby frowned thoughtfully. 'I didn't know his mum kept livestock here.'

Debbie jerked her head towards the brick wall and adjoining building. 'Len, the greengrocer next door, told me the old biddy dyed knackered-out greyhounds a different colour, so she could sell them to race under another name. She even trapped wild birds and kept them in cages. He said she'd sell anything with a heartbeat. If anyone had offered a good price for Larry she'd probably have taken it.'

'Poor Larry. No wonder he flogged everything when she died.'

'What Len objected to was the stink of the animals as it drifted over the wall. She wasn't exactly known for her hygienic standards.'

Ruby shuddered at the horror story. 'Not like Larry, then?'

'No, Larry even carries a lady's lace hanky to blow his nose with.'

'Yeah, he's dead fussy about his looks,' Ruby agreed.

Debbie raised an eyebrow. 'We're more or less running the business for him, you know. Not making millions, but enough to cover the overheads and for them to trot off abroad every year.'

'Don't blame 'em.' Ruby shrugged. 'I like Stuart. He's always got a smile.'

'And more!' Debbie snorted. 'He's a dish.'

Ruby thought of Larry's boyfriend who breezed in occasionally to flatter and charm. Tall, dark and exotically handsome, he'd be snatched up by any girl if he was available. Stuart must have been a real catch for Larry who was nothing out of the ordinary. Short and plump and in his early thirties, he was already losing his hair.

'You off soon?' Debbie removed her wellingtons and slipped on her shoes at the back door.

'I'm going to have me hair done at two.'

'No rush, love. Larry never calls till late, so take your time. And I've only got the Pekinese to trim.' Debbie smiled, her blue eyes twinkling. 'By the way, there was someone trawling past us in a blooming great car this morning. It stopped, then moved off and must have gone around the block as it came back again.'

'Did you see who was driving?'

'No, why?'

'I saw it too. Just now. Thought it might be Larry. But it wasn't.'

Debbie frowned. 'Here, it ain't Bernie, is it? Up to his old tricks again, following you.'

Ruby despaired at the thought. Bernie had once or twice tried to meet her from work until she'd told him in no uncertain terms to get lost. 'He don't have expensive wheels like that,' Ruby dismissed. 'His car is a rust bucket.'

'Well then, it might be Jack the Ripper for all we know.' Debbie laughed at her own joke. 'Watching two pretty girls and waiting for his chance to strike.'

But Ruby didn't find the joke funny. 'Don't say that. It's scary.'

'On the other hand it could be a posh geezer sussing us out,' Debbie remarked with a teasing grin. 'Some good-looking chancer with hidden assets.'

Ruby frowned. 'You'd better not let Rog hear you saying that.'

'Why not? We're not hitched yet.'

'As good as.'

Debbie tapped the side of her nose. 'A girl's got to have some fun occasionally.'

Ruby laughed though she still felt unsettled. There weren't many cars around like the one that had waited outside the parlour. Why should anyone want to stare in if they weren't a dog owner? And if they were, why hadn't they brought in their pet?

'How do you fancy coming out with me and Rog next

Saturday?' Debbie enquired. 'Bring your boyfriend too. We'll make it a foursome.'

Ruby pulled a face. 'You know I'm not seeing anyone.'

'In that case, come on your own.'

'It's Kath's birthday,' Ruby said with a shrug. 'We're going to a pub up Hoxton way.'

Debbie wrinkled her nose. 'Hoxton's not my cup of tea, I'm afraid.'

'I can't cancel, Debbie. Not at the last minute.'

'Please yourself.' Debbie glanced in the big mirror, flicking her blonde fringe with her long painted nails. 'But you'll be missing out. We're off to the Manor, in Hampstead.'

'The Manor?' Ruby repeated incredulously. 'The new club everyone's talking about? But it's membership only.'

Debbie nodded, a smug look on her face. 'Rog sold the manager an insurance policy. In return Rog got complimentary tickets to the club. Rog said the place is loaded with antiques and old paintings, not like your usual grungy venue. There's a good cabaret and dancing too. So, as I say, you'll be missing a good night out.'

Ruby was sorely tempted. Compared to sitting in a dingy, stuffy pub eating fish and chips, it was no contest. 'How much would I have to pay on entry?'

'Told you, it's free.'

Ruby felt a real thrill. The Manor was said to be very high class and memberships were like gold dust.

Debbie lifted her big blue eyes. 'Wouldn't offer if I wasn't sure. Anyway, it's up to you.' She raised her neat eyebrows.

Ruby hesitated then quickly nodded. 'Okay, I'll come.'

'What will you tell Kath?'

'Dunno yet.'

Debbie looked satisfied. 'We'll pick you up about nine. You can stay at my place if you like. That is, if you don't mind kipping with me.'

'What about Rog?'

'Blimey, I never take him back home, except for a quick cuppa. Don't want him getting the third degree from Dad. Even though we're engaged and I am twenty-one!'

'I forgot, you're a big girl now.'

'Big enough,' Debbie added with a rueful smile. 'Anyway, my parents could sleep through an earthquake. The twins, Desmond and Derek, are only ten. Mum and Dad are knackered out before their heads hit the pillow. But I warn you, two little ruffians running around the place means you won't get a lie-in.'

Ruby shrugged. 'Okay. But don't call for me at the bedsit. I'll meet you at the Bricklayer's.'

'Blimey, you are in a bad way,' Debbie responded drily. 'You was always going on about how your life would be different if you left home. But now you've got a ball and chain round your ankle in the form of the Riglers.'

'No, I have not,' Ruby disagreed at once. 'But I don't like to break a promise.'

All the same, there was a grain of truth in Debbie's assumption. When Ruby had first started work at Larry's after Pete's death, moving in to Kath's bedsit had felt liberating even though the room was tiny. Life at home in the prefab had become depressing. Her mum kept the place as a shrine to Pete; his room and all his belongings were exactly as he had left them. The doctor said it was her mum's way of grieving and she would pull out of it. But time had passed and even her dad had given up trying, preferring the normality of work in the docks and his social club. Even so, Ruby still felt guilty about leaving home.

'So what are you wearing on Saturday?' Ruby asked, changing the subject.

'A brand-new dress,' Debbie boasted. 'An off-the-shoulder cocktail gown.'

'Was it pricey?'

Debbie beamed smugly. 'Rog isn't short of a few bob. I think I deserve looking after.'

'I might catch a bus up to Oxford Street on Saturday afternoon after work,' Ruby decided. 'I've got a bit put by.' She hadn't of course. But the rent could wait another week. She would never again have another chance like this to go to the Manor.

# Chapter Three

Ruby gazed around at the sophisticated interior of the Manor. Whoever had lived here once, if they didn't live here now, must surely have been gentry.

Wooden beams criss-crossed overhead and the walls were papered in thick, embossed wallpaper. A huge log fire sparkled and crackled in a hearth that held a pair of ancient bellows, blackened metal tongs and a fringe of horse brasses. Just like she'd seen on the films.

'Well, what do you think?' Debbie enquired, raising her eyebrows as they stood in the grand entrance.

'It's stunning!' Ruby stared at the plushly carpeted staircase. Beneath, a set of impressive double doors was thrown open to the lower floor. She could hear music and laughter. Her eyes widened when she saw the formally dressed men and elegant women in evening gowns. Was her new dress going to stand out like a sore thumb?

'Quite a sight, isn't it?' Rog peered round Debbie, his blue eyes full of salesman's confidence. 'With the manager of this place as my client I clinched my bonus for the month.'

'Rog, you are clever,' Debbie flattered, clinging to his arm. 'Do you think my dress looks all right?'

In answer, Rog bent and kissed her full on the lips. A little embarrassed, Ruby made her excuses. 'I think I'll find the cloakrooms.'

'I could do with a drink.' Debbie pulled Rog's sleeve. 'Let's find the bar.'

'Meet you there,' Rog called over his shoulder as they walked away arm in arm.

Ruby saw a member of staff by the staircase. She was wearing a figure-hugging black blouse and skirt, and a pair of white gloves, and greeting the visitors with a polite smile. Ruby waited for her turn.

'Can you direct me to the cloakrooms, please.'

'The Powder Room is upstairs, madam,' the girl told her politely. 'Turn right down the hall and second left.'

Ruby thanked her, though by the time she reached the top of the staircase she had forgotten the instructions. There were so many things to see. The carpet she trod on was luxuriously thick. She felt as if she was walking on air. The walls were covered in huge oil paintings with ornate gilt frames. There was even a suit of armour. She stared, fascinated, at the shining metal. Had someone really worn this cumbersome suit for battle?

By the time she reached the end of the hall, she was lost. Unfortunately she opened the first door she came to and at once realized her mistake.

A smooth green-baize table filled the room. Groups of

distinguished-looking older men wearing formal evening suits were talking around it.

Ruby felt like dying on the spot. Her cheeks burned as she stood, gawping at her surprised audience. Words of apology tumbled from her lips.

'The other direction, my dear,' one of the men said in a deep, somewhat amused tone. 'Would you care for an escort?'

Ruby shook her head firmly. 'Oh no! No, thank you,' she mumbled, and backed away, closing the door softly. Why hadn't she read the sign on the door, *Billiard Room*?

She turned back to the hall. Most of the oil paintings were of aristocratic-looking men and women.

There were also paintings of nudes. Ruby couldn't help staring at the well-endowed, naked young males and full-breasted girls. She had to tear away her eyes. The Manor certainly was surprising!

She passed the *Library* and the *Study* and finally arrived at the *Powder Room*.

She gasped as she entered the lavish, exquisitely decorated room, lined with gilt-edged mirrors on apricot and blue walls, not a rust-spot between them. Fragile paper tissues, fluffy white towels, squares and ovals of pastel-coloured soaps and even a scented spray stood on the marbled tops. The floor was carpeted in thick blue pile, to match the four velvet chairs in a small annexe to her right. She cautiously pushed open the white door of a cubicle and took another gasp. The toilet was an apricot wonder, with a golden chain hanging from the gilt-embossed cistern above.

This was just heaven!

A few minutes later Ruby was studying her appearance in the full-length mirror.

Though she wasn't as tall as she would have liked to be, the beige chiffon gown showed off her full bust and small waist of which she was very proud. The purchase of the dress had cleaned her out. But the sacrifice was worth it.

Suddenly the door opened and two women entered. They glanced briefly at Ruby and without acknowledging her took their places at the row of mirrors.

Ruby sat in the little annexe on one of the blue velvet chairs. The women continued to converse in cut-glass accents, as they studied their reflections and attended to their make-up. When eventually they left, Ruby thought about the places the women had mentioned; the Champs-Élysées in France, the basilicas of Venice, Rome's Vatican City. They had bought fashions from world-famous designers, eaten at sumptuous restaurants, spoiled by their rich husbands who had flown them to all corners of the earth.

Ruby sat anxiously, uncertain if she was ready for the Manor. Did she really have the nerve to go downstairs and mix with these people? She was wearing a cheap off-the-peg dress and hadn't ever been further than Devon. What would it be like to live the life of luxury that those women had taken for granted?

The door opened again. A tall, attractive brunette of about thirty walked in.

Ruby noted the stylish pearl slide in her thick dark hair and creamy pearls at her neck. She wore a deep green satin gown which – much to Ruby's relief – was of a similar design to her own.

The woman was so striking that Ruby found herself staring. Much to her embarrassment, their gazes met.

'Do we know each other?' the woman asked in a friendly fashion.

Ruby went crimson. 'N-no,' she stammered. 'I was – er – just admiring your dress.'

'Thank you. I see we have similar taste.'

Ruby was taken aback. Not only was this woman pleasant, but she had just paid her a compliment too. With large green eyes full of warmth, she came over to where Ruby was sitting. 'Do you mind if I join you for a few minutes?'

'No,' Ruby replied in surprise. 'Not at all.'

'I'm Annabella Charnwood-Smythe.' A slim hand was extended and Ruby took it.

'I'm Ruby Payne.'

'Call me Anna. May I ask, is this your first time at the Manor?'

'Yes.' Ruby blushed. 'Can you tell?'

'It's just that I know most of the faces,' Anna said as she took a black satin case from her purse. With long, mani-cured fingers, she shook out a cigarette. 'Do have one, won't you?'

Ruby was about to say she didn't smoke, but changed her mind as it seemed unfriendly to refuse. She slid the cigarette between her lips, leaned forward as Anna flicked on her lighter and then began to cough.

'Why, my dear, you're not a smoker, are you?' Anna said with an amused expression as she slid the cigarette from Ruby's fingers and ground it out in the coffee-table ashtray. 'You should have said, you know. It's not a crime not to smoke. Only, perhaps, a little unfashionable these days. Have you never succumbed to this terrible habit?'

'No. But smoking does look very smart.'

Anna laughed lightly. 'Believe me, once you start it's very difficult to stop.'

'That's what Mum always told me.'

'Your mother is a smoker?' Anna enquired.

Ruby nodded. 'At least forty a day and Dad likes his Old Holborn. But my brother and me never took it up, though.'

'That is a surprise,' Anna said, frowning.

'Pete was very particular,' Ruby found herself explaining as the green eyes regarded her curiously. 'He was always – well – dead worried about his appearance, always eating healthy and looking after himself. He used to say you've got to look after number one in life, or who else will?' Ruby stopped and looked down at her tightly clenched fingers. Talking about Pete always made her sad. She didn't know why she had even said his name.

'My dear, is something wrong?'

'No. It's just that he – he died two years ago. And I still miss him.'

'Oh, I am so sorry,' Anna replied softly, placing her hand on Ruby's. 'How indelicate of me to question you.'

Ruby sat up straight. 'No, it's all right. We were really close, you see. Even when he left home, he'd always come back to stay when he could. But then suddenly he was gone. And as I said, I still miss him so much.'

Anna sighed. 'Only time will heal, so I'm told.'

Ruby remained silent. She didn't want to talk about Pete any more. It was too painful.

'So what do you think of the Manor?' Anna asked, discreetly changing the subject as if she'd guessed how uncomfortable Ruby felt.

'I haven't seen much of it yet.'

'Have you come with your date?'

'Oh no. Just some friends.'

'So there's no romance in your life?' Anna said, looking surprised. 'I would have thought a pretty girl like you would have suitors falling over themselves to woo you.'

Ruby looked crestfallen. 'I wish there were. Instead I'm playing gooseberry to the two people who brought me.'

Anna hesitated. 'Listen, I've an idea. I know we've only just met, but we seem to be in the same situation. I'm with two couples and feel a little redundant. Why don't you join me at my table? At least for a while and we can get to know each other better.'

Ruby was so shocked, she just sat there. Why would someone like Anna want to get to know her?

'It is rather impertinent of me, I'm afraid,' Anna said before she could reply. 'I'm sure you'd prefer to be with your friends.'

'Oh no, not at all,' Ruby said hurriedly. 'I'm sure they won't miss me.'

'In that case, let's make the most of this evening.' Anna laughed, her green eyes sparkling as she stood up. 'This really is fun, isn't it?'

Ruby couldn't believe her good fortune. This evening was turning out to be more fun than she'd ever had before.

# Chapter Four

Although Ruby looked for Rog and Debbie as they passed through the bar, there was no sign of them. However, Ruby's attention was on Anna, who drew many glances as they made their way through the crowded room. She was so flawlessly elegant that women as well as men seemed to be taken by her appearance.

This place is so much more than Roger described, Ruby thought as they passed groups of people knotted together in conversation; men dressed formally in dinner suits and women wearing evening gowns like the couple she had seen in the Powder Room.

A buzz of conversation came from the bar, its shelves fitted with more optics than Ruby could count. White-coated barmen with black bow ties served the drinks while black-uniformed waitresses brought glasses on silver trays to those who were seated. Ruby's heart thumped as Anna turned to crook her finger, gesturing to a pair of double doors.

Together they passed through them and into a semi-darkened area, where individual orbs of light cast glows across the many low tables arranged around a dance floor.

The music, Ruby realized, came from a softly tuned tannoy as there were instruments on a raised platform: a black piano, double bass, saxophone and set of drums.

'The band is taking a break,' Anna explained, coming to stand close to Ruby. 'Do you like jazz?'

'I'm not sure,' Ruby replied, feeling very unworldly.

'Then you are in for a pleasant surprise.' Anna nodded to a table in the far corner. 'There's my party. Come along.'

But Ruby didn't move as she saw the circle of distin-guished-looking men and stylish women seated in comfortable bucket chairs laughing and talking together. Instinctively she felt as though she wouldn't be welcome.

Anna smiled knowingly. 'My friends won't bite, you know.'

Ruby managed to smile but she still felt nervous. What if Anna's friends were like those other women? She wouldn't be able to engage in conversation and was sure to embarrass both herself and Anna.

Moving backwards rather than forwards, Ruby bumped against a chair. 'Oh . . . s-sorry,' she stammered, aware that the man carefully returned the glass he was holding to the table, disguising the fact that he'd spilled some of its contents. His companion, an attractive young woman dressed in a deep blue cocktail gown, took a handkerchief out of her bag and wiped his jacket.

Ruby wanted to die of embarrassment. She wanted to run. Run far away from the Manor where she felt so out of place. Everything was going wrong. She should never have agreed to Anna's invitation. The Manor and the people there were out of her league. She daren't even open her mouth or she would betray her cockney accent.

'We've met before, haven't we?' the man said.

With a gasp she was unable to disguise, Ruby stared into the handsome features of the mysterious stranger she had met at Fortuno's.

'Nick!' Anna was swiftly at Ruby's side, a smile on her lips. 'Do you two know each other?'

'Indeed we do,' he replied, standing up and smiling charmingly. 'Although it was, I regret to say, a very brief meeting.'

'I see.' Anna's soft fingers gently tucked under Ruby's arm. 'Well, as nice as it is to see you again, Nick, Ruby and I must take our seats before the cabaret begins.'

'Of course.' Nick met Ruby's gaze. 'I'm glad we met again.'

Ruby felt Anna pulling her gently away. 'I'm sorry to hurry you, but we should be in our seats. It's only fair to the band.'

Ruby nodded. She tried to glance back, but Anna urged her on. 'Is Nick a friend of yours?' Ruby asked as they made their way forward.

'An acquaintance,' Anna replied. 'As I told you, one knows most of the faces at the Manor.'

When they arrived at Anna's table, four faces looked up at them.

'Gwen, Paula, Charles, Taylor, meet Ruby,' Anna said and the man called Charles stood up, offering his hand and his seat to Ruby.

'Thank you, Charles,' Anna said, and after shaking his hand Ruby sank onto the cushioned chair. 'We'll talk more after the cabaret,' Anna whispered. 'I've ordered champagne. I take it you've no objection to a little refreshment?'

'No, not all. But—'

'With my compliments,' Anna told her. 'Let me spoil you a little.'

There was sudden applause as the musicians sat at their instruments. The atmosphere was so exciting that Ruby forgot entirely about Debbie and Rog though she did glance over her shoulder to see if she could see Nick Brandon.

Ruby was feeling the heady effects of the expensive champagne. As she listened to the energetic rhythms of the music – at first so unfamiliar to her – it seemed as if she had been enjoying that type of music for years. Bubbles of alcohol danced on her tongue and flew up into her nose. All her tension had slipped away. She had looked for Nick, but hadn't caught sight of him again.

The tall American called Taylor had said very little but Charles, an older man, had given her friendly smiles. Gwen and Paula had both asked her if she was enjoying herself. And much to her own surprise she was.

She was talking to Anna when the pianist spoke into the microphone. 'Let's get you all dancing,' he said, running his fingers over the keys. 'We'll start with a catchy little number you all know from Charlie Parker, the ever-green "I Got Rhythm!"'

An applause drowned his voice and Ruby watched the couples file onto the small dance floor. She smiled to herself. There was no way she could dance here like she did at Fortuno's.

As Ruby watched Anna's friends take to the floor, she wondered if they were very rich. The two men looked it, with their air of confidence and the rather old-fashioned way in which they danced.

Paula, a stunning redhead, was closest to her own age, she decided, while Gwen and Charles must have been in their forties. How long had they all known each other? Ruby wondered. And why didn't Anna have a partner? Once again Ruby craned her neck round to see if Nick was there.

'So, tell me more about you,' Anna said suddenly. 'What do you do for a living?'

A little reluctantly, Ruby told Anna about her job at the poodle parlour. To Ruby's surprise, Anna seemed inter-ested and listened attentively as she explained that coming here tonight had only been made possible by Rog's job as an insurance salesman and the free tickets he'd been given by the management.

'How kind of him,' Anna said. 'Has the Manor lived up to your expectations?'

'Oh yes, and more,' Ruby replied. 'Do you come here often?'

'Rather too much, I'm afraid. Even though the Manor is quite new on the scene, it's only the cabarets that interest me.'

'I don't think I'd ever get bored with a place like this,' Ruby sighed. 'Although at first I was scared I wouldn't fit in. That was, until we met in the Powder Room.'

'Oh, my dear, all eyes have been on you. Haven't you noticed?'

Ruby blushed. 'No. I thought they were on you!'

Anna laughed. 'How charming! Now tell me – I'm curious. Where did you meet Nick?'

'Well, we just bumped into each other really,' Ruby said, feeling awkward. 'I was out with my friends at a local dance hall. He came over and gave me his card with his telephone number. Then asked me to phone him.' Ruby deliberately left out the argument with Bernie. She didn't want it to sound cheap.

'And did you phone him?'

'No, as I wouldn't have known what to say.'

'He attracted you then?'

Ruby hesitated. 'Well, for an older man he is very good-looking.'

'Do you like older men?' Anna pressed.

Ruby giggled. 'I don't know. I've only been out with boys of my own age.'

Anna smiled. 'Then may I give you a word of advice? From someone a little older and perhaps a touch wiser?

You see, if I had a daughter of your age, I would be concerned.' Anna paused, appearing to choose her words carefully. 'Nick Brandon is a man of the world, charismatic and charming. But he did, after all, try to pick you up. It's obvious you're not that sort of girl, so I consider the gesture quite reprehensible.'

'I'm not looking for a man,' Ruby said with a casual shrug, at the same time remembering the feelings Nick had stirred in her and which she hadn't been able to forget. 'I want to enjoy life, travel and see places.' She thought of the two women in the Powder Room. 'Like Paris and Rome.'

Anna's green eyes twinkled. 'Let's drink to that.' Her expressive eyebrows lifted. 'Now, a little more champagne while we sit back and watch these lovebirds.'

Ruby took a sip from her refreshed glass. She was happy to sit with Anna and watch, even though Nick hadn't come over. She didn't fancy dancing with Charles or Taylor, and she certainly wouldn't have wanted to be asked to dance by anyone else here.

Despite Anna's warning, she couldn't stop thinking about Nick. He was definitely more mysterious and handsome than any other man at the Manor. Anna's advice had only served to make her even more curious.

'So this is where you've been hiding!' Debbie's voice boomed suddenly into Ruby's ear. 'We've been looking all over for you.'

Ruby looked up at Debbie. 'I couldn't see you at the bar.'

'We sat in the lounge.'

'Debbie and Rog, this is Anna,' Ruby said quickly.

'Anna? Anna who?' Debbie's voice rose.

'We met upstairs in the Powder Room,' Ruby continued, glancing apologetically in Anna's direction. 'I was just coming to find you.'

'Don't bother!' Debbie interrupted sulkily. 'You seem to be getting on all right without me.'

'We'll be in the bar,' Rog called as Debbie flounced off, tugging him with her. 'I'll order your usual, right?'

Ruby nodded, but she felt ashamed. Debbie had been very rude.

Ruby sank down on her chair. 'I'm sorry,' she apologized to Anna who was sitting quietly, watching. 'There was no call for Debbie to speak like that, even though, perhaps, I should have gone to look for them.'

'Not your fault but mine, Ruby,' Anna said graciously. 'I've had the most wonderful time.'

'Have you really?' Anna looked amused.

'I'd like to stay with you longer. But I'd better go.'

'Of course you must. Good friends don't grow on trees.'

'Perhaps I'll see you again?' Ruby said, wondering if this was the end of what had felt like the beginning of an exciting new friendship.

'Yes, indeed,' agreed Anna. 'Perhaps we could make a date? Do you ever travel up to town?'

'Oh yes,' Ruby said eagerly. 'I go shopping in Oxford Street sometimes. Mostly on Saturday afternoons after work.'

'Well, I am busy in October but less so in November. Come to see me then and over coffee we'll make plans for an evening together at the Manor. I live at 10 Dower Street, just off the Edgware Road. Press the little red button and I'll let you in.'

Ruby felt elated. She had actually received an invitation to Anna's home!

'I will,' Ruby finally agreed.

'That's settled then. Now go off and enjoy the rest of the evening with your friends.'

Ruby smiled gratefully. She didn't want to leave. But she knew that Debbie would be waiting.

Anna smiled her beautiful smile. '*Au revoir*, until we meet again.'

Ruby thought Anna's words sounded like poetry. If only she could express herself in the same way.

'Say goodbye to your friends for me,' Ruby said as she moved away.

'I will.'

Ruby made her way past the tables and thought how well-mannered Anna had been. She hadn't criticized Debbie for being rude and unfriendly. In fact she'd said how important friends were.

Ruby passed by Nick's table and saw his chair was empty. The woman he was with had gone too. She looked around, but couldn't see him. Had he forgotten her existence already?

'Did you get home all right?' Debbie asked on Monday morning. 'The buses from our road to Poplar don't run very often on Sundays.'

'Yes, one came eventually.'

'Who was that woman you were with on Saturday night?' Debbie asked pointedly as she swept the parlour floor.

'I told you, I met her in the Powder Room. She was very nice and made me feel welcome,' Ruby replied, hoping Debbie was in a better mood. 'Thank you for taking me. It was a great night out.'

'Even though we didn't spend much time together,' Debbie couldn't resist adding.

Ruby was relieved when Larry and Stuart walked in the parlour door. 'Girls, girls! We have some interesting news!' Larry waddled over, his plump skin smelling of something fresh and spicy as he greeted them.

'You're giving us a rise,' Debbie said hopefully.

'Sadly not yet,' Stuart chuckled. 'But you'll have an increase as soon as the parlour makes it big.'

'One day in the not too distant future,' Larry sniffed, darting a glance at Stuart. 'Now, girls, as I was saying, we've got a surprise in store.'

Ruby looked down on Larry's bald pate surrounded by a thatch of black wiry hair. He gazed at her through his thick, horn-rimmed lenses. He was barely her height but dressed immaculately in his hand-tailored suits. He looked up to Stuart who was Latin in looks and taller by a foot. They made an odd, but happy couple and Ruby felt deep affection for her boss who had shown her such kindness when she'd started the job just after Pete's death.

'Ruby, you and Debbie and your young men are invited to a party,' Larry told them. 'This coming Saturday at eight. Chez Larry and Stuart.' He batted his short eyelashes. 'No excuses – you're coming.'

'What's the party for?' Debbie asked, obviously feeling left out.

'We've moved!' Stuart informed her before Larry could reply. 'And, darlings, our new pad is delicious!'

'But you had a nice flat in Hackney,' Debbie protested.

'Hackney is old news, pet. Soho is the place to be.'

'Soho!' Ruby and Debbie exclaimed together.

Larry crinkled his eyes. 'Aren't we the lucky ones? Now, all you have to do is turn up looking spectacular as always.'

'Can't wait, Larry,' Debbie responded eagerly. 'My Rog will find it wherever it is.'

'We're just off Dean Street. What about you, Ruby? How will you get to us?' Larry asked.

'We'll call for Ruby,' Debbie cut in, eager to seal the arrangement. 'Poplar is on our way.'

'I'm sorry, but I'm going out with Kath, my roommate, that evening,' she said apologetically. 'I can't let her down.'

'Then bring the lovely Kath too, my darling,' Larry insisted. 'The more the merrier. I should be most upset if you weren't to be there,' Larry told her. 'We have a delicious buffet. And plenty of these arty types for you to meet. Soho is so bohemian.'

'What does that mean?' Debbie said with a frown.

'Quite out of the ordinary,' Stuart explained. 'You'll adore it.'

'So, all settled.' Larry patted his ample stomach under his Jermyn Street shirt. 'Now, girls, it's down to business. What fortune have we taken today?' He drew Ruby to the till.

She listened as her boss counted the takings while describing the food, entertainment and booze he intended to provide for his party guests.

But she wasn't listening. She had only been to Soho once before and that was with Pete. She couldn't wait to go again.

# Chapter Five

Ruby watched squeamishly as Kath served the fried food from the greasy blackened pan. Kath tried her best, but healthy food wasn't Kath's scene. Not that Ruby refused anything served up to her. She was always hungry and had the appetite of a horse.

Kath slid out the wooden stool next to Ruby and sat down. There was no room to spare at the folding picnic table, even though Ruby had tried to make the eating space look bigger by partitioning it off from the rest of the room with a curtain.

'Sorry it's fried again.' Kath pushed back her long black straight hair. 'At least it's hot.'

'Does it have a name?' Ruby enquired.

'Three guesses,' Kath offered. 'But you'll probably get it in one.'

'Spam *à la carte*?' Ruby suggested. 'Makes a change from sardines on toast.'

Kath prodded the greasy lumps with a fork. 'I can't bear the sight of me own cooking.'

'It's better than what we was given in Devon,' Ruby

said as she began to force the fritter down her throat. 'Remember the whale meat? I was put off fish for life. The vicar's wife soaked the meat overnight and steamed it the next day. The stink was in my hair and clothes and even followed me to school.'

'We didn't have whale meat on the farm,' Kath remembered. 'But the veg and spuds drove us bonkers. We was out in the fields from dawn till dusk. My back ached and my hands were always bleeding. It was the final straw when we were made to peel and eat the bloody things.' She sighed, staring into the distance. 'Not that food was any better when we came back to the Smoke. Mum and Dad lived up the pub, so me and Bernie got a job at the pie and mash shop, remember? The gaffer let us have the leftovers before the pig-bins arrived.'

Ruby nodded sadly. Poor Kath was still thin as a rake. Food didn't know how to operate in her body. Her stomach had shrunk to such a degree she couldn't eat a decent meal if she saw one. She also hated her height as it made her feel conspicuous.

'What have we got for afters?' Ruby asked.

'Same as always. Tinned fruit and evaporated milk. Or there's some bread and cheese I bought on Saturday. Though the cheese is a bit ripe. Even Bernie didn't fancy it.'

Ruby glanced at her friend. 'I thought you were going to eat at the pub in Hoxton.'

'I didn't want to go without you. So Bernie went without me. He called in on the way back, though, so I wasn't alone. Talking of Saturday, how was your mum?'

'Same as always.'

'Is she still a bit doolally?'

Ruby nodded. 'Some things never change.' She couldn't meet Kath's enquiring gaze. It was too late to confess the truth, that she'd lied to Kath about going home in order to go to the Manor. Her guilt was mounting up.

'It's really good of you to stick by her, considering,' Kath said softly.

'Oh, I don't go round very often.'

'Well, some girls just wouldn't bother at all with her being the way she is.'

Ruby hung her head, idly drawing a pattern with her finger on the sticky plastic tablecloth. 'Kath, would you like to go to a party? I want to make up for missing your birthday.'

'You don't have to do that. And anyway, you know I don't like parties.'

'My bosses are having a house-warming,' Ruby explained. She had decided she wasn't going to ask Kath but now she felt it would help to ease her conscience. Although she'd have to warn Debbie not to say anything about the Manor.

'Where is it?' Kath asked suspiciously.

'Larry and Stuart have moved to Soho.'

'But why would they invite me?' Kath queried. 'I don't know them.'

'They know you're my best mate,' Ruby urged. 'I'm always on about you at work.'

'Really?'

'Really.' Considering that only a minute ago she had shelved the idea of mentioning a party at all, this was a complete turnaround. Ruby was beginning to wonder if lies were addictive if you told enough of them.

Kath shrank back. 'But I won't know anyone.'

Ruby shrugged. 'Nor will I. It's a chance for us to make new friends.'

'I'm not very good at mixing. You know that.'

'I'll be with you. We'll have a good laugh.'

Kath pulled the tips of her hair as she always did when she was worried. 'I don't know, Ruby. You'd be better off going without me.'

'Listen, you'll love Larry and Stuart. They can't wait to meet you.'

Kath smiled hesitantly. 'Well, all right, then. If you think—'

'I do,' Ruby decided. 'We both need to get out more. Pete always used to tell me to give new experiences a go. This is the perfect opportunity.'

Kath smiled wistfully. 'Pete was very wise.'

Ruby nodded. 'Yes, he was.' She looked at Kath. 'I'm glad we were all best mates and have the same memories.'

Kath's gaze was far away. 'Yes, though some I wish I could ditch. I still have nightmares about Dad.'

Ruby's heart squeezed in sympathy. Even though Kath had missed the East End while they lived in Devon and evacuation was the only peace she'd ever known, her dad had made up for lost time when she'd come home. A violent drunk, he'd made Kath and Bernie's lives hell. 'He can't hurt you now, Kath. He's dead and gone. He'll never touch you again.'

'I know that, but at the back of me mind, he's there.'

Ruby touched her friend's arm. 'All the more reason for you to see new people and go to new places. We can't live at Fortuno's forever.'

'What about transport? I don't want to be hanging round Soho, trying to catch a bus in the early hours.'

'No, neither do I.'

'I could ask my brother for a lift. But you'd better be nice to him and turn on the charm.'

Ruby grinned. That wouldn't be difficult at all.

Making her way home from work on Saturday, Ruby paused to window shop. Normally she would bus up West, to Harrods and Selfridges, dreaming of buying their fashions. Often she'd visit the HMV shop to listen to the records that were at the top of the hit parade. But mostly she'd seek out the smaller shops around the interchange with Regent Street.

Today she was saving her money even though she was hungry and the smell of pies, muffins and bagels from the street traders' stalls was tempting. But when she came to Patterson's, the small boutique where she had bought her new dress, she paused. She had been very lucky to see exactly what she wanted on the model.

'Lovely shoes, those,' a small voice said beside her. Ruby realized she had stopped by Patterson's after all. A young girl was standing close by, a baby in her arms.

'Yes,' agreed Ruby, 'they're very nice.'

'Make yer mouth water, don't they?'

Ruby stared at the footwear arranged attractively with a black handbag and floaty grey chiffon scarf. 'Yes, I like the peep-toes.'

The girl nodded her agreement. She was dressed in an unbelted brown mac that was far too thin, Ruby decided, for an autumn day. Suddenly the drooling infant's dirty face crumpled into an alarming scream.

'You gonna buy 'em?' the girl enquired as she rocked the baby.

'No, I'm afraid not.'

'You got kids?'

'I'm not married.'

'Well, I tell you this for nothing,' the girl shouted above the screams of the child, 'I'd give my right arm to be single again. My old man is as tight as a drum. Yet he's down the pub every night, boozing. Don't reckon I'll ever wear a nice bit of kit like those again.'

Ruby stared at the girl's once-pretty face. She was about the same age as herself. It was then Ruby noticed her large belly and the thick, ugly stockings that sagged around her swollen ankles.

'When is the baby due?' Ruby asked.

'Just before Christmas,' the girl replied. 'This will be me third.'

'Christmas must be difficult for you,' Ruby commiserated as the baby refused to be silenced.

'Don't get me wrong, I love my kids. But your life

ain't never your own after you have a family. Mustn't grumble, I suppose. There's people don't have roofs over their heads. At least my old man has put one over ours. Even if I have to climb four flights of stairs to get to it.'

The baby's screaming grew unbearable. 'Better be off. Time for another feed,' the girl said. 'If I was you I wouldn't hesitate to buy them shoes. Go on, spoil yerself.'

Ruby watched the girl walk off, shopping bag in one hand, infant in the other. The heels of her dirty boots were worn down and Ruby could hear the scuffing of the many Blakeys hammered into their soles.

She turned back to Patterson's window and shuddered. What had the girl said that had upset her so much? *Your life ain't never your own after you have a family.* And the fact that the young mother could never see herself wearing a smart pair of shoes again.

Ruby's eyes fixed on the shoes. They were very smart. And the notice said they were her size. They would go perfectly with her dress. She had worked hard all week. There was no harm in looking.

Ruby opened the shop door and went in.


'How much were those shoes?' Kath demanded the moment Ruby unwrapped the brown paper parcel.

'Not much.' Seeing the disappointment on Kath's face, Ruby began to regret her impulse purchase.

'Oh, Ruby, you can't be trusted where shops are concerned.'

Ruby flopped down in the chair. 'I know. I shouldn't have.'

'Oh well, we'll just have to forget the taxi.'

'I really am sorry.' Ruby gazed at the shoes. 'I'll take them back on Monday.'

Just then there was a knock at the door.

'Who can that be?' Kath whispered, her face ashen. 'Do you think it's the landlord?'

Ruby looked into Kath's frightened eyes. 'But Bernie's been paying the rent.'

'He might have forgotten.'

'That's all we need.'

Another knock came. Kath got up. 'What are we going to do?'

'Open the door, I suppose.'

'I saw him once when he came with his men to the bloke upstairs. They went inside and knocked the old boy about.'

There was silence until they heard a friendly voice calling.

'Bernie?' Kath and Ruby ran to the door together.

'What's going on?' he demanded as he strode in.

'Why did you pound on the door like that?' Ruby asked angrily.

'Because it's bloody cold out there. And you both moan if I let meself in.'

'You scared your sister half to death.'

Bernie touched Kath's shoulder. 'Sorry.'

Kath took out her hanky and blew her nose. 'We didn't know if you'd paid the rent.'

'Of course I have. Though that's more than I can say for you two. I'm not a bleeding charity, you know.'

'We ran a bit short, that's all,' Ruby said, hoping Bernie wouldn't spot the shoes.

'I bunged you three quid a couple of weeks ago.'

Kath stared down at her lap. 'We're not good with money. It just seems to disappear.'

'You're supposed to be females, do the shopping and all that,' Bernie complained. Nevertheless he took out his wallet and peeled off several notes. 'For God's sake, feed yourselves. Fill up that cupboard and when I come here again, I expect to see something in it. Or else I'll be asking for my money back. Understand?'

Kath and Ruby nodded.

'There is one thing more,' Kath said as she smiled at her brother. 'You don't fancy giving us a lift up West tonight?'

Bernie looked at them, shaking his head in disbelief.

But Ruby only smiled. She knew they could wind him round their little fingers.

Ruby sat in the back of Bernie's car, gazing out at the streets of the West End. She felt very excited. People were silhouetted by the lights and brilliantly lit billboards overhead portraying images of famous film stars like Deborah Kerr, Burt Lancaster, James Mason and Tony Curtis. Queues snaked out from the busy theatres: Drury Lane and the Opera House, the Duke of York, the Apollo, the Lyric and the Strand.

A woman walked out of one of the grand hotels on the arm of a tall, handsome man. She was wearing a deep red cocktail dress, high heels and a silver fox-fur stole. Her escort looked like Marlon Brando, who Ruby had worshipped ever since seeing *A Streetcar Named Desire*.

When they arrived in the narrow streets of Soho Bernie parked the car. He steered them past the working girls and noisy nightlife of the clubs and bars towards the address Larry had given them.

Ruby looked for the street where Pete had once brought her one Sunday afternoon. A tall, terraced house beside a bookshop and opposite a small green park. 'This is my boss's bolt hole,' he'd explained. 'He's not here now. So I'll show you round.' The house had many rooms set over three floors. Pete had served her tea: real scones from Lyons with thick red jam. There was a light, airy kitchen, a modern lounge and, up the winding stairs, several bedrooms, one with a four-poster bed. She'd never seen a bed like it before.

Now, as Bernie led the way, Ruby looked around expectantly. But the bustling streets all looked the same in the dark. Nowhere could she see that park or little bookshop.

Bernie stopped outside a rather grimy door. 'Well, you two, I'll pick you up later. And be good.'

'Thanks for the ride, Bernie.' Kath kissed his cheek.

Ruby did the same, smiling. Everything had worked out all right in the end. She couldn't wait to join the party!

# Chapter Six

'What's this we're drinking?' Ruby enquired several hours later, as Larry tilted the chrome cocktail mixer over Ruby's glass.

'Gin and sin,' Larry told them with a sly wink.

They were squeezed into the small kitchen where bottles of wine and spirits were lined up by the buffet. Most of the snacks had gone, but the alcohol seemed to be endless. As empty bottles disappeared, full ones took their places.

'What's a gin and sin?' Kath asked, taking a big gulp.

'Just what it says, my lovely.'

Kath laughed. 'It's delicious.'

'And so are you, dear girl.'

'Larry, we don't want a hangover,' Ruby admonished. She had lost count of the orange- and lime-flavoured cocktails they'd drunk.

'Stick to the one poison and you'll be fine.' Larry flipped the lid of a silver cigarette box. 'Do try one, Kath.'

'Are they poison too?' Kath giggled.

'Not at all,' Larry assured her. 'Try one and you'll see.'

Ruby watched as Kath took one of the cigarettes. After Larry helped her to light up, she inhaled, closing her eyes as she did so. 'They're amazing!'

Larry chuckled. 'I'm here to please.'

'I could get used to these very quickly.'

'Feel free.' Larry gave her a wink. 'Experimenting is such fun, don't you think? Anyway, do enjoy. I'll be back in a jiffy.'

'What did he mean by experimenting?' Kath whispered to Ruby when he'd gone.

'I think you're about to find out.'

They both burst into laughter again. Ruby sighed with pleasure. This was turning out to be a very good night.

'I'm Penny,' a very tall girl said later that evening. 'I'm a dancer at the Windmill.'

'I'm Kath,' Kath said shyly. 'And I work in a factory.'

'I'm Ruby. I work for Larry at the poodle parlour.'

The conversation turned to dancing, and as Penny and Kath seemed to hit it off immediately, Ruby moved off to join Larry who was talking with an older couple. 'This is Bruno Cuthbertson and his delightful wife, Marianne,' he introduced. 'They run a studio on Wardour Street.'

'Charmed,' said Bruno flirtatiously.

'Likewise,' breathed Marianne in a husky, almost masculine voice.

Ruby smiled at the casually dressed older man with long white hair tied back in a ponytail and his brunette wife who had a boy's haircut and wore trousers.

'Have you ever posed for a professional photographer?' Bruno asked.

Ruby blushed. 'There's not many of those in the East End.'

'Then you should come to the studio,' Bruno invited. 'I can see great potential.'

'Leave the poor girl alone, you monster,' Larry broke in. 'Goodness knows what would happen if she walked into your cave!'

Ruby wasn't sure if Larry was serious or not. Marianne saw her doubtful expression and took her arm. 'Take no notice of these men, *chérie*. I'm afraid you are in disreputable, but adorable company. You see, here in Bohemia, anything goes!'

Ruby giggled. She stood still, swaying a little, moving her hips from side to side as she drank her cocktail. This was such a different world to hers.

And she was loving it.

It was towards midnight when Ruby noticed a hush in the room. 'It's Lady Granger,' Stuart told her as he placed yet another cocktail in her hand. She watched intrigued as Larry met the latecomer and her escort, carefully slipping the fur stole from the older woman's shoulders. She had short, grey-blonde hair and her slight figure was tightly encased in a slim black gown. But it was the young man she was with who took Ruby's attention. He was extremely handsome, with coffee-coloured skin, fine features and short black curly hair. For a moment their eyes met across the room.

'Are they married?' Ruby asked Stuart.

'No, she has a husband, albeit an absent one.' Stuart sighed. 'Johnnie Dyer is rather a dish, don't you think? But I would never be tempted away from Larry.' Stuart gave a sudden tinkling laugh.

Ruby had grown to accept that Larry and Stuart were romantically involved. They made no secret of it and she admired them for that. They had taken her under their wing after Pete's death and were always there for her if she needed to talk.

Ruby glanced again at the couple. They were certainly the most intriguing guests of all. Lady Granger must be very rich, she decided. Did her husband know about Johnnie?

A few minutes later, Ruby felt a little light-headed. She guessed the cocktails were having an effect. So she found herself a small space on a sofa and sank down. This type of partying was exciting but also very exhausting!

'There you are!' Kath said, flopping down beside her.

Ruby giggled. 'Yes, here I am. But where are you?' She waved her hand. 'No, I mean, where were you?'

Kath pointed a crooked finger. 'Ruby Payne, you're tipsy.'

'So are you,' Ruby spluttered.

Kath hiccuped and frowned under her fringe. 'I wish tonight would go on forever.'

'So do I.'

'Is it midnight? Has our coach arrived?'

Ruby kept a straight face. 'Bernie's car might turn into a pumpkin.'

They burst into laughter. Ruby thought how funny it would be when Bernie had, somehow, to get them home at the end of the evening.

When Ruby woke up the next morning, she couldn't remember the drive home at all. Thank goodness, she didn't appear to have a hangover from hell. But she did have a raging thirst.

'Could you pour me some water?' Kath croaked from the single bed, as Ruby hauled herself up from the bed-settee and stumbled to the sink.

'People say you should have a hair of the dog,' Ruby mumbled as she filled two tumblers. She shakily made her way back to Kath. 'But we've only got sherry.'

Kath took the tumbler. 'You look as though you've had a night out on the tiles. Do you know you've only got your bra and knickers on?'

Ruby looked down at her full, rounded figure. 'Well, it's better than me birthday suit.' She nodded to Kath's naked shoulders. 'And you're almost starkers.'

Kath peeked under the eiderdown and giggled. 'Oh, so I am.'

'Can I get in with you? It's taters out here.'

Kath threw back the cover and, careful not to spill the water, Ruby climbed in. There was no room to move in the single bed. But it was much warmer snuggled together.

Ruby laughed. 'This is nice.'

'It's almost worth the hangover.'

'We don't have to get up as it's Sunday.'

Kath sighed. 'That's lucky because I couldn't face the factory.'

'How many gin and sins did we drink?'

'I didn't count. I was too busy talking to Penny. She lives up the road at Mile End and said we should all get together again.'

'She did seem like a nice girl.'

Kath nodded. 'We were the same height too.'

'As long as you had a good time.'

'I did until I saw Bernie,' Kath complained. 'He was Mr Grumpy when he picked us up.'

Ruby suddenly remembered Bernie grabbing hold of her before the party. She could hear him shouting at her, telling her what a little tart she'd turned out to be.

'He said we were drunk,' Kath continued indignantly. 'When all we was doing was singing in the back of his car.'

'P'raps we'd better learn the words next time.' Ruby giggled.

Kath snuggled close. 'Thank you so much for taking me.'

'It was a belated birthday present, after all.' Ruby quickly brought the conversation round to Lady Granger and her escort.

'He was drop-dead gorgeous,' Kath agreed. 'But who knows what someone like that is really like?'

'I know you don't trust men,' Ruby replied. 'But they're not all like your dad.'

Kath went very quiet.

They were silent once more, lost in shared memories. Ruby yawned, blinking her eyes and stretching. 'I'd give my right arm for a hot bath.'

'Me too,' Kath agreed. 'We could boil up a few kettles and squeeze in the sink. Only you'd never manage. Not with those huge knockers of yours.'

Ruby took hold of the thin pillow and swung it at Kath. Soon they were in hysterics until, once again, they snuggled down.

'We are a bit of an odd couple,' Kath remarked. 'You small, blonde and all busty. Me tall and as flat as a pancake. But I wouldn't want anyone else for a best mate.'

As Ruby, too, drifted back to sleep, she thought of Lady Granger and Anna. They had the same class and style. She knew they were in a league of their own but would it ever be possible to be like them?

She made a promise to herself to find out.

# Chapter Seven

It was a foggy November afternoon when Ruby got off the bus at the Mallard Road Estate. Her last visit home had been just before her nineteenth birthday in September. She hadn't stayed more than an hour. Long enough to be given her card and present; stockings, a bottle of Evening in Paris perfume and a white cotton blouse her mother had made for her.

It had been an uncomfortable hour. Ruby knew that Pete's birthday in August, when he would have been twenty-three, had been very hard for her parents. Her mum was still living in the vain hope he would walk in the door. Despite having seen his dead body with her own eyes, she couldn't accept he was gone. As for her dad, he'd wished her a happy birthday and then promptly left for the working men's club.

Ruby pulled her coat around her and shivered in the grey drizzle. The long lines of prefabs looked even more gloomy than usual. In 1945 when they'd moved in, the prefabs were cutting edge. Then, they were called box bungalows. The council's answer to the post-war crisis in housing.

Some hopes! she thought as she passed roof after sunken flat roof. Eight years down the line and damp was eating up the flimsy asbestos walls, slowly corroding the steel windows. The gardens were overgrown and neglected.

Ruby came to a halt at number 24. Butterflies filled her stomach. What mood would her mum be in? She hoped her dad hadn't gone out.

Even from where she stood, she could hear the clatter of the treadle. Day and night, her mum worked at the Singer sewing machine. One reason why her dad went to the club, he'd told her. The noise was deafening.

Dad used to love this garden, she thought sadly. Flowers had grown here, even a little tree. But with Mum being so depressed, he'd lost interest.

Ruby paused at the front door. She wanted to turn and walk down the broken path. She knew the moment she saw her mum's face she would be filled with guilt. But living at home was as impossible for her as it was for Dad. She feared that he'd leave one day too. Then what would happen to Babs?

Ruby knocked loudly and repeatedly on the door. If her dad happened to be out, it was the only way to gain her mum's attention.

'Ruby?' Babs Payne opened the door. 'I wasn't expecting you.'

'Hello, Mum. Are you busy?' Ruby kissed her mother's cheek and stepped inside.

'Never too busy for you.'

For a hopeful moment Ruby looked into her mother's eyes. Was she any better? Babs wore her khaki sewing overall with its many pockets and a turban tied over her frizzy fair hair. Her pale face, once youthful a few years ago as she turned forty, was now lined and aged. 'I thought I'd call by. Is Dad in?'

'He's out the back. Trying to mend the guttering. I told him Pete would do it. Your Dad's no good at jobs around the house.'

Ruby's heart sank. 'But, Mum, Pete's not coming home.'

'Not this weekend, no. The guttering could wait though. Your dad just gets restless. Go and make yourself a cuppa. I'm on the machine in the front room.'

Ruby watched her mother scuttle back to her work. She'd deliberately misunderstood about Pete. But Ruby knew if she were to press the point, Babs would get upset. Their conversation would end in tears and her dad wouldn't thank her for that.

Ruby stood in the hall, looking around the dark, depressing prefab. The damp was getting worse. The cloying smell turned her stomach, but her mum never noticed. Once more Ruby fought the urge to leave. Even the fog smelled better than this. But she knew she must stay. At least for an hour.

'Ruby, is that you?' her dad called as she walked through the kitchen door and into the back yard. A tall man, thinner now than he'd ever been but still with a full head of wavy fair hair, he had Pete's broad shoulders and her

brother's beautiful brown eyes. Ruby could see the suffer-
ing had left its mark on his wizened features, as it had on
her mum's. She knew Pete had meant everything to him.
And nothing would ever change that.

'Hello, Dad.'

'Come here and give us a kiss.'

Ruby smiled as she hugged her father. He still felt the
same strong man, yet he was changed. He'd not only lost
Pete but her mum too. Or at least, the woman he'd
married.

'What brings you over?'

Ruby shrugged. 'You and Mum of course.'

Dave Payne nodded. 'I'm glad you caught me in. It's
billiards this afternoon.'

'Are you going to the club? I thought Mum said you
were doing the guttering.'

He shook his head. 'It was only a nail needed.'

'Is she any better?'

'What do you think?' He patted his jacket pockets nervously. 'I've had me fill, gel. I can't take much more. Pete's
always there, for her anyway. For me there's just a bloody
great nothing. She feeds me and washes the clothes and
cleans the house. Then she's back at her sewing machine,
driving me nuts.'

'Oh Dad, I'm sorry.'

'It ain't your fault. You did the right thing, moving out.'

Ruby didn't feel any the less guilty. She'd left her dad
to live in a madhouse. But it was sink or swim and she was
still young enough to swim.

'I'm going round the side way,' he told her, stamping his boots on the crazy paving and loosening the dirt in their soles. 'Tell your mum I'll be back in a couple of hours.'

'Ain't you coming in for a cuppa?'

'I'll catch a game with the boys if I hurry. Don't mind, do you?'

'Course not.' She did mind. A lot. She wanted to talk to her dad. To listen to his deep voice and see him sitting next to her mum in the kitchen, his arm around Babs's shoulders, and Pete standing there, making them all laugh like he used to. But what she wanted and what she had were two different things. She had to settle for at least having a dad to hug, even if only for ten minutes. And a mother who was more than a screw loose, but at least still functioned enough to keep the house going in some sort of order.

'Take care of yourself,' her dad said, giving her a quick pat on the arm. 'And give Kath me love. I take it you and her are doing all right?'

'Yes, Dad, thanks.' She knew he wanted to get away. To leave while the going was good. Before emotion got the better of him. Before they were forced to acknowledge the truth. That things wouldn't be, couldn't be, the same as they were. Not by a long shot.

'I'll be off then.'

She wanted to hug him again, to be safe in his arms, but instead she watched him walk over the weeds and brown grass, ignoring the pile of rust and rubbish that had accumulated, that once he'd have disposed of in the blink of an eye.

When she heard the chink of the side gate, she gave a soft sigh and turned back to the prefab. The kitchen door had a broken pane of glass in its frame, and the greying net curtain hanging behind drooped. Once upon a time, Pete would have helped Dad replace the glass and Mum would have hung a new curtain.

Babs walked into the kitchen as Ruby went in.

'Dad's gone for a game of billiards at the club,' Ruby told her mother.

'Your brother will see to the repairs,' Babs said cheerfully. 'Now, I'll put the kettle on. Why don't you go in the front room and warm up? There's a nice fire going.'

Ruby watched Babs busy herself over the stove. The kitchen was in need of a scrub. There were patches of mould on the walls and the table and chairs had been worn down to the bare wood. She couldn't bear to look any more, so she did as Babs told her.

But when she arrived in the front room, Ruby gasped. There were clothes strewn everywhere. Over the chairs and sideboard, hanging from the picture rail and old leather sofa. Labels were attached to materials. Hems were tacked up, others had patterns attached. The sewing machine took up most of the dining table.

It was chaos.

'What's all this?' Ruby asked as Babs walked in with two teacups balanced on their saucers.

'Business is brisk, dear. Let me clear one of the chairs.'
Babs put the cups down on the sideboard. She shuffled
the clothes from a seat. 'Park yourself there, love. You
can talk to me while I work.'

'Mum, the fire's almost out. It's very cold in here.'

'Is it? I wrap up warm. Lots of layers under me overall.'
She sat down at the sewing machine. 'I have to have this
ready for Monday. You don't mind if I carry on, do you?'

'S'pose not.' Ruby shivered. Apart from the cold, the
smell of mould was overpowering.

Babs slipped on her round spectacles and off went the
treadle. Her slippered feet went up and down. Ruby
flinched as the noise grew louder.

'Are you keeping well, Mum?' Ruby shouted above
the treadle.

'Not bad.'

'Does Maggs Jenkins still pop by?' Ruby knew that her
mum had one good friend in the street who lived a couple
of doors down.

'Not so much these days.'

'Why's that?'

'I'm very busy, you know. I have customers to please.'

Ruby sighed as her mum continued to thread the material under the needle of the sewing machine. No wonder
her dad had gone out. What sort of life was this for him?
Did her mum really have all these customers? Or were
they just another figment of her imagination? Her poor
dad. How could he live in this?

'I'll take the cups out.'

Babs just nodded.

Ruby threw away the cold tea and rinsed the dirty china. When all was clean and tidy she went out to the hall. She realized she hadn't even taken off her coat. But it wasn't just cold, it was freezing.

The door to Pete's room was ajar. She went inside. Why did it surprise her every time she saw the interior? It was just as Pete had kept it.

For a boy, Pete had always been very particular, Ruby reflected as she stood gazing around. He'd disliked untidiness and clutter in any shape or form. From very young, he had cleaned his room himself. Kept it spotless. Unlike me, Ruby thought with a rueful smile. She was only too ready to leave her mess to Mum, who had, once every month, turfed out the debris and swept the lino.

Dad had put up the dividing wall between her bedroom and Pete's. It was very thin hardboard. She remembered listening to Pete's music through the partition, echoing from his Dansette record player. Frankie Laine, Jo Stafford and Kay Starr. Pete couldn't play enough of them.

Now she looked at the record player and her heart gave a twist. It stood silent on the lacquered black-and-cream sideboard supported by thin, splayed legs. His collection of records was stacked under the set of teak shelves screwed to the wall. Slowly she walked over to browse Pete's books. He'd had his favourites; *The Little Grey Men*, *King Solomon's Mines* and *The Three Musketeers*. Well-thumbed copies, too old or too flimsy to stand upright, steadied by plaster Scottie dog bookends. A volume of poetry, *The*

*Ballad of Reading Gaol,* which she'd read once and not understood; a man had killed the thing he loved most, the meaning of which – as Pete had predicted – was lost on her.

Ruby drew her fingers over the polished sideboard, moving slowly to stand by the small settee. Next to it stood the wardrobe, far too large for the room. But Pete had thought nothing of spending a fortune on clothes. Ruby smiled as she recalled his many suits and pairs of shoes.

'You're as vain as any girl,' Mum often told him and she was right. Pete would occupy the bathroom for hours, until Dad hammered on the door, wanting to use the lav.

Ruby inhaled as she opened the wardrobe. Pete's particular smell wafted out. An unforgettable mixture of wood and spice that was his favourite Floris cologne. His clear image suddenly danced into her mind, bringing with it both pain and pleasure.

All his suits were hung neatly on sturdy wooden hangers. Some were even marked *Savile Row.* His best shoes were lined neatly below, all polished to perfection. She reached down, sliding out one of the brown suede loafers. It was hardly worn, the sole almost without a scratch. Then, as she was about to replace it, her eye fell on a small catch at the back of the wardrobe. Taking hold of it, she pulled gently.

To her surprise the floor shifted. Was there something beneath? Should she look? Ruby listened for the sewing-machine noise. It was still clattering away as noisily as ever. With haste, she lifted the wooden base. Below was a book, and one she recognized.

Pete's diary.

Ruby's heart was racing as she sat on Pete's bed, diary in hand. No larger than a school exercise book and bound by a flimsy grey cover. 'You're too young to read it,' he'd said as he'd taken the book from her wandering hands as she'd sat idly in his room. 'One day perhaps, when you know more about life.'

'I'm old enough now,' she'd insisted, but Pete had only chuckled and she'd noticed how quickly he'd slipped it out of sight.

Now, about to open the diary, she hesitated. But how could she resist seeing inside?

'Jan 4 1950. Today R. Westminster, then Harrow. Will call Joanie later,' Pete had written on the first page in his clear, familiar handwriting. More dates followed. Some of the entries made her smile. 'Collect suit a.m. Barber's. Full works this time. Joanie likes me smooth as a baby's bottom.'

Joanie? Who was this Joanie? It must be his girlfriend. But Ruby had never heard Pete mention her. She read on. 'Mr R to the House of Commons today.' And, 'Collect clients from Heathrow. Tight bastards. No tips.'

There was a quote from someone with the initials WC: 'If you're going through hell, keep going.'

She studied the walls of his bedroom. There were no pictures of girls, or even a girlie calendar, much less a photo of Joanie. But there was a poster of a film that Pete had raved about. And on the wall by the wardrobe a picture of an ugly white dog wearing a black top hat. Ruby smiled. Pete's sense of humour had been crazy.

Who was this Joanie? Ruby wondered again. Pete had lots of girlfriends. None had stood the test of time. Was Joanie one of Pete's secrets? A special girl he'd really liked?

Ruby read on. Some entries weren't dated. There were random thoughts and even poems. Suddenly she realized the house was quiet. Replacing the shoes, she closed the wardrobe door quietly. There was no sewing-machine noise. Quickly she slipped Pete's diary under her jumper.

A few steps later and she was safely in the bathroom.

'Oh, here you are,' her mother said, looking in. 'I went outside to see if you was in the garden.'

'Would you mind if I had a bath?' Ruby asked. 'I ain't had a good soak for ages.'

'Course not. There's plenty of hot water. The council put in a new boiler to cure the damp. Just turn the knob and it'll come through.'

'Thanks, Mum.'

'There's a towel behind the door,' Babs said, frowning. 'I'll go and find some Lifebuoy.'

After she'd gone, Ruby turned the knob. Soon the cold, musty bathroom was warm. At least there was constant hot water now.

She wondered if her mum knew about Pete's diary. Would she look for it, then find it gone? No. That was unlikely. The catch in the wardrobe was hidden.

'Here you are, ducks.' Babs returned with the soap.

Ruby couldn't undress as the diary was inside her jumper. But her mum just stood there.

'It's nice to have you home,' Babs said sadly. 'Just like the old days.'

This gave Ruby a jolt. Her mum had never said she missed her before. It had all been about Pete. Now Babs stood there, staring through puzzled eyes. As if, looking at Ruby, she had suddenly remembered something she'd lost.

Ruby knew it was still all about Pete. The son Babs had loved so dearly and was now gone. But where? This question was in her mother's gaze, the mother who couldn't leave grief behind.

'Pete will be pleased to see you.'

A shiver went over Ruby. It was as if Pete's ghost was trapped in the prefab. Babs kept him prisoner, refusing to allow Pete his escape.

'Better get on with me sewing,' Babs said in a distant voice, and, to Ruby's relief, went out.

# Chapter Eight

It was early in December and most shops had already put up their decorations. Ruby left the bus in Oxford Street, eager to window shop as she made her way to Dower Street. The lights strung overhead were not yet alight. Everyone was busy shopping, enjoying the Saturday afternoon. She gazed in all the shop windows. There were tall artificial green Christmas trees, decorated with silver balls and glitter. Lifelike models of children wearing winter coats and hats with brightly coloured scarves. Over it all was a dusting of white fake snow.

Carols were being played by a Salvation Army band and Ruby paused to listen. She dug in her purse for a copper to give to the worthwhile cause. After listening to 'Silent Night', Ruby moved on. Once again she saw her reflection in the windows as she passed through the crowds. Her new outfit, bought at the Co-op last week to cheer herself up, looked very smart. The three-quarter-length coat and straight skirt looked classy, a definite plus. She wanted to impress Anna. Unfortunately, she was broke again, but she was in no hurry to settle the rent. Not after Bernie's unforgivable behaviour!

Her extravagance quickly forgotten, she continued to admire her reflection. The plum-coloured coat with its high rolled collar marked her out from the crowd. Her black suede peep-toes, leather gloves and fashionable beret were the perfect accessories.

Ruby paraded on, her bottom swaying from side to side. She felt top dollar, as Pete would say. For a few seconds she thought about his diary tucked safely away in her drawer. Every so often she'd take it out and read it. But only when Kath wasn't there. And that wasn't very often.

It was now almost three, according to the clock above a tobacconist's. As Debbie had left early to meet Rog she'd closed the parlour at twelve and caught the first bus up to the West End. She'd just had enough money for a coffee in the El Cabala in Oxford Street.

Would Anna be at home? she wondered. And even if she was, would she be too busy to see her?

Ruby turned off at Marble Arch and made her way to the Edgware Road. As she didn't know where Dower Street was, she stopped to ask the way in a corner shop selling hardware. She was given directions to a small square which led to Dower Street. Ruby walked along the rows of white stucco terraces, admiring the pillared front doors and their shining brass letterboxes. Other houses were not quite so impressive. But peeling paint or not, they all had charm.

Number 10 had broad white steps, gleaming long windows and a basement. Her heart raced.

Following Anna's instructions, she pressed the red button. Would Anna answer?

The door opened and there stood Anna, just as Ruby remembered her. Tall and slim, with her dark hair swept up at the back of her head. Her green eyes were emphasized by a set of jade earrings and a chunky glass necklace. The tangerine dress she wore might not have suited everyone, Ruby thought, but against Anna's creamy complexion it looked wonderful.

'I thought you had decided not to visit me,' Anna said, kissing her cheek and drawing her into the beautifully decorated hall. 'I was beginning to feel forgotten.'

'We were busy at work,' Ruby said, surprised by such a warm greeting. 'Or I would have come sooner.'

'Never mind, you're here now. What a wonderful surprise.'

Ruby followed Anna into a large room furnished with two white brocade sofas scattered with silk-covered cushions. Pale, thick rugs lay on the floor. To the rear of the room was a set of white doors and Ruby could hear voices beyond.

'You're entertaining,' Ruby said, glancing anxiously over Anna's shoulder. 'I don't want to interrupt.'

'Not at all.' Anna took her coat. 'In fact, this is perfect timing.'

Ruby didn't quite believe her as Anna placed her hands on her hips, studying Ruby carefully. 'May I say you look charming today.'

'Thank you.'

'You have a good figure, my dear. Have you ever done any modelling?'

'No,' Ruby replied. 'But I always wanted to work in fashion.' She sat on one of the sofas. It was like sitting on a cloud. 'This is a lovely room.' She couldn't take her eyes from the glass chandeliers sparkling like hundreds of jewels.

'Thank you,' Anna said. 'Would you like tea or coffee?'

'No, thank you,' Ruby answered politely. 'I wanted to phone you first. But I didn't have a number.'

Anna tilted her head as she sat down and crossed her long legs. 'Did you enjoy your evening at the Manor?'

'Yes, very much.'

'A few of us are going on the 19th. Are you free to come?'

Ruby nodded eagerly.

'And of course, you'll stay the night.'

Ruby felt dizzy with excitement. 'Are you sure?'

'We've plenty of guest rooms upstairs.'

Ruby took a shocked breath. She'd thought this was just a flat. 'You mean this whole house is yours?'

Anna chuckled. 'I use it as my office too.' She reached for a small green box on the long ornate glass coffee table. 'I know you don't smoke, but you don't mind if I do? It's a dreadful habit. But I can't seem to kick it.'

'No, of course not.' Ruby felt flattered that Anna had remembered.

'Tell me more about yourself and this poodle parlour.' Anna flipped open the top of a silver lighter and held the flame to the filter-tip cigarette.

'Actually, it's the only one in the East End.' Ruby was proud of that.

'Who runs it?' Anna asked interestedly.

'Larry Dickens, a very nice man, and his business partner, Stuart.'

'How long have you been working there?'

'Nearly a year,' Ruby explained. 'I saw the advert in the *Gazette* and applied.'

'You must like animals.'

'Not especially,' Ruby admitted shyly.

'A curious choice then, for a smart young woman like you. If animals are not your thing,' Anna said with a frown, 'then why are you working there?'

Ruby hesitated. 'It was just something different to try. And Larry's a very good boss. He lets me and Debbie run the place just as long as we make enough money for him and Stuart to go on all their holidays.'

'I see. So, do you have any long-term goals?' Anna enquired after a short pause. 'For instance, could you be tempted into a new career?'

'Well, I might,' Ruby replied, a little flustered at the unexpected question. 'I'm saving up for my own place, you see. The bedsit me and my friend Kath live in is very small. One day I want a nice flat, with a bathroom.'

Anna smiled, sitting quietly for a few moments. 'Well, I may be able to help you there.' Her green eyes met Ruby's with confidence. 'You see, this is a modelling agency. My girls are trained for such stores as Harrods and Debenhams. It's not unusual for an international costumier to request our services.' Anna paused, tilting her head as Ruby's eyes grew wider. 'Sometimes the girls are asked to escort our clients. Wealthy businessmen visit the capital, and attend many important functions. They like to be seen with stylish women who wear elegant gowns. And we like our models to be seen with them. These days, the newspapers can make or break a reputation. So if we are linked to a famous name, everyone wants to hire a model from the Charnwood-Smythe Agency.'

Ruby nodded, trying not to look as ignorant as she felt.

'Our recruiting programme is very strict,' Anna continued. 'I only employ girls I can trust, and demand absolute discretion. As do our clients of course.' She paused. 'In fact, I'm interviewing at this very moment.' As she bent forward to put out her cigarette, she slid her beautiful green eyes towards Ruby. 'So, my dear, does the idea appeal to you?'

Ruby gulped in a breath. 'How much would it cost to be a model?'

'I'm not suggesting you pay me,' Anna laughed in surprise. 'The training is automatic if you sign with the agency. How do you feel about that?'

'But, why me?' Ruby asked, puzzled.

'When I first saw you at the Manor, I knew you were very special,' Anna explained. 'Your taste and grooming impressed me. Then, as we talked, I realized you had an open and charming personality, perfect for our agency. However . . .' Anna paused, raising her perfectly curved eyebrows. 'It would have been very remiss of me to talk business and interrupt your evening. Especially as you told me it was a very special night for you and your friends. That's why I gave you my address and hoped to see you again.'

Ruby didn't know whether to be flattered or disappointed. What had she imagined that Anna wanted with her? Why would a woman such as Anna seek her friendship? But even as she thought this, Ruby was overwhelmed by the thought of Anna's offer.

'Do forgive me, Ruby,' Anna said with a soft pout.

'There's nothing to forgive,' Ruby replied quietly. 'It's just that I'm a bit surprised.'

'If your answer is no, we shall still be friends. And look forward to another evening together at the Manor.'

'But even if I accepted your offer, I'd have to give Larry a month's notice.' Ruby hesitated. 'And travelling here each day would be a problem. I had to change buses twice and walk from the Edgware Road. Also, I haven't really got any good clothes.'

Anna began to laugh, waving her hand again as if none of these concerns mattered. 'Ruby, these are very small issues. It makes no difference to me when you start, just as long as I have your assurance you are seriously interested. Otherwise I would hire someone else. As for taking buses – there will be none of that. You'll stay here at the house until we find you your new accommodation. And you will be pleased to hear it's the agency's policy to supply their staff with a comprehensive new wardrobe. After all, you will be representing the firm.'

Ruby's pulse raced. Was she dreaming? This was everything she had ever wanted – and more.

Anna smiled, raising a slender finger. 'One warning. Modelling may sound glamorous but it's also exacting.

Clients can be demanding and often difficult. You will be expected to humour them and use tact. The hours are long and can be unsocial. You may well find you have little time to yourself. However, you will be given a good wage. A flat basic of £10 a week and you will often receive tips. I don't want to paint a perfect picture. But I think you would enjoy the challenge.'

Ruby caught her breath. In just a couple of months she would earn more than she did in a year.

'Take your time and think about it. We'll talk again on the 19th,' Anna promised.

Just then, a slender figure walked towards them from the far room. Dressed in an exquisite powder-blue suit, the redhead smiled. 'Hello, Ruby.'

Anna rose to her feet. 'Paula, do take Ruby in to meet the other girls.'

'Nice to see you again, Ruby.' Paula extended her hand. 'Do come along.'

'I'll join you shortly,' Anna called, but Ruby had no time to reply as she was shown into a large, perfume-filled room where two young women reclining on lemon sofas gazed up at her and smiled.

Enlivened by her afternoon at Anna's, Ruby made her way home in what was turning out to be a pea-souper. As the fog engulfed her she began to wish that she had accepted Anna's offer to stay the night. But she had been worried about Kath – as usual. What would she have told her? This time she couldn't use her mum as an excuse.

Now she had missed her bus, one of the few in service. All hope of getting home quickly had vanished as the bus's lights disappeared in the eerie yellow mists. She stood, cold and confused, having almost walked under the wheels of an oncoming car.

The driver pulled into the kerb and wound down his window. 'You were lucky I missed you back there,' he called.

Ruby peered through the fog. 'Sorry, I didn't see you. I wanted to catch my bus.'

'That's Ruby, isn't it?' the familiar voice said and he waved her closer.

Ruby was startled when she saw his face. 'Oh, it's you!'

'Yes, now that is a coincidence. Where are you off to?'

'I live in Poplar, near the Bricklayer's.'

He pushed open the door. 'Jump in. I'll save you the bus fare.'

Ruby hesitated. She remembered Anna's warning. Was he to be trusted?

'Come on,' he coaxed, grinning. 'I assure you I won't bite.'

She climbed in and sat stiffly on the comfortable leather seat. 'What are you doing round here?'

'I was on my way to the Jester. Do you know it?'

'No. Is it a club?'

He chuckled as he drove away from the kerb. 'Yes. Nothing to get excited about though. And what brings you out in this pea-souper?'

'I've been to visit a friend,' she said after a brief hesitation. Perhaps it wasn't wise to mention Anna.

'Sit back and relax,' he said, swerving the car around a large truck. 'Let's get away from the river and this damned weather.'

A remark that immediately worried her. As he drove, she looked out of the window for familiar landmarks, but could recognize none. This didn't look like the direction to Poplar. Where was he taking her? Anna's warning came back to mind. Who would ever know that she'd accepted a lift in the fog from a stranger?

Then another thought came; it wasn't just Nick's voice she recognized but the car too. The vehicle's shiny black paint, its ornate chromium grille and heavy-duty bumper bar. She'd seen the car before and now she remembered where.

Ruby sat up. 'Please stop.'

'Why? What's wrong?'

'I'd like to get out.'

'What, here?'

'Yes, I'll go back to my friend's.'

'Ruby, you're not making sense.'

Ruby squeezed herself against the door. 'Your car – I've seen it outside the poodle parlour. You were driving up and down. Even my friend Debbie saw you.'

He slowed the car down and stopped the engine. 'Listen, this is a short cut to the City Road. And as for seeing me outside your shop, yes, hands up, it was me. You see, I counted on the fact you'd phone me. And when you didn't, I asked around at Fortuno's. I was lucky. You and your friends are regulars there and it wasn't difficult to look you up.' He paused. 'I just wanted to talk to you. And I couldn't do that with your boyfriend present.'

Ruby sat up. 'Bernie isn't my boyfriend.'

'Had I known that I would have been more up-front.'

'Why didn't you come in the parlour?' she asked uncertainly.

'Pride?' he suggested with a rueful grin. 'I'd waited all Sunday for your call. I was certain I had your attention.'

Ruby's feelings were confused. Of course she was flattered, but she was also a little frightened. He was very persistent. Did she like that? She wasn't sure. He was certainly much older than any of the boys she knew. But now she looked at him closely, he was also far more handsome than she remembered. He had warm, unblinking eyes, a nice smile and a dimple on his chin. His overcoat looked tailor-made with a row of meticulous hand-stitching on its lapel. There was something very charming about this man.

'It's getting late,' he said. 'And if I'm to get you home before the cock crows, we'd better get going.'

She smiled. Now she felt embarrassed. She had made a fuss over nothing when he was only trying to do her a good deed.

Starting the engine he drove them out of the darkened street.

Ruby sat back and enjoyed the rest of the journey. She was even mildly disappointed when it came to an end and they drove into the mist-shrouded light of Poplar.

★   ★   ★

When Ruby got home Kath was saying goodbye to her new friend, Penny Webber, the dancer she had met at Larry's party.

'Ruby, do you remember Penny?' Kath said as Ruby came up the stairs. 'We've been enjoying warm bagels and wine that Penny brought. And we saved a glass for you.'

Ruby smiled at the tall, reed-thin girl with curly dark hair. 'I could do with that. It's very cold out there although the fog is clearing now.'

'It's nice to see you again, Ruby,' Penny said. 'It's a shame you couldn't join us.'

'Perhaps another time,' Ruby replied.

'Penny's been telling me how she got into dancing,' Kath explained. 'And lots of wonderful stories about the Windmill.'

'Well, that does sound exciting,' Ruby said, shivering a little on the freezing landing, her mind still on Nick and her interesting drive back to the East End.

'I'd better go,' Penny said. 'Would you like to meet up again, Kath?'

'Yes, I'd love it,' Kath replied eagerly.

'You'll have to come over and meet Mum and Dad.'

Ruby watched Kath and Penny go down the stairs together to the front door. She was very surprised to see Kath so happy. The bedsit was warm when she got inside, the one-bar fire having been on. But Ruby didn't begrudge the expense tonight. She had had such an exciting day and night that she wanted to tell Kath all about it. But how could she, without mentioning the Manor?

'Did you buy anything nice?' Kath asked when she came in, rubbing her hands together in the cold.

'No, but I did a lot of window shopping.'

'I was a bit worried when you didn't come home,' Kath said, taking the chair beside her. 'But as it was foggy, I guessed you'd find your way eventually.'

Ruby looked at the half-full bottle of wine. 'Shall I pour?' she said with a grin.

'Yes, I only had one glass. It went to my head.'

'Don't worry, we won't get another hangover.'

'Penny is such a nice girl,' Kath said as she sipped her drink. 'She lives up Mile End with her parents who are in the rag trade.'

'How did she get to work at the Windmill?'

'She was an usherette first.'

'You're not thinking of leaving the factory, are you?' Ruby asked in surprise.

'No. But I can dream.'

Ruby grinned. 'I'm glad to hear it. Just don't go packing the factory in, till we've paid your brother back.'

Kath rolled her eyes. 'And that will take a while.'

They both ended up giggling as they finished the last of the wine.

When Ruby lay in bed, she snuggled under the covers and let her thoughts turn to Nick Brandon. Before leaving her, he'd asked to see her again. In reply she'd said she would be at the Manor on the 19th. To her surprise, he had told her he would be there too.

Ruby smiled as she closed her eyes hoping to dream of what the future might hold.

# Chapter Nine

It was the morning of the 19th and Ruby couldn't wait to leave work. Just ten minutes more and it would be midday. Then she would close the parlour and catch the bus to the West End, arriving at Anna's for the lunch that Anna had invited her to.

Ruby could hardly believe everything was smoothly going her way. Kath was staying overnight with Penny Webber, so no explanations had been necessary, or even the smallest fib about where Ruby herself was going. And Debbie had been whisked off by Rog after her last customer had left. Ruby had stowed her suitcase containing a change of clothes under the counter so she was ready for a swift departure. But, just as Ruby was about to leave, a small white van drew up outside the shop. Emblazoned on its side was *J. Henry & Sons, Florists of Distinction, Bayswater Road*. The driver, a middle-aged, moustached man clad in a green overall, opened the back doors and took out a spray of flowers. He made his way into the parlour. 'I'm looking for "Ruby",' he told her with a cheerful smile. 'Sorry, but I haven't a surname.

However, the gent said there would be only one Ruby here.'

Ruby blushed. 'That's me.'

'Pleased to meet you, m'dear,' the man said with a flourish. 'One dozen red roses and note attached.'

'Who sent them?'

'It should say in the note.' He indicated a small white envelope slipped between the tiny red buds and green fern.

'Could you hold them for me while I read it?'

He grinned, opening his arms. 'Service with a smile, m'dear.'

Ruby passed back the bouquet and opened the note. Inside was a single sheet of paper. It read, *Two weeks have been two weeks too long. Nick.*

Ruby's face felt on fire as she looked at the driver and folded the note into her pocket. 'They're from a – friend,' she said, feeling she owed an explanation.

'Perfect choice, I would say.' He gave Ruby the roses. 'Cut the stems before you put them in water.'

'I'm just closing. And I can't leave them here. But I can't take them with me either as I have my suitcase to carry.'

'Where are you going?' the man asked.

'To Dower Street. Off the Edgware Road. And my bus is due any moment.'

'I can drop you at Portman Square,' he suggested. 'I've two deliveries on the way, mind. But we can put the flowers and your case in the back.'

'Is Portman Square near the Edgware Road?'

'Ten minutes' walk at a guess.'

At the sight of a red bus through the window, gliding slowly along, Ruby's mind was made up. 'There goes my bus, anyway.'

'Then we'd better be on our way. Here, I'll give you a hand with the case.' He picked it up and hurried out.

Ruby clutched the flowers to her as she locked up and slipped the keys in her pocket. By the time she was seated in the florist's van and heading towards the city centre, Ruby was smiling at the thought of the red roses and note from Nick. He was letting her know he intended to be at the Manor.

'This dress is beautiful, Anna. But I ain't—' Ruby corrected herself. 'I've never worn anything like it before.' The gown was so glamorous it had taken her breath away. The floor-length pastel-blue silk-chiffon evening gown had a waterfall of soft pleats at the waist almost too small to see. Encased in firm intricate drapery, her full breasts were discreetly covered under a fitted bodice. Together with the elbow-length white satin gloves, Ruby could hardly recognize herself.

'I've seen to it that your wardrobe will be well stocked with an outfit for every occasion,' Anna was saying as they stood in the upper rooms that were to be Ruby's. 'Although very often the stores will want you to model their own stock.'

'But what if I'm not the right size?' Ruby asked worriedly.

'You're a favourable size twelve, you'll do,' Anna assured her.

'I always thought models had to be tall and thin.'

'Some are, of course,' Anna agreed as she worked at the waist of Ruby's dress, sliding a pin from the bracelet pin-cushion on her wrist. 'But there is a demand for all sizes. Hold still. Your small waist needs another tack. There! I shall have Janet make the alteration before we go out tonight.'

'Is Janet your housekeeper?' Ruby had seen a tiny, middle-aged woman working in the kitchen downstairs. She had cooked their omelette and prepared salad, which had been delicious.

'I couldn't do without her,' Anna replied, then frowning at Ruby she asked, 'What did your mother have to say about your new job?'

'I haven't told her yet,' Ruby said evasively.

'Are you having second thoughts?'

'No, not really.'

'I was hoping you would come here today without doubts.' Anna narrowed her eyes. 'Would this change of heart be connected to those roses?'

Ruby blushed. On arrival, she hadn't told Anna the flowers were from Nick. Instead she'd said they were from a friend. Anna hadn't asked who the friend was but had taken them to the kitchen for Janet to find a vase. 'Could your roses be from Nick Brandon?' Anna asked.

'How do you know that?'

'They are rather his style.' Anna just shrugged. 'Now, you're all finished. So why don't you change into something more comfortable? There are plenty of outfits in the wardrobe. And when you're ready, join me for coffee downstairs. I think it's time for us to have a chat. Perhaps there are questions you'd like to ask?' She hesitated, her warm smile making Ruby feel very welcome.

'Thank you,' Ruby said, beginning to peel off her gloves.

'Paula is staying with us, too,' Anna explained. 'She's in the room at the end of the hall. So if you feel lonely, just tap on her door.'

When Anna was gone, Ruby looked around her. What a sumptuous room! Furnished with a big sofa and contemporary furniture, it was twice as large as the bedsit she shared with Kath. The second room contained a double bed covered by a delicate silk throw. Resting against the maple-wood headboard was a tasselled bolster of the same pale lilac shade. Just off the bedroom was her very own bathroom.

But it was the wall-length built-in wardrobe, with its contents of silk-satins, taffetas, chiffons, velvets, wools and tweeds, that really took Ruby's eye. Blouses, skirts, dresses, coats and hats together with slide-out drawers full of accessories of every colour. There were also three generous drawers of underwear, corsetry, slips and lingerie.

Ruby gazed into the long mirror sitting squarely on four bronzed feet as she examined her reflection.

Her fingertips brushed the soft folds of the gown and a ripple of excitement went through her. Anna had said she could be a model. And, at this very moment, she felt like one.

Janet served coffee and although Ruby was pleased to find she was Anna's only guest, she was told Gwen and Paula would be joining them later.

'Charles is driving us,' Anna told her as they sat on one of the sofas.

'Will Taylor be coming too?' Ruby asked as she enjoyed the soft silk comfort of the Japanese wrap-over she had found in the wardrobe. Anna was dressed in a dark suit and fawn blouse, her lustrous hair drawn up into a pleat behind her head. As usual she wore the eye-catching jewellery she favoured.

'That client had to return to the States,' Anna explained. 'We only see Taylor when he travels to England on business. But Charles Fowler is based in London and something of a name. And, I have to admit, a favourite of Gwen's.'

'Oh,' Ruby said shyly. 'I didn't realize they were clients.'

Anna smiled. 'The agency strives for an intimate atmosphere. We are more like a family, you see. Once you begin to work here, you'll understand what I mean. But first, let's talk about Nick. What, exactly, does he mean to you?'

Ruby put down her cup, aware that Janet had arranged Nick's roses in a discreet glass vase and positioned them over the hearth. 'I don't really know much about him.'

'If you work for me, your private life is still your own. I should have made that clear.'

'He does seem very nice.'

Anna trapped her bottom lip with clean white teeth. 'He's an older man and experienced with women. Have you ever had a steady boyfriend?'

Ruby looked away from Anna's perceptive gaze. She was afraid her dark secret would show in her eyes. She'd never told anyone, not even Kath, about what she and Bernie had done in the alley.

'Forgive me, I don't mean to pry,' Anna continued before Ruby could answer her question. 'But you are very young.'

'Yes, and I want to concentrate on my career.'

'In that case, I can see you're a sensible girl and will keep a level head when dealing with men. In this industry you'll find many challenges. In my view, it's better to develop your independence first before getting into a relationship.'

'I'd like that too.'

'Good. I think we understand one another.' Anna opened the cigarette box and took out a filter-tip. Lighting it, she inhaled, her red-varnished fingernails curling around the cigarette. 'I shall always be here if you need me. As for Nick, you must be the judge of his character. Only time will tell.' Anna tilted her elegant head to one side. 'Is there anything else you would like to discuss?'

'No.' Ruby smiled quickly. 'I would like to join your agency.'

'Are you sure?'

'But for meeting you, I would never have had the chance.'

Anna smiled. 'Then it's settled. I have your contract and terms in the other room, so after you've signed them we can look forward to an evening full of fun.' Anna stood up. 'May I say you looked divine in the pale blue. You are going to turn every male head at the Manor by wearing it.'

Ruby was brimming with happiness. She had no doubt now and accompanied Anna to the polished oak desk where the papers were spread out. Her fingers were trembling as she took the pen from Anna and signed on the dotted line.

# Chapter Ten

The Manor was decked throughout with red, white and green Christmas lights. The ceilings and walls were strung with tinsel and garlands of holly. A tall spruce stood by the wide staircase, every green branch entwined with glitter and colourful glass baubles. A grinning elf with tiny golden horns leered down from the pinnacle, giving the tree a distinctly mischievous air.

Ruby stood by the hearth enjoying the warmth of the roaring log fire, as Anna, Charles and Gwen paused at the bar.

Ruby felt confident, but a little anxious in the powder-blue gown. What would Nick think of her appearance? He'd first seen her at Fortuno's, wearing the polka-dot skirt she had thought looked so classy. She'd never worn it since. Now all her old clothes seemed cheap and vulgar.

'Let's take our seats,' Anna said demurely, touching the slim shoulder straps of her black evening gown. 'The waiter will show us to our table.'

Ruby found herself being escorted by Charles. He was tall and dark and gave her an intimate smile, sliding his hand around her waist. During dinner, he made easy conversation as they ate. 'Good wine is like a beautiful woman, Ruby. To be savoured,' he whispered flirtatiously in her ear.

She was relieved when the meal ended and the women went upstairs to the Powder Room.

'How are you getting on with Charles?' Gwen asked as she studied her appearance in the mirror.

'He's very polite,' Ruby said diplomatically.

At this, Gwen frowned. 'Yes, he can be.'

'Come now, Gwen,' Anna reproved, turning from the mirror and frowning, 'Charles is a dear.'

Gwen shrugged. 'If you say so.'

Quickly Anna took Ruby's arm. 'Charles is a superb dancer. As you'll soon find out.'

Back at the table again Ruby tried to enjoy the music. But Anna and Gwen had met some other people and left her with Charles. He was drinking heavily and making suggestive remarks.

She moved away from him several times, but his hand kept touching her thigh.

'Come along. I need a bit of exercise,' he said, pulling her up.

Ruby looked for Anna and Gwen. They were nowhere to be seen. And where was Nick? Why hadn't he come to her rescue?

On the dance floor Charles roughly pulled her against him. 'You're a strange one,' he said sulkily. 'Are you playing hard to get?'

'No, of course not.'

'You know, I quite like this. You make a change from types like Gwen, always ready to give it up.'

'Charles, I want to sit down now,' she said, trying to break out of his hold.

'A breath of fresh air will do us both good.'

She pulled away. 'No thank you.'

'You lazy bitch. You'll do as you're told and come with me.'

Ruby gasped as he increased the pressure of his fingers on her wrist. Now she was truly frightened. What had he in mind? Anna couldn't know what kind of a drunk he really was. Is this why Gwen had left him?

'You've put on your little show, but now that's the end of it,' he told her. 'I'm not a patient man, girlie, as you'll find out.'

Ruby winced as he breathed into her face. 'My name is Ruby, not girlie,' she told him.

Charles just laughed.

'Put a smile on your face as if you're enjoying yourself,' Charles said under his breath as he took her upper arm and thrust her through the couples. His grip was very firm.

'Let me go,' she protested as they left the dance floor. 'Where are you taking me?'

'If you make a fuss I'll tell the staff you're a whore and touting for custom,' he said in her ear as he forced her through reception.

Ruby tried not to panic. Who would believe her against Charles?

She looked for help. But the doormen were greeting new arrivals and the other staff were busy waiting at tables. There was no one she knew. There were no friendly faces she could call on.

A cold blast of air and Ruby was forced out into the night. She was entirely alone with Charles and she gave out a scream as he pushed her across the darkened car park.

'Shut up, you little wretch,' he shouted and gripped her arm so tightly that tears sprang to her eyes.

'W-where are we going?' she cried as he dragged her along.

'For a nice quiet ride in the Bentley.'

'No!' she shrieked, but he pulled her even harder.

When they got to his car, she remembered how exciting it had felt to sit on the leather seats and watch Anna and Gwen drink the champagne from the bottle in a small walnut compartment. But now, as Charles fumbled to open the door, she knew what awaited her inside.

'Get in,' he yelled as she screamed again, but the flat of his hand soon silenced her.

'Do as you're told!' he stormed, hitting her again. But this time, she managed to lash back, tearing the skin of his cheek with her nails. 'What have you done to me?' he howled, looking furious. 'I'm bleeding!'

His face creased in agony and, as he cupped his cheek with his hands, Ruby bolted. She ran towards the Manor but the heel of her shoe snapped. She shook both her shoes off and ran barefoot. But before she'd gone far Charles caught up with her. He began dragging her back towards the woods, hitting her when she tried to resist.

Ruby found herself in a daze and suddenly crashed to the ground. Charles climbed on top of her, pulling up her dress and clamping his hand over her mouth as she tried to scream.

'You'll pay dearly for what you've done to me,' he threatened as he pushed open her legs.

Ruby fought hard, but he was too strong. Pinning her wrists above her head, he slapped her again sending her head to the side with a snap.

She could only sob bitterly as he ripped away her clothes.

Nick Brandon drove up to the Manor and parked the Buick by the ivy-covered walls. He was later to arrive than he'd planned. Trade at his warehouse had been brisk. He'd made a killing on his latest deal, selling the bankrupt stock at knockdown prices; solid teak Danish furniture, stylish upholstered classics, radios, telephones, clocks, mirrors, cameras and a host of household appliances. A little cash Christmas bonus the taxman would never know about. Then closing up shop, leaving no trace behind him.

As he left the Buick, his thoughts turned to Ruby. Would she be waiting for him? He hoped Anna wasn't about to make life difficult. The irony was, Anna could have recruited any pretty face she happened to fancy. But, of all people, she'd found Ruby Payne. Now, that was uncanny!

Nick nodded to the staff who welcomed him as he entered. He slid off his navy-blue overcoat and handed it to the cloakroom girl, then straightened his black bow tie in the wall-sized mirror behind her desk. Flipping open the buttons of his dinner jacket, he double-checked his gold cufflinks on his white dress shirt.

Making his way to the bar, he dug in his pocket for his Gauloises. Then realized he'd left them in the Buick.

Returning the way he'd entered, he hurried back to the car, unlocking and sliding his hand along the dashboard to retrieve the soft package. He lit up and stood for a moment, enjoying the thick taste of the tobacco. Noticing how bright the stars were, he listened to the silence as he filled his lungs.

Music drifted from the building, lights glimmered. There was an occasional hoot of an owl in the tall firs. And now, something else.

A scuffling. A muffled cry. A woman's scream.

He dropped the cigarette, turned towards the sound and saw a movement. 'Hey!' he shouted. 'You there! What's going on!'

The cry came again, the shadow evaporated and Nick hurried forward into the trees.

Ruby's scream came out like a gurgle. Charles's fingers tightened around her throat, slowly crushing her windpipe.

As if from outside herself, she saw her eyes bulge, her mouth gape open. Little dots of light speckled the darkness, until finally she lay limp on the ground.

How long she fought him, she didn't know, but suddenly, unbelievably, he was climbing off and she was gasping in oxygen. She went on all fours and retched. Her throat felt very sore. Where was he? Why had he let her go?

The moon shone an eerie light through the trees. She could smell the damp undergrowth. Her arms and knees and legs felt bruised, her dress was ripped. Charles had tried to strangle her.

Suddenly she heard footsteps. The crackling came through the undergrowth, closer and closer. Once again terror filled her. Was it Charles?

'Hello?' a voice called.

She peered fearfully into the night, at the trees and a small crack between them that must have been the lights of the Manor. She could see his silhouette.

'Is someone there? Do you need help?'

'Here!' she called on a sob, recognizing the voice. 'I'm here, Nick.'

The figure came through the darkness. 'My God, Ruby?'

'Is he there? Did you see him?' she asked in panic, certain Charles would appear.

'Who?'

'Charles. He tried to—' She swallowed. She couldn't say what sounded so bad when put into words.

'Are you hurt?'

'Only a bit,' she sobbed.

He took off his coat and put it round her. 'Stay here. He can't be far off. I'll find the bastard.'

She grabbed hold of him. 'Don't leave me. Let him go.'

'But he attacked you—'

'Stay with me, please,' Ruby pleaded.

'He didn't—'

'No. You scared him off.'

'Thank God for that.' He gently cupped her face and stroked the hair from her eyes. 'My poor Ruby.'

Ruby stifled a sob. She could feel her bare toes poking through her laddered silk stockings and Anna's lovely dress was ruined. What would Anna say when she saw it?

Suddenly she burst into tears.

Nick drew her into his arms. 'You're all right now. I've got you.'

She couldn't stop shaking and clung to him.

After a few minutes, he said softly, 'You'd better come home with me.'

Ruby nodded. She couldn't face going back into the Manor and confronting Charles. After all, Charles would deny what he'd done and who would believe her anyway?

# Chapter Eleven

Ruby lay in a narrow bed in Nick's spare room. Her head, although going round and round, was comfortable on the spongy pillows. The piping-hot water of the bath she had just taken had soothed her. She had put back on her petticoat, knickers and bra and Nick had given her his bathrobe to wear.

She could hear sounds coming from the kitchen.

'Hot soup,' he told her as he pushed open the bedroom door. 'From a tin, I'm afraid. How are you feeling?'

'The aspirin and hot bath helped. And the cream stopped the grazes on my knees from stinging.'

'My poor little wounded soldier.' He sat down on a chair and crossed one leg over the other as Ruby sipped the hot soup. 'Thank you for the roses,' she said. 'They were beautiful.'

'My pleasure.' He tilted his head enquiringly. 'Do you want to talk about what happened tonight?'

Ruby put the mug on the bedside cupboard. 'I'll never forget that horrible man Charles.'

He frowned. 'How did you meet him?'

'He's a friend of Anna's and drove us to the Manor. At first he was all right, although very boring. Then he started to drink and wouldn't stop.'

'Drinking is no excuse for what he did.'

'He forced me to go outside, then tried to get me in his car. But I fought him off.'

'Good for you.'

'But if you hadn't come along I dread to think what would have happened.'

'This man should be reported.'

Ruby shook her head. 'But who would believe me? He threatened to say I was a working girl and touting for custom.'

Nick dug in his pocket for his cigarettes. 'Tell me about yourself. Have you family – sisters, brothers?'

'My mum and dad live on the Isle of Dogs. My older brother Pete – he died.' She stared down at the bedclothes. 'He was only twenty-one.'

Nick nodded thoughtfully and passed the lit cigarette from one hand to another. 'That's very tragic.'

'Life hasn't been quite the same since.'

'Was his death an accident?'

'It might have been.' Ruby looked into his steady gaze. 'You see, I found Pete one morning with a bottle of aspirin and some alcohol in his bedroom. We were told it was a combination of both that killed him. But the mysterious thing is, Pete wasn't a drinker and he never took drugs. He was a very clean-living person.'

Nick was silent, then leaned forward, resting his elbows on his knees. 'I was a kid when I lost both my parents in a flu epidemic. My late gran brought me up but I know what you mean about things never being the same. It did, however, make me realize you have to live for the day. I grew a tougher skin from then on.'

'Yes,' Ruby said eagerly, 'I do feel like that sometimes. But others—'

'You are resilient, Ruby,' he interrupted. 'Pete would be proud of you.'

'I hope so.' She lifted her chin and said tearfully, 'If he'd told me what was worrying him, I'm sure I could have helped him.'

Nick smiled regretfully. 'It's often painful to discover that we're not as important in someone's life as we imagine.'

Ruby wondered if he was thinking of someone special in his own life. But rather quickly he ground out his cigarette, stood up and walked to the window. He stood, staring out at the dark night. There were no curtains to draw, Ruby noticed. It was a rather cheerless flat. But it would only take a woman's touch to improve it.

Nick gestured to the hall. 'I'm sleeping in the far room. The bathroom is opposite. If you need me, just give a shout. I'm a very light sleeper.'

Ruby smiled. 'Thank you.'

'Sleep well,' he said and turned off the light, closing the door behind him.

Ruby stared into the darkness. Her whole body ached and her mind wouldn't stop ticking over. She thought about what Nick had told her about himself. She thought about Anna and what she would say in the morning when she heard about Charles. She also thought of Anna's beautiful dress which was now in the dustbin. And of her lost shoes somewhere in the grounds of the Manor.

This wasn't a good way to start her new career. Her last thought was of Nick's rescue. If it hadn't been for him, things tonight would have turned out very differently indeed.

Ruby was still asleep the next morning when Nick came in. She opened her painful eyes to see him standing beside the bed. He placed a cup of tea on the cupboard. 'Did you sleep well?'

'Y-yes, I think so. But I do feel a bit bruised.'

'I'm afraid you have an impressive black eye.'

She put her fingers to it. 'Ouch.'

'Before I take you to Anna's we'll put a cold compress on it to reduce the swelling. There's a toothbrush and clothes on the chair and a mac and jumper. They will be rather large on you, as will the bedroom mules, but as you'll only have to go from my car into Anna's, no one will see you.'

Ruby tried to smile but her face was very stiff. 'Thank you.'

'Give me five minutes to have my shave, then help yourself to the bathroom.'

She sat up after he'd gone and drank the hot tea. A pain went through her face. How many times had Charles hit her?

Slowly, aching all over, she climbed out of bed and looked in the small wall mirror. Her hair was full of tangles. She was white, except for the ugly black eye. Below the collar of the bathrobe was a purple-and-yellow bruise.

Her eyes filled with tears. But they soon dried, as it was very uncomfortable to cry.

'Ruby, where are your clothes?' Anna stood in the hall of 10 Dower Street, her bright red nails going up to her face.

Ruby choked back a sob. 'There's so much to tell you.'

Anna took her in her arms. 'Where have you been? Did you leave the Manor with some friends?'

'No, I would never have done that.'

'There, there, come along. We'll talk in the drawing room. You can sit here and tell me everything.'

Ruby dried her eyes on a handkerchief Anna gave her. Taking a deep breath, she began to explain about Charles. When she came to the part where Charles had almost strangled her, she pulled down the collar of the jumper. 'He did this.'

Anna gasped. 'You poor girl!'

'He was very drunk.'

'You must have been frightened.'

'I couldn't see you or Gwen anywhere. He said if I didn't do what he wanted he would tell everyone I was a tart touting for custom.' Ruby began to cry. When she finally drew a breath, she mumbled, 'If Nick hadn't come along, I think Charles would have raped me.'

'So you've been with Nick?'

'He put me up in his spare room.'

Anna stared at her, eventually nodding. 'I hope he behaved himself?'

'He was very kind,' Ruby said at once. 'And gave me this mac and jumper to wear as I'm afraid Charles ruined your dress.'

'I can't believe this of Charles,' Anna said, shaking her head.

'He said I was there to please him. He thought I was playing hard to get.'

'But that's ridiculous!' Anna exclaimed. 'Why would he think that?'

'He said some very nasty things about Gwen. I thought they might have fallen out and that was why he was drunk. Perhaps I should have left him earlier, but you said he was an important person.'

'He is. But that doesn't give him the right to attack you.' Anna gave a long sigh. 'My dear, I had no idea this was happening. I would have called the police if I'd known. Did Nick report Charles?'

'I didn't want him to. There would only have been a fuss. And no one would have believed me.'

'You poor, poor girl.' Anna sat closer, patting her arm. 'I'll get Janet to bathe your bruises.'

'Nick put some cold towels on my face. It is a little easier.'

'What Charles has done to you is inexcusable. I shouldn't have left you alone with the man. But he's never shown the slightest inclination to – well, be violent.'

'Not even with Gwen?'

'Especially not Gwen. She is very particular. Charles has never put a foot out of place. I can only think the drink got the better of him.'

'I'm sorry about your dress.'

'Think nothing of it.' Anna held her close again. 'We must be grateful for your timely escape. I'll have Janet put out some fresh clothes for you and make sure you are comfortable.'

Ruby listened to Anna's comforting words but fear began to creep in. Was Anna just being polite and pretending to believe her? He was, after all, someone she had known for some time.

Ruby looked away. 'After last night, I don't think I'm cut out for the agency.'

Anna took her hands. 'Don't let one ghastly experience upset you.'

'I might attract the wrong type.'

'What nonsense! Charles is to blame here. Not you. I'll make certain you have an apology.'

'I never want to see him again.'

'Listen, tomorrow you'll feel much better. Last night's incident was regrettable but not insurmountable. I assure you that you will recover given a few days of rest.'

Ruby sniffed. She still wasn't certain what Anna really thought of her. Charles could easily say that it was she, Ruby, who had led him on.

'Enough for now,' Anna said, helping her to her feet. 'Let's not think about last night. I want to see you looking ravishing again and dressed in something other than men's clothes.' She smiled encouragingly. 'We'll go upstairs and Janet will help you change. After which, I'll make up your face so well that no one will see the bruises. Then I'll join you in a light lunch. How does that sound?'

Ruby nodded. Anna was sympathetic and kind. But what was she really thinking?

Ruby was still very unsure of the situation as she waited for Janet to join her upstairs. Did Anna really still want her for the agency? Only time would tell, Ruby decided, putting her hand up to her sore face.

Ruby sighed and looked around. This room was so beautiful. Pale winter sunshine flooded in from the tall windows. The polished wood sparkled, the walls gleamed. Even the smell of the room was luxurious. She didn't want to forfeit all this because of one night's bad experience.

Well, not entirely bad, she corrected herself. She had made a friend in Nick. He had told her he would see her again if she wanted.

And yes, she wanted – very much indeed.

# Chapter Twelve

It was Christmas morning and Bernie lifted the PLA grain sack out of the car. He swung it as he sang an old Perry Como number, 'Frosty The Snowman', and opened the creaking ground-floor door to the stairs leading up to Kath's.

He was in a good mood, as the sack was stuffed with presents. He was wearing his best navy suit, white shirt and dark tie to celebrate the most unseasonal Christmas he could ever remember. Dry, mild and overcast, it was more like a spring day. As usual at Christmas, he'd put on a silly red hat and done his impression of Santa to all who cared to listen. His audience being the blokes at work, his landlord, his mates down the pub on Christmas Eve and now, hopefully, Kath and Ruby.

As he mounted the stairs to the bedsit, he thought guiltily what a dump this place was. Well, next year he was thinking of buying a new gaff. It wouldn't be luxury, not by a long shot. But he'd seen a two-up, two-down over Chrisp Street. And if Kath was up for it, he could do it up and see her all right. As for Ruby, she was Kath's best mate. He'd look out for her too if she let him. But Ruby had a mind of her own, always had had. Still, if Pete would want anything from him, it would be to watch over his kid sister. But Bernie knew he'd blown it with Ruby all those years ago. When they'd fooled around in the alley it had been the death knell to their friendship. What the hell had he been thinking? He knew he was to blame. He was just so nuts about her he couldn't stop himself. Ruby had been willing enough, but it had been her first time. He'd wanted to make her his steady girlfriend. But Pete would have blown his top if he'd found out. They'd both known that. So that was the end of a beautiful friendship, as the old song says.

Puffing, Bernie paused on the landing. The radio he'd given Kath for her birthday was playing loudly. He recognized the voice of Bing Crosby singing 'White Christmas' and his thoughts turned to Christmases of the past. Well, for him and Kath, they weren't Christmases, were they? They were bloody nightmares. Staying anywhere close to home was asking for trouble. Their dad was always on a bender in the holidays. Come to think of it, he was out of his skull the whole year round. Boozing began the moment he woke up to the time he blacked out. Woe betide anyone within arm's reach; man, woman or child. Their mum always ended up the worst off. No wonder she did a bunk. Well, wherever the old man had washed up these days, Bernie hoped he'd found his own private hell.

With a start, he came back to reality and the drab surroundings that were frighteningly like the slum they'd existed in as kids. Yeah, next on the list was the two-up, two-down terrace, ideal for himself and his sister.

He hiked the sack over his shoulder more firmly, cleared his throat and prepared to shout out his seasonal greetings.

Ruby and Kath were in the kitchen, or at least one of them was, Ruby thought as she recalled Janet's large workspace at Anna's. Fitted out with all the mod cons you could think of and a dining table large enough to seat six people easily. Leaving behind her the cramped and dingy bedsit was going to be no hardship at all in exchange for that gorgeous room at Anna's.

But what was Kath going to do, if she left? Kath probably wouldn't eat at all, knowing Kath. But it would be Bernie's responsibility then to see that she didn't starve, Ruby told herself firmly.

She took hold of the pan of boiled potatoes. No matter how much she tried to convince herself that she was entitled to a life of her own, she still had a guilty conscience.

'Tip the potatoes into the dish, there,' Kath said through the steam that billowed up into a thick cloud and soaked into the airless walls. 'It's cracked on the rim so be careful. I'll arrange the chicken bits. The carrots you sliced are cooked and on the table.'

Ruby nodded, trying to avoid both the steam and the sharp chip on the china. She couldn't afford to cut herself now. Her hands had to look perfectly manicured for her first assignment directly after New Year. Her black eye had soon faded with help from Anna's make-up. And much to Ruby's delight, she was going to be modelling the new type of figure-hugging 'roll-ons' in a small boutique. Ruby had been flattered too, by the fact that she had been chosen for her curves, whereas the other girls had been too thin.

'Practise over Christmas,' Anna had instructed her. 'When you pause, straighten your back and place your hands lightly on your hips. Put one leg across the other, foot turned out. This allows the buyers to see the garments at their best. And last of all, tuck in your tummy and chin up.'

Thinking of Anna's advice, Ruby straightened her spine as she tipped the steaming potatoes into the dish and carried them to the small table. Modelling wasn't quite so easy when you were cooking!

Three places were laid, since Bernie was joining them. She wasn't looking forward to seeing him; the atmosphere between her and Bernie was still tense. Besides, she wanted time with Kath to break her news.

'So what do you think of my dress?' Kath was standing beside her, looking intently into her face. 'Penny gave it to me. We're about the same size.'

Ruby came out of her reverie. Gone were Kath's worn apron and turban. Her long straight black hair was shining and pulled back behind her head. The deep blue colour of the dress suited her. 'It's very pretty.'

'Blue looked lovely on Penny. I'm not sure about me.'

Ruby smiled. She was pleased Kath had made a friend

in Penny Webber who was always talking about her apprenticeship as a dancer at the Windmill.

'Ruby?' Kath hesitated.

'What?'

'Nothing. It doesn't matter.'

'Have I forgotten something?' Ruby glanced at the table she had set: cold chicken slices so thin you could see the plate underneath. Slightly grey, boiled spuds and carrots she had sliced a little too thickly to compensate for the chicken. For decoration she had added holly, a few sprigs from the bush that grew in the lane by the Bricklayer's. The dinner was nothing by comparison to the celebratory meal Janet had begun planning for Anna's guests on Christmas Day. But next year, Ruby had decided, would be very different to this.

'No, the table looks very nice. So do you.'

As the weather was mild, Ruby had chosen a blouse and plain black skirt. She hadn't dolled herself up as it was only Bernie who was coming. She couldn't wait for the new year to arrive and the promise of all that glamour and luxury at Anna's.

The knock at the door along with Bernie's familiar, 'Yo-ho-ho, let me in. Santa's brought the gin!'

Ruby and Kath laughed. For all their ups and downs, Ruby knew this would be their last Christmas together and one she would always remember.

Kath delivered her news. Bernie stared in disbelief at his sister.

'You're kidding me!' he exclaimed as they sat together after dinner. 'You're going to quit your job?'

'I've given in me notice.'

'Without telling me?' He didn't know how to hide his hurt feelings. His little sister, chucking in her job, without even consulting him!

'I thought you'd be pleased.'

'Do you realize what you've done? You've chucked in a sound job.'

'I've been making tents and tarpaulins since I left school, Bernie.'

'My point exactly.' Bernie turned his gaze on Ruby. 'And what part do you play in all this? Have I got you to thank for putting me sister up to this?'

'Ruby don't know, either,' Kath interrupted. 'I haven't told no one.'

'So what is your master plan?' Bernie heard himself demand. 'You can't even manage on the money you earn at the factory.'

'I know,' Kath answered shortly. 'But all that's about to change.'

'And pigs might fly,' Bernie retorted, pushing his plate away. 'Listen, this is a major development, Kath. I'm your brother. We discuss things, right? Like we always do. I can't believe you've been so bloody stupid.'

Kath straightened her back. 'My friend Penny, who I met at Larry's party, works at the Windmill. She's got me a job as an usherette.'

Bernie almost choked. 'You must be crazy! You know what the Windmill is, don't you? The women all dance around starkers. And then get raided by the fuzz.'

'You're quite wrong, Bernie,' Kath argued. 'I've done my homework. They are completely law-abiding. That's how they've kept open all these years.'

Bernie felt the breath leave his body as he thought he must be going bonkers. This was his little sister and she was telling him she'd got a job in a glorified knocking shop.

'I've watched a performance and spoken to the girls,' Kath continued. 'My interview was successful and Penny has asked me to move in with her—' She stopped and looked apologetically at Ruby. 'Sorry, I didn't mean it all to come out like this. I wanted to talk to you first.'

Bernie stared disbelievingly at his sister, then looked at Ruby who for once was silent. For a Christmas Day this was turning out to be a right balls-up. And when he'd walked in here this morning, he was going to deliver his own news, about the Chrisp Street terrace and a fresh start for him and Kath in the new year. All the bells and whistles he could think of to put a smile on her face.

'Think again, Kath,' he tried reasonably. 'Ruby, tell her she can't. You're her best mate. Tell her she's flaming crackers!'

But Ruby just sat there, her mouth slightly open.

'I've made up me mind,' his sister told him. 'I don't want to stay at the factory till I'm old and grey.'

'The factory has been good to you, gel.'

'Yes, and I've been good to it. I've shed blood, sweat and tears on the assembly line and never had any thanks.'

Bernie shook his head wearily. 'Well, in that case, I'll leave you two to discuss your grand plans for the future. Me? I'm off to find one of me mates and try to celebrate the happy season.'

He stood up, reached for his coat and slung it round his shoulders. 'Merry Christmas to one and all,' he said as he opened the door and closed it with a bang.

He hurried down the stairs and out onto the street but, before he'd got very far, his steps slowed and he stood in the mild evening, looking up at the star-filled sky. As he stared at the brightness, his anger cooled. The air soothed his confused feelings and the silence of the Christmas night with not even the sound of a distant ship's hooter was a balm to the upheaval inside him.

He had to admit that he had been caught on the hop tonight. Kath had sprung one on him. But he should have held his tongue and thought it through before reading her the riot act. She was entitled to make a change in her life if that was what she wanted. He couldn't protect her forever. She was beginning to live her life. Who was he, Bernie-bloody-nobody, to throw a damper on it?

'Well, that was a turn-up for the books,' Ruby said after Bernie had gone.

'I'm sorry,' Kath said. 'I hope you don't mind.'

'You certainly gave us a Christmas surprise.'

'I hope I'm doing the right thing.'

Ruby smiled. 'An usherette's job sounds exciting to me.'

'Penny says it's a good way to get into the chorus line.'

'You've certainly got the legs for a dancer.' Ruby would never have guessed that Kath would be the one to move out of the bedsit first. And with a job lined up too.

'I was going to tell you after Christmas, but the wine must have gone to my head.'

'Well, I wish you luck. You deserve it.'

'I don't want us to split up.'

'We'll never do that.'

'We can meet at the El Cabala. I can tell you all about me exciting new job and not all the boring news from a factory.'

Ruby was very impressed. 'Are you nervous?'

'I'm dead scared really.'

Ruby giggled. 'It was a laugh seeing Bernie's face.'

'Yes,' Kath agreed, stifling a grin. 'He'll come round. He always does in the end. But Bernie's always been me big brother who knows best.'

'Like Pete was mine,' Ruby mused.

There was a long pause until Ruby asked, 'Have you got a nice uniform?'

Kath nodded. 'A white blouse and black skirt. Oh, and a little hat. But what about you? What will you do?'

Ruby took her opportunity. 'As a matter of fact I've got a bit of news of me own.'

Kath sat bolt upright. 'What!'

Ruby nodded to the bottle of gin on the table. 'Let's pour ourselves one. Then I'll tell you.'

'It's really Bernie's gin. And we've already drunk wine.'

'Who cares?' Ruby dismissed. 'This is a celebration.'

Kath gasped. 'You're not going to leave Larry's, are you?'

'Well, I might.'

'Now who's the dark horse!' Kath said excitedly.

Ruby sloshed large measures of gin into their glasses. Now she could tell Kath *everything* – well mostly everything – and not feel as if she was letting the side down.

This Christmas had turned out the very best – ever!

# Chapter Thirteen

'Almost New Year.' Nick raised his glass of champagne in a toast. 'I hope all your dreams come true, darling.'

Ruby blushed. 'Yours, too.'

'Oh, they have already,' he assured her.

Ruby tried to look away from his gaze but she couldn't. He was so handsome her tummy turned over. In his formal dinner suit, white shirt and dress tie, he seemed so assured, so familiar with everything around him, that she felt at ease in the restaurant too.

Everyone in Angelo's was excited, letting off crackers and counting the minutes to midnight. She'd never been to such a classy Italian restaurant before. The waiters had brought her flowers to begin with, another gift from Nick. Tiny red roses, his trademark gift. Then Nick had ordered the finest champagne. Which, Ruby was pleased to hear from the head waiter, left Dom Pérignon in the shade. That name still gave her the shivers. When Nick had called by the parlour to ask her out, she'd accepted. On one condition. They didn't go anywhere near the Manor!

Even though Ruby felt safe with Nick she still could not forget what had happened with Charles. So tonight Nick had brought her to Angelo's, a small restaurant in Camden where she'd enjoyed her first taste of real pasta. As they ate she was aware that Nick knew all the staff, calling them by their first names and asking them how their families were. He told her he used the restaurant quite often. He liked to think they served the best pasta in London.

Ruby had never before eaten food like this. Nick had even shown her how to eat spaghetti properly. They'd laughed as she tried to curl it over the fork without much success. He'd reached across, using his napkin to wipe the sauce from her chin. They'd spent most of the evening eating, laughing and talking. After the final dish of whipped Italian ice cream sprinkled with nuts and chocolate, it was now time to toast in the new year.

Nick stood up and amid the streamers cascading around them, he helped her to her feet. 'Happy New Year,' he whispered, sliding his arm around her waist.

'And to you,' she said, gazing into his eyes. She had bought a dress especially for the occasion, a deep blue taffeta and silk with an enormous underskirt. She'd coiled her hair up as Anna had shown her. Nick had threaded one of the small red roses over her ear. Her new high heels made her taller and were perfect for practising her model walk. As she'd entered the restaurant on Nick's arm, she'd remembered everything she'd learned: how to move, stand and sit gracefully. And now here was the result.

When the clock in the restaurant struck twelve everyone cheered. All the couples kissed one another. Some were Italian and shouted in their native tongue, as did the waiters. '*Felice anno nuovo!*'

Nick folded his arms around her and brought her close. Stroking a pink streamer away from her face he smiled. Then with gentle fingers he tilted up her chin. 'I made a mistake,' he said softly. 'Beautiful doesn't do you justice. You're exquisite.'

Before she could reply he kissed her. The noise around them was nothing to the pounding of her heart. Her arms slid around his neck. Every single part of her body tingled.

'Larry, I've got something to ask you. Well, two things actually,' Ruby said as Larry was counting the takings at the close of a dark January day.

It had been quiet at the parlour for the first two weeks of the year, but Larry as usual was full of gossip. Ruby had been trying for the last half-hour to gain his attention but he'd been eager to tell them about Stuart's audition for a television programme to be filmed at Elstree.

'The poor lamb has been in a real tizzy,' he recounted drily. 'Costing me a fortune in clothes and he might not even get the part.' Larry giggled affectionately.

'It's about this Friday,' Ruby tried once more.

'Going out on the town, are you?' Larry asked, licking his fingers as he counted the ten-bob notes from the till and stuffed them in his wallet. 'How much do you want to borrow?'

'It's not money.'

'Well, that's a first!'

Ruby hesitated. 'Could I have the day off? I expect it to be docked from my wages of course. But as we're quiet, I think Debbie will cope on her own.'

Larry closed the till, a frown pleating his bald forehead. His eyes looked large and concerned under his glasses. 'Are you going to say what you want the time off for? Or keep me in suspense?'

Ruby took a deep breath. Although she had thought this would be easy, it wasn't. 'I've signed a contract with a modelling agency.'

'A what?'

Ruby laughed nervously. 'Larry, I'm going to be a model.'

Larry took out a handkerchief from the top pocket of his fur-collared coat and mopped his forehead. Even though it was a gloomy, dark and cold night, Larry was sweating. 'Darling, forgive me, but do my ears deceive me?'

Ruby ran her fingers nervously down her white overall. 'It's always been my ambition to work in fashion. You know that, Larry.'

Larry just stared at her, looking up from under his thick lenses. 'Does this mean you're leaving us?'

'I'm sorry, Larry.'

'Don't I pay you enough?'

Ruby shook her head. 'It's not that. This is my big chance.' She found herself telling him about how she'd met Anna and her subsequent visit to Dower Street when Anna had offered her the job. 'I've already modelled underwear in my spare time. And on Friday I'm working at Steadman's near Regent Street. That's why I need Friday off.'

Larry sank down on the chair beside the counter. 'Oh Ruby, I'm heartbroken.'

'I'm so sorry, Larry, really I am. Especially as you took me on just after Pete's death and I was a mess. I owe you, I know. But this new job means an awful lot to me.'

Larry nodded slowly. 'I can see that.'

'I'll stay on till you find a replacement.'

'Stuart will be very upset.'

'As I'll be working and living in the West End, perhaps I could call by your flat sometime?'

Larry nodded, once again using his handkerchief. He looked up at her with lap-dog eyes. 'Have you told Debbie?'

'No, I wanted to tell you first.'

Larry slowly rose to his feet and took hold of her hands. 'You've become very dear to us. I shall let you go, angel, but you must promise to stay in touch.'

'What's going on? Who's to stay in touch?' a voice said and they turned to see Debbie with Delilah in her arms. The white poodle gave a little struggle, but Debbie held on tightly.

Larry sighed, letting go of Ruby. 'We are about to lose Ruby to the big wide world.'

'What!' Debbie looked at Ruby. 'Is this a joke?'

Ruby took another deep breath, suspecting that Debbie wouldn't be as eager as Larry to wish her well.

'As you can see I'm not laughing,' Larry said in a sober tone. 'But I want whatever makes you happy, Ruby.'

And with that he hugged her and wiped a tear from his eye.

After Larry had gone and Mrs Freeman had collected Delilah, Ruby sat down with Debbie to explain. She deliberately avoided any reference to Nick and her fated second visit to the Manor. Even so, she could see the envy in Debbie's pretty face as she described Anna and Dower Street and the modelling work she hoped to make her career.

'Is this the woman you met with when me and Rog took you to the Manor?' Debbie asked.

'Yes, Annabella Charnwood-Smythe.'

'Is she legit? You don't know with these type of places. It's said they're just a front to find girls.'

'Not in Anna's case,' Ruby replied evenly. 'I've already had one assignment. It was very enjoyable. Next, I'm modelling rainwear at Steadman's in the West End. That's why I asked Larry for the day off.'

'I'm amazed,' Debbie said sullenly, 'that you've kept this all secret.'

'I needed to be sure.'

Debbie stood up. 'Well then, I suppose congratulations are in order.'

'Thanks.'

'You'll have to starve yourself, you know. And with your appetite that will be a challenge.' It was Debbie's parting shot, but Ruby ignored the sarcasm. After all, Debbie needed to feel that she was still the centre of attention.

'You'll have to get Rog to bring you over,' Ruby invited.

But Debbie was already taking off her overall and shrugging into her winter coat. She grabbed her bag and checked the clock. 'Better be off. As you know, Rog is never late.'

Ruby sat alone in the parlour. She looked around at the mirrors, the many pairs of scissors and pictures on the walls of black and white poodles. She could smell the animal must and talcum powder mingling with the disinfectant. She had been very upset to see Larry distressed. As for Debbie, they had never really become close.

Would she regret leaving? she asked herself.

Not in a million years.

The changing room was filled with half-naked girls wearing only their bras and knickers. Ruby had already put on her raincoat, a rather dull brown belted affair, and was dodging the arms and legs as everyone tried to dress. Paula was sliding on a beautiful silvery cocktail dress with a low neckline and balloon skirt. 'Zip me up, will you?' she asked Ruby and turned her back.

'Hold still.' Ruby fought with the fasteners. 'There, that should do it.'

'How do I look?' Paula asked from under her pageboy-styled red hair.

'Dazzling.'

'Chin up, lovie,' Paula said, grinning through crimson lips, 'you'll have the glam stuff next time. Steadman's want to plug their wet-weather stock before the spring when the new designs arrive. Pull this one off and they'll ask for you again.'

Ruby smiled nervously. 'I don't mind.'

'Mr Steadman junior sits in the front row, a middle-aged man with a moustache, and squinting eyes. He'll have his personal assistant by him, a stuffed shirt, excuse the pun, who wears a grey pinstripe suit every day of the year. Give them your full attention as you come to the end of the catwalk.'

'I thought we are supposed to look up,' Ruby said, panic-stricken. How was she going to identify someone in the audience when she had been practising keeping her nose in the air?

'It's an old trick. If he likes you he'll ask for you again.'

Ruby swallowed, joining the line of girls waiting to leave the room and walk out to the shop floor where the audience was gathered. Some models were wearing expensive winter coats, but most rainwear like her. How was she to catch anyone's eyes dressed so frumpily? It was stock they needed to clear at reduced prices. She felt a bit tacky in comparison to the others. But she mustn't think like that. She was lucky to be here.

Just then the line moved up and Ruby felt slightly sick. She had forgotten everything she was supposed to do. Her pulse was banging hard at her temples and a slight veil of sweat had formed under her fringe. She smoothed it away quickly, hoping her severely drawn-back hairstyle didn't reveal how nervous she was feeling.

And then her turn came. The girl in front of her walked out and through the curtains. Ruby paused until a little woman in black called Elsie, who was the dresser, thrust her forward.

'Hurry up,' Elsie barked. 'And don't forget to show off the pockets.'

Ruby found herself walking along the catwalk. All around her there was a sea of faces. And they were staring at her. She tried to remember how to hold herself, pretending she had a pile of books on her head. She tucked in her tummy and gracefully performed the turn. Then, revolving her body, she pulled gently at the pockets in order to show off the garment to its best. Just as Elsie had reminded her. But there was so much to remember! Had she remembered it all?

As she turned on her heel, she remembered Paula's advice. Quickly she glanced down into the audience. All she could see was a blur. Her nerves were so bad, she was shaking from head to toe. Then she suddenly saw Mr Steadman junior, a middle-aged man with a moustache and narrow, close-set eyes. He was sitting with his personal assistant, a man in a pinstripe suit, just as Paula had described. It was only sheer fright that caused her to smile, her lips trembling as she did so.

Quickly she moved on, her head in the air and her bottom swaying under the mac. She reached the safety of the curtains and the tiny lady in black pulled them apart.

Ruby wanted to run out to the lavatory. Her tummy was in turmoil with fear. She had forgotten everything Anna had taught her. Had she managed to smile at Mr Steadman?

A hand gripped her arm. 'Good for you, ducks,' Elsie said in a sharp cockney accent. 'Now, don't rush off as I'd like to see you in something else. Go over to Margaret and ask for the cream linen with the semi-fitted bodice. We'll squeeze you in later at the beginning of day wear.'

Ruby nodded, forcing herself forward, searching for this Margaret, unable to believe she had been given approval, when she had felt such a disaster.

'You see, that smile did the trick,' Paula said as she drove them in her car to Dower Street.

'So I did smile?' asked Ruby, still in a daze.

'You certainly did. Making eye contact with the boss was a shrewd move,' Paula said with a cheeky grin.

'I was very nervous.'

'You didn't look it. And you were given another outfit to model. That doesn't often happen with first-timers.'

'I thought I was awful.'

'No, not at all.'

Ruby turned to look at Paula who had changed into a black-and-white two-piece suit. 'How did the silver dress go down?'

Paula just shrugged. 'Same as usual. I don't think I'll be working stores much longer.'

'Why not?' Ruby asked.

'The pay is a pittance. And with no extras.'

Ruby shook her head. 'I didn't know there were any.'

Paula turned slowly. 'How sweet. I suppose I used to be innocent too.' She sighed. 'A long time ago.'

Ruby sat thinking. What did Paula mean about extras? And even if there weren't any of these so-called extras, Ruby couldn't ever imagine wanting to turn down work. Once the fear had left her and she had paraded down that catwalk in the gorgeous cream dress to die for, she had been in her element. And eager to repeat her performance. There had been smiles and whispers from the audience. A little clap came at the end, which she hadn't expected at all. Even Elsie had nodded approvingly as she'd walked through the curtains for the second time.

# Chapter Fourteen

It was a freezing-cold February day when Bernie helped
Ruby to take her few possessions to Anna's. He was now
sitting opposite her in the El Cabala, a frown on his face.
'You sure you're doing the right thing?' he asked once
again. 'It's the big city you're moving to. And full of sharks.'

Ruby sighed, rolling her eyes. 'Anna isn't one of those.'

'Because she talks with a posh accent?'

'No, because she has offered me the chance I've always
wanted.'

'I wouldn't like to see you stitched up,' Bernie
complained. 'There's something about that woman I
don't trust.'

Ruby laughed. 'Anna was very polite to you.'

'Yes, because she has to be.'

'What do you mean by that?'

'Well, she's on to a good thing and wants to keep you
sweet.'

'Anna only wants what's best for me,' Ruby said,
becoming irritated by Bernie's unsupportive attitude.
When he'd moved Kath out a few weeks ago, he'd been

full of smiles and jokes, telling his sister he now realized she was making a change for the better.

'Just don't say I didn't warn you,' Bernie continued, pushing away his empty coffee cup. 'And when your life goes tits-up, don't blame me.'

Ruby wondered what it was that Bernie didn't like about Anna. When she had introduced them, he'd been cold and unfriendly from the off. Yet Anna, like the lady she was, had greeted him warmly. Much to Ruby's embarrassment Bernie had carried her luggage up the stairs to her room at 10 Dower Street without a word or a smile.

Anna had ignored his rudeness and suggested that, as Bernie had taken time off work, it was only fair that Ruby spend the rest of the morning with her friend.

That was how considerate Anna was, Ruby thought as she looked at Bernie's solemn face.

Now Ruby wished she had said goodbye to Bernie in Dower Street. His gloomy mood was getting her down.

'All I'm saying is,' Bernie persisted as they sat by the misted window overlooking the busy pavements of Oxford Street, 'you needn't have moved your clobber out so quick from the bedsit. I'm keeping the digs on for a bit. Just in case the usherette job don't work out for Kath.'

'I'm sure it will.' Ruby took a sip of the scalding coffee and smoothed her finger around the edge of the glass cup. 'But it is very lonely there without Kath.'

'Beats me why you girls had to leave.'

'Because everything changes, Bernie. And if you don't grab the chance when you can, you ain't living life.'

'Yeah, I know,' admitted Bernie dolefully.

'You've got dust on your coat from my stuff.' She reached out to brush the marks off.

Bernie looked into her eyes and smiled. 'Thanks.'

'You always were a messy bugger.'

'You ain't supposed to swear any more, remember? Or Madam will clip your ear.'

'Don't call Anna that.'

'Why not?' He laughed. 'It's a wonder she let the likes of me into that posh house of hers.'

'You're just in a bad mood.'

'She was flitting around you, almost up your a—'

'You didn't even bother to talk to her.'

'She put the mockers on me,' Bernie snorted, sitting back and smoothing his hand over his greasy black brilliantined hair, 'just with that snobby look of hers.'

Ruby laughed. 'It's what's called sophistication.'


Bernie dug out an empty packet of Woodbines from his pocket and threw it on the coffee table. Drumming his fingers, he squashed the paper with his palm. 'Well, this is it,' he said, heaving a long sigh. 'There's been enough goodbyes since Christmas and I hope this is the last of them.'

'It's not goodbye,' Ruby said evenly. 'We'll still see each other.'

'Don't suppose you want to go to Fortuno's this Saturday?'

She smiled. 'You should get yourself a decent girl and settle down.'

'I've been too busy doing what Pete would have wanted, trying to keep an eye on you.'

'Yes, and you have,' Ruby said, feeling a little sorry for Bernie now. He had done his best for her and Kath.

'I saw a book in one of them boxes of yours,' Bernie said suddenly. 'It brought back a lot of memories. Pete wrote in the bloody thing all the time.'

Ruby was surprised. 'How do you know that?'

'I was his mate, wasn't I? He'd say, "Oh, that's one for the diary," or, "That's one for posterity." I never understood the long words he used, but he did show it to me one day and I kidded him about it.'

'Did he let you read it?'

'No. He just had this big grin on his face. He said he'd sell his memoirs to the newspapers one day.'

'I thought I was the only one who knew about the diary,' Ruby said, a little upset. 'I found it in his wardrobe.'

'Did you read it?' Bernie asked curiously.

'Yes, there was a girl in it called Joanie,' Ruby explained. 'Do you recognize the name?'

Bernie thought for a moment then shook his head. 'Haven't the foggiest.'

'I was a bit upset,' Ruby admitted. 'If he had a special girlfriend, why wouldn't he have told me?'

'Just goes to show,' Bernie said, 'you was his sister and me his best mate and neither of us knew about Joanie.' There was a drawn-out silence before he added, 'Dunno if she had anything to do with it, but Pete was acting strange towards the end.'

'How do you mean?'

'He was quiet one minute, then the next he was all over the place. He'd say that when he was in the money he was gonna get away from all this. I never knew how to take him. He used to love the East End once. Before he moved up to the city and worked for the rich guy. After that, all we shared was small talk.'

'He thought you was jealous, probably,' Ruby accused.

'Maybe I was,' Bernie admitted, shifting on the chair. 'But he started mixing with a different set, not my type at all.'

'What sort of types?'

'Foreigners by the looks of 'em.'

'What didn't you like about them?'

Bernie shrugged. 'Dunno. It's me sixth sense, I expect.'

'Didn't know you had one except when it comes to chasing women.'

'What I mean is, I never saw Pete with any of our old crowd. One night, when we was back on the island and drinking at the Quarry, I said to Pete, why did he want to meet there? I like the pub, mind, it's our old turf. But Pete mixed in different circles and I had accepted that. So this night he said, "You've been a good mate but I may have to go away for a while. So I want you to watch out for Ruby." I asked where was he going. "Spain," he said. And that was it.'

'Did you ask why he was going to go to Spain?'

Bernie nodded. 'Said he needed the sunshine.'

'So it was a holiday?'

'What else could it be?'

'Why didn't you tell me this before?' Ruby was annoyed with Bernie for having kept this to himself. Pete had never said anything about Spain to her. As far as she knew Pete had never been out of the country.

'Because the minute I tried to talk to you about Pete, you got miffed. Like that night at Fortuno's. So I just shut up.'

'Yes, but this is important.'

'Because he told me and not you?'

'No,' she replied impatiently. 'Because someone going on holiday wouldn't want to top himself.'

Bernie was silent, then nodded. 'You've got a point there.'

Ruby thought about the empty bottle she had found beside Pete and the aspirins spilled on the bedcover. 'The coroner said he had been drinking and as a result took too many aspirin. That it was an accident.'

Bernie sighed. 'Yes, but Pete wasn't a boozer, as we both know. We never drank more than a couple of beers together.'

Ruby frowned, leaning her elbows on the table and rubbing her aching temples with her fingers. Was what Bernie told her true? And if so, what did the information mean? All these new questions seemed to gather inside her brain and fill it so much it hurt. Bernie had never expressed his doubts before. No one had about Pete or the last months of his life, which to her hadn't seemed much different to normal. He had a good job with a rich boss and was away a lot. He came home to the prefab odd weekends, but he never was anything other than happy. Or so she thought.

'Did you tell the police all this?' Ruby asked, looking up sharply.

'Course I did.'

'So you told them and not me?'

'They were a bloody sight easier to talk to.'

'I'm going back to Anna's,' Ruby said, getting to her feet. 'Thanks for the coffee.'

'What's all the rush?'

'There has to be something in Pete's diary that I'm missing.'

'Like what?' Bernie demanded.

'Don't know. But you can come with me if you like. We could look at it together in my room.'

'Not on your nelly. Not with Madam giving me the evil eye.'

'Then I'll fetch it and we'll go back to the bedsit to read it.'

Bernie frowned. 'Still feel it's a liberty,' he muttered, but all the same he paid for the coffee and followed her outside onto the icy street.

'It's taters in here. I'll bung a bob in the meter.' Bernie dug in his pocket for a shilling and returned to the table where Ruby was sitting, shivering.

'There might be a bit of paraffin left in the heater,' Ruby said hopefully.

Bernie lit the ancient appliance and slowly the oily wick flickered and flared into action. 'What does it say?' he asked as he looked over her shoulder.

'Come and read for yourself.'

He slumped down on the chair, rubbing his hands for warmth. 'A diary's supposed to be private.'

'How else are we going to find out about Pete?'

Bernie stared at the diary.

'For goodness' sake, it ain't going to bite you.' Ruby opened the pages of the well-thumbed exercise book. He saw Pete's handwriting, neat and bold with commas and full stops into the bargain. That was Pete all over. He was the clever one, always quoting bits from books and coming out with surprising facts.

'Read it,' Ruby said, her elbows on the table and her eyes fixed on his face. 'I want to hear what his voice sounds like.'

He stared into her clear hazel eyes. 'Hey, come on, gel, you're giving me the creeps.'

'Go on, just try.'

Bernie heaved in a breath. He knew he was going to do what she asked. But it was unnerving. '"Jan 4 1950. Today R. Westminster, then Harrow. Will call Joanie later."'

'So who do you think Joanie is?' Ruby said.

Bernie shrugged. 'Never had the pleasure.'

'Turn over. She's mentioned again.'

'"Collect suit a.m. Barber's. Full works this time. Joanie likes me smooth as a baby's bottom."' Bernie chuckled. 'Christ, Pete must have fancied her something rotten.'

'But who is she?'

'Does it matter?'

'Yes, course it does,' Ruby insisted. 'She might be able to tell us something.'

'Does it say any more about her?'

'Read for yourself.'

'"Mr R to the House of Commons today. Collect clients from Heathrow. Tight bastards. No tips." And this, by a WC, "If you're going through hell, keep going." What did he mean by that?'

'Don't know.'

Bernie didn't want to read any more. It was depressing. 'We shouldn't be doing this.'

'What do you suggest, then?'

'Let sleeping dogs lie.'

'Bernie, answer me straight,' Ruby demanded, giving him a stern look, 'does this sound like your best friend and my brother talking? Or rather, writing? Who is this Joanie he never told us about?'

'Dunno.'

Ruby gave out a long sigh. 'I don't really blame him for not telling me about her. I think he wanted to make certain Joanie was his girl. One thing I do know, he was happy. He had a smile on his face as wide as Greenwich Reach. So why would he do something silly like taking all them aspirin?'

'What if this Joanie gave him the elbow?' Bernie suggested. 'So he got down in the doldrums and wrote that bit about going through hell.'

'Then he went drinking and bought the pills,' Ruby continued. 'But he never meant to take so many. Just enough to take the edge off his heartache.'

'Aspirin don't cure heartache.'

'No, course not. But it was just a gesture.'

'True. This Joanie could have had him by the—' Bernie corrected himself. 'Specially if he'd fallen hard.'

'Oh, why didn't he tell me?' Ruby wailed miserably.

'Because you're all screwed up when you're ditched,' Bernie said knowingly. 'Trust me. I've had a few rejections in my time. And then you find out there's another face in the frame. You ain't sensible about it. You're either bloody mad, or depressed. Which, it turns out, he was.'

Ruby nodded slowly. 'Poor Pete. Joanie must have hurt him badly.'

Bernie sighed. 'Don't suppose we'll ever know the half of it.'

And don't want to, Bernie thought to himself. In his own private opinion, Pete was too canny to go in for all that female drama. Rather, he'd moved up in the world, obsessed with making it big, and mixing with a dodgy crowd, Arabs, Russians and Chinese. Mr R kept him busy earning his wedge. And though Pete had only ever hinted at it, never actually said, there were a few A listers too from closer to home. Every one of them with fingers in Mr R's dodgy pie. As for being in love with this Joanie, Bernie couldn't see that at all. It was the old bees and honey Pete lusted after.

'So now we know,' Bernie said, hoping to put an end to further speculation. 'You can put the book back.'

But Ruby was shaking her head. 'No, it's all I've got of his.'

'Yeah, but Pete never meant it to be read.'

'Not when he was alive, no.'

'You're too hung up on this Joanie.'

'So what if I am?' Ruby argued. 'She was a big part of his life that he kept secret.'

Bernie rolled his eyes. 'Look, Pete was a good-looking bloke. He mixed with the toffs. He was bound to have a girl. And this girl, well, she might not have been your sort.'

'What do you mean by that?'

'I mean, there are chicks and chicks. Birds you take home to meet the family and others you don't. So let's say they had a tiff. Maybe they'd had a few. We don't know why, but it's enough to send Pete on a bender. So he takes an aspirin for his hangover – first thing you bung down your throat when your head's splitting. But your brother is hungover and can't get rid of this damn pain, so he takes more. And what happens? He's topped himself. The poor bugger don't know it, but he has. This much we've worked out. Reading through this book ain't gonna reverse the fact that Pete didn't want you or me to know what he was doing. If he'd wanted to tell you about Joanie, he would have, right? So put the book back where you found it, Ruby. Where Pete meant it to be.'

Ruby glared at him. 'How can I? I want to know who she is.' Tears glistened in her eyes and Bernie knew he wasn't going to get through to her today. He'd have to leave it for now. Hope she'd forget.

'All right, all right,' he conceded. 'What do you want me to do?'

Ruby sniffed back her tears. 'Just ask around, that's all. See if any of his old mates knew anything. Knew *her*.'

Bernie nodded, although Pete didn't have any old mates, did he? He was even thinking of changing his name, hated any reminder of who he'd once been. He'd moved on, shunned his roots. And had been in the process of shunning me, Bernie thought morosely, except I wouldn't let go.

Ruby reached out and touched his hand. 'Thanks, Bernie.'

'Don't get excited. I dunno where half of our old pals are.'

'No, but you might turn up something.'

'I'll do me best.'

'Look, if you want to drive me back to Anna's, we could have a drink on the way.' She smiled and looked into his eyes in the way that she knew melted his heart. 'It would be nice. Like old times.'

It would be, he thought, if she wanted to be with him for the right reasons. His reasons. But he knew better than to hope for a miracle. He knew she was seeing a bloke, not just seeing, but crazy over, so Kath had told him. And he knew who he was. The geezer from Fortuno's who'd fronted up to him that night. Well, what was he going to do about it? he'd asked himself a hundred times. Sod all, that was what. It was her choice, not his.

While she put the diary back in her bag, Bernie turned off the heater. As he did so, he had a gut feeling he'd never set foot in here again. As soon as he was shot of the bedsit, he was going for that terrace. A little house with a small garden. Quiet families either side who didn't live up the pub and create bedlam every Saturday night.

There was another life out there for him. A girl he had to find, a family to rear. A wife and kids he could call his own. A family who would love him and stick by him. Just as he had loved and stuck by Ruby.

Like Ruby had said, it was time to make changes.

# Chapter Fifteen

Ruby left the small shop in Frazer Street, pleased to see the Buick waiting for her on the other side of the road. She was wearing a light wool suit of black and white, black patent high heels and a small black hat that she had been given as a perk by the shop manageress. For March, it was still chilly but the freeze was over and the two-piece suit was summer weight. She would soon be in the warmth of the Buick and sitting next to Nick.

Her pulse raced at the thought of seeing him. They had been together almost every Sunday since she'd moved to Anna's and some weekday nights too. Anna had not commented on this, although Ruby knew that she had been observed climbing into Nick's car.

'Hello, gorgeous,' he said and kissed her when she got in beside him. 'Where to?'

She grinned. 'Anywhere so long as it's not the Manor.'

He jerked an eyebrow. 'The Jester?'

'Yes, I like it there.'

'That's settled then.' He leaned across and kissed her again. 'Sit back and relax. My, you do smell good.'

'It's called Forbidden. Anna gave it to me.'

'And are you?'

She blushed. 'Am I what?'

'Forbidden to see me?'

'Of course not,' she said, knowing this was a small lie.

'Tell me what you did today,' he said as they drove. 'How many dresses you wore. And just how much the customers liked you.'

Ruby laughed. 'How do you know they liked me?'

'Anyone who didn't would be out of their minds.'

'You should come to one of the shows and see for yourself.'

'Maybe I will.'

Ruby told him about her day. 'Rule number one is to please the customers,' she explained as though she'd been a model for years. 'The next is to show off the garment, indicating the best features. For instance, a roll-neck collar, side pockets or flared skirt. Needless to say the way we walk is important, as if we had a book or two balanced on our heads. My favourite designer is Norman Hartnell who created Queen Elizabeth's wedding gown.'

Nick turned slightly towards her. 'I'm thinking of going into the fashion business myself. The rag trade is the one area I've never invested in.' A small smile touched his lips. 'And you'd be my perfect model.'

Ruby blushed. 'And I'd love to be your model.' Nick always said something to make her feel wonderful.

When they arrived at his club, Nick parked the car and helped her out. 'Hungry?'

'Very!'

'That's what I like about you, Ruby.'

'What?' she asked as they walked hand in hand towards the stately building in the heart of London's West End.

'You'll try anything once. You're a very good sport.'

'My brother used to tell me how important new experiences were.'

'Your brother was right.'

Ruby thought of how proud Pete would be if he could see her now. And wouldn't any girl want to visit such an important place? The Jester Club was very old, Nick had told her. He hadn't yet taken her to the casino on the top floor but they had visited the bar and restaurant. On the last occasion she had eaten her first Dover sole. The fish had been mouth-watering as was the fragrant wine that Nick chose to go with it.

Nick was always the perfect gentleman; they would end the evening at his flat and enjoy home-brewed coffee. The flat had seemed cold and empty at first, but she had soon brightened the place up. She had arranged vases full of freshly cut flowers and scattered brightly coloured cushions about the place. They kissed and cuddled on the sofa and she knew that one day he would want her to sleep with him. What would she do then? She didn't want to get pregnant.

Nick's voice broke into her thoughts as they stood at the bar. 'Would you like a Tom Collins?'

She nodded. 'Yes, please.'

Soon a tall glass was placed before her, this cocktail was now her favourite drink: a blend of gin, lemon, sugar and soda mixed with ice, a cherry on a stick and little paper umbrella.

'You look very lovely tonight,' Nick told her as they sat in the lounge before dinner.

Ruby thought Nick was the most handsome of all the men in the room. He wore an elegant dark grey suit tonight and his brown hair was trimmed short above his white shirt collar. She was so proud to be with him.

She sipped her cocktail and crossed her legs elegantly. A few men glanced her way, but she hardly took notice.

Who, a year ago, Ruby thought to herself, would ever have guessed she would be dining out in a place like the Jester Club with a man like Nick Brandon?

It was early in April and Ruby was excited to be working with Paula again at Steadman's. Despite Paula's intention to give up the stores, she had changed her mind. In part, Ruby suspected, because Steadman's were Anna's top clients.

Ruby liked Paula and, since they often worked together, they had become close of late. Now that the evenings were getting lighter they would explore the city: Bond Street, Covent Garden, and eat al fresco at the Dorchester. At lunchtimes, they would enjoy succulent olives with a glass of red wine. Very often, when the weather was fine, they would walk down to the Serpentine to watch the swimmers brave the cold water. Ruby always felt sophisticated and worldly in Paula's company.

As Ruby gazed into the floor-length mirror of the dressing room, she almost had to pinch herself. Was this reflection really her? A dazzlingly beautiful young woman with spun-gold hair that the stylist had set in a loose bob style, braiding her crown with lemon rosebuds. The pale lilac bridesmaid's gown was full-skirted and the capped sleeves were embroidered to match the braid on her bodice.

'You look enchanting,' Paula told her, attending to the last details of her satin-silk wedding gown with sheer straps attached to a bodice that showed off Paula's bust to its best under a sweetheart neckline. Ruby liked the simple design. And most stunning of all was the discreet white veil that flowed down to Paula's shoulders, inset with tiny white pearls.

Paula turned briefly to smile at her. 'Ready?'

Ruby nodded, feeling very nervous.

They passed the girls just coming off the catwalk. A combined gasp of surprise came from the audience as a shower of confetti rained down from above. The wedding march boomed out from the public address system and everyone rose to their feet. Even the shop assistants had been allowed to watch the show.

Ruby heard the applause as they began their entrance. It seemed much louder than usual.

Her heart raced as she and Paula paused at the end of the long plinth. Mr Steadman had told them that many of the customers were brides-to-be. There was a reception afterwards downstairs where orders would be taken. It rested with her and Paula to show off these gowns to their best, encouraging the young women to buy their wedding dresses from Steadman's.

Suddenly, as Ruby gazed into the sea of faces, she recognized two in particular. Debbie and Rog were staring up at her, wide-eyed.

Debbie waved her glove. 'See you after,' she mouthed as Rog raised his hands in applause.

Ruby beamed them a smile. She felt so very proud.

The show was over and Ruby changed into her own clothes.

'See you outside,' called Paula, who was being assisted by Elsie in removing the pins that had secured the wedding dress and veil in place.

Ruby nodded and made her exit. She knew Rog and Debbie would be waiting for her. After the rapturous applause from the audience she was eager to hear their remarks.

Debbie hugged her. 'You looked amazing, Ruby.'

'Thank you.'

'You should have worn the wedding gown, not the other girl,' Rog said, giving her a sloppy kiss on her cheek. 'You'd make a much prettier bride than the redhead.'

'How did you come to be here?' Ruby asked.

'Well, Steadman's is well known for its bridal wear,' Debbie said shyly, looking up at Rog.

'Yes, and the brochure said that the Charnwood-Smythe Agency was modelling the gowns. So we hoped you might be here.'

'And there is another very special personal reason,' Rog added as he squeezed Debbie's waist.

Debbie blushed, looking under her eyes. 'We're getting married in August.'

'Oh, that's wonderful!' Ruby kissed her friend's cheek. 'Congratulations.'

'I'm going to order a bridal gown just like the one I saw here today. It's very expensive according to the brochure prices. But Rog insists I have it.'

'Anything for my princess,' Rog said, giving Ruby one of his winks.

'That's enough, Rog! Stop teasing the girl,' Debbie said, pulling his sleeve.

'Are you still going to work at the parlour?' Ruby asked.

'Yes, but only until we start a family.'

'That won't take long,' Rog laughed. 'So you'd better give in your notice now.'

'Shut up, Rog,' Debbie giggled. 'Ruby, are you enjoying your new job?'

'Very much.'

'I love your outfit too,' Debbie said as she studied Ruby's fashionable plum-coloured skirt and white cotton cardigan. 'You look amazing. I see you haven't put on too much weight.'

'Nor have you,' Ruby said a little sharply, thinking that Debbie had put on weight. But in all the wrong places.

'Larry and Stuart are having another party,' Debbie told her then. 'They said to tell you if I saw you that you're invited. And to bring Kath too.' Debbie pulled a face. 'I suppose you still see her?'

'Yes. She's working at the Windmill.'

'The Windmill?' Rog repeated, unable to hide his surprise.

'She's an usherette,' Ruby said proudly, 'and training for the chorus line.'

'But don't those girls dance naked?' Debbie gasped, hand over her mouth.

'Too right, not a stitch, just feathers,' Rog said, then realizing his mistake added quickly, 'Not that I would know, of course.'

'Then how do you know?' Debbie asked suspiciously.

'Only from some of my mates at work,' Rog mumbled as a scarlet flush filled his face.

'So you discuss naked girls, do you?' Debbie demanded.

'No, princess, why would I do that, when I've got you?'

'I'm sorry, but I have to go.' Ruby was relieved to see Paula coming out of the dressing room. 'It was nice to see you both. Good luck with the wedding gown.'

'Are you coming to Larry's party?' Debbie called after her.

'When is it?'

'The third Saturday in May. Can I tell Larry and Stuart you'll be there?'

'I'll do my best.'

'You'd better,' shouted Rog.

'Can we leave quickly?' Ruby whispered as she joined Paula.

'What's all the rush? Mr Steadman has invited us to the reception.'

'I don't want to get involved with that couple over there.'

Paula grinned. 'Not surprised. The creep was giving me the eye the whole show. And anyway, listening to all those brides-to-be would be very boring indeed.'

Ruby nodded. Marriage was not what she wanted just yet. But one day, with the right man, she would be proud to wear a diamond on her finger.

'Was Mr Steadman satisfied?' Anna enquired as they walked in the front door of 10 Dower Street.

'Elated,' Paula replied with a smile. 'He said it was the best show Steadman's had ever put on.'

'Do you know how many orders were taken?' Anna asked, looking immaculate in a silver-grey suit and white silk blouse.

'No, I'm afraid not. But I think there will be quite a few.'

'I'll find out when he telephones. Ruby, did you enjoy your first bridal show?'

'It was wonderful.' Ruby wished she had been with Paula in the dressing room when Mr Steadman had praised the models.

'Excellent.' Anna looked satisfied. 'This evening I'm having drinks in the lounge. A few clients are stopping by and I'd like you to join us.'

'We'll be there,' Paula said, glancing quickly at Ruby. 'But we need to powder our noses first.'

'Of course.' Anna smiled, running the palm of her hand down Ruby's arm. 'I'll see you about seven.'

When they reached the next floor and Ruby's room, Ruby at last found the courage to ask Paula about the things she had on her mind. 'Paula, could I ask you something?' Ruby said, blushing.

'What is it?'

'Will you come in for a moment?'

Paula smiled. 'Have you any cigarettes or alcohol?'

'No, I don't smoke. And no, I've nothing to drink.'

'I'll be back in a moment.'

Ruby left the door open and went to the sash window, lifting it to gaze down on Dower Street. She should have bought cigarettes and perhaps some gin. But other than Bernie, no one had visited her here.

She slipped off her jacket and kicked off her shoes. It was late afternoon and the pavement was busy with commuters. Early-season tourists and vehicles made their way to and from the West End. Ruby thought how she loved this room and everything about it. Even though she spent a lot of her time at Nick's, this was her sanctuary.

'Addictive, isn't it?' Paula stood beside her, a long, slim cigarette holder between her two fingers, as she too gazed down on the street. Her red hair was now loosened and fell to her shoulders and she wore a black silk robe and mules. A bottle of whisky and two glasses stood on the coffee table next to a silver cigarette box.

'Do you mean London?' Ruby asked, walking barefoot to the sofa.

'No, I mean this life of luxury.' Without asking Ruby if she wanted a drink Paula poured two measures and handed a tumbler to Ruby. 'Chin-chin!'

Ruby didn't like the smell of the whisky, but she took a small sip. Wrinkling her nose, she thought it tasted like syrup of figs.

'You'll acquire the taste,' Paula assured her, curling herself into the cushions of the armchair. Inhaling the smoke, she took it deeply into her lungs and closed her eyes. 'You have to admit, we work hard so we must play hard.'

'How long have you worked for the agency?' Ruby asked curiously, feeling the warmth of the alcohol soothe her stomach.

'Eight years. Since I was nineteen.'

'The same age as me.'

'Yes, and as green as you.' Paula laughed. 'We all have to grow up in the end.'

Ruby felt her cheeks grow hot. 'That's what I wanted to ask you about.'

'Feel free.' Paula drank heartily.

'It's about, well – about—'

'Men?' Paula said for her, crooking a well-defined eyebrow.

'Yes, how did you guess?'

Paula shrugged. 'Answer me honestly. Did Charles have you?'

Ruby was so startled her jaw dropped open. 'How do you know about Charles?'

'How do you think, my dear? This is a house of women.

News travels fast. Besides, dear Gwen wasn't slow to add her version of things. Which, I have to say, is quite different to yours.'

'Gwen? But I thought—'

'Listen,' Paula said softly, leaning forward and refilling her glass. 'You're new here and you love it, don't you? Just as I did. But there will come a time when you wake up to reality. Charles is a drunk. A wealthy drunk, which is why Anna tolerates him. And why Gwen continues to insist he's the perfect gentleman. When, in fact, he's quite the monster. Unfortunately, he took a liking to you. Hence my question, were you raped?'

Ruby went cold from head to foot. She felt sick with shame. Everyone seemed to know what happened with Charles.

'Don't blame Anna,' Paula said as if reading her mind. 'We are her girls and she takes care of us. Charles isn't on the scene now, so be grateful to her for that. And, if you are pregnant, Anna will take steps to end it.'

'But I'm not,' Ruby insisted. 'He didn't – I wasn't—'

'Good enough,' Paula interrupted with a dismissive wave. 'You certainly don't look it. But an accident can happen. And Anna wouldn't want you to go to just anyone, if you see what I mean.'

Ruby looked blankly at Paula. 'No, I don't really.'

Paula smoked and drank, then said softly, 'The agency has a doctor. He's discreet and he's safe. It's not just pregnancy a girl has to guard against. It's other things too. Now do you understand?'

It took a while before Ruby did, then she too reached for her glass. The whisky burned her throat, and when she had finished her drink, Paula refilled her glass.

'So, if you're not pregnant, then what is it?' Paula continued, lighting another cigarette.

'It's personal,' Ruby said hesitantly, 'nothing to do with the agency.'

'*Everything* is to do with the agency,' Paula corrected her. 'This is a demanding business you're in and owns you lock, stock and barrel. Now tell me, you're going out with Nick Brandon, aren't you?'

Ruby knew she couldn't hide the truth from Paula, who was looking steadily into her eyes as if sucking out all her most intimate thoughts.

'And he wants you to sleep with him,' Paula suggested.

Ruby looked away. 'He hasn't actually asked me—'

'But he will,' Paula broke in, flicking her ash into the square art deco ashtray beside the bottle of whisky. 'Have you had an affair with a man before?'

Ruby thought of the night Bernie had taken her virginity. Could that be counted as an affair? 'I did once,' Ruby admitted. 'Years ago, but we weren't together for very long.'

'And you didn't take any precautions?'

'No.'

'But you want to now?'

Ruby nodded hesitantly. 'Yes, I suppose so.'

'Come on, drink up.' Paula waved her hand at the whisky. 'Being inexperienced is nothing to be ashamed of. And you're sensible in thinking ahead, especially as you're involved with – shall we say, an older man.'

Ruby listened with growing dismay as Paula explained how to wash out her vagina with a douche and a mixture of vinegar and water, accompanied by a kind of jelly or paste that would act as an agent of death to the male sperm. Or there was, of course, the ring inserted inside a woman by the agency doctor which caused only moderate pain, yet was considered to be the most effective.

But at the end of it all, Ruby decided this wasn't for her. Not just yet, anyway.

# Chapter Sixteen

Kath hugged Ruby close. The last time they'd met at the Frith Street coffee house, Ruby hadn't stopped talking. Her cheeks had been pink and her eyes bright. But today she looked tired and was unusually quiet. 'Are you all right?'

'Yes, I'm fine,' Ruby assured her. 'Where shall we sit?'

'Over here. It's nice and cosy.'

They made themselves comfortable on the plastic chairs and Kath took out her cigarettes. She lit one as the waitress took their order of coffees and macaroons. When they were alone, Kath studied Ruby's distracted expression. 'I'm giving these up tomorrow.'

'Why's that?'

'I need all me breath for dancing.' They laughed but Kath's forehead drew into a frown as Ruby distractedly undid the buttons of her coat.

'Did you get into the chorus line, then?'

'Yes, but it's hard work. I've another month of selling ice creams and cigarettes. Meanwhile, I practise after my shifts.'

'Do you wear any clothes?'

Kath grinned. 'Enough to be respectable.'

Ruby idly turned the spoon in her coffee. 'Do you like living with Penny?'

'Yes, but I miss the long chats you and me used to have. Penny's schedule is very strict. She has to go to bed and rest as soon as she comes in. Working as a dancer is much harder than you would think.'

'What are the Windmill girls like?'

'They're very talented and friendly. Sometimes I can't believe how lucky I am. And it all started through you taking me to Larry's party where I met Penny.'

'Talking of parties, Larry's having another one on the third Saturday of May. You're invited of course.'

'Saturday?' Kath repeated doubtfully. 'I'd love to, but I can't take time off.'

'Not even one night?'

'It would be very difficult.'

Kath thanked the waitress who brought them their order. But she saw Ruby wasn't interested. Her attention was on her wristwatch.

'Do you have to be somewhere?' Kath asked curiously.

'I've got an appointment for seven o'clock.'

'Is it close by?'

'Not far, the Strand.'

'Are you going to a modelling job?' Kath sipped her coffee. Ruby was just staring at hers.

'No. Something else.'

Kath waited, watching Ruby's lowered eyes. 'You're being very mysterious.'

Ruby at last looked up. 'I'm meeting an agency client. An American.'

'I thought you was a model,' Kath said in surprise.

'I am. But we have to act as escorts sometimes. It's written in our contracts.'

'So what's this American like?'

Ruby shrugged. 'Don't know yet. He was supposed to turn up at one of Anna's cocktail parties last week. But his plane was delayed.'

'He's rich, then?'

'Yes. And Paula says you can earn good money in tips, or extras like gifts.'

'Who's Paula?'

'She's a model and is staying at Anna's too.' Ruby looked at her watch again.

Kath put out her cigarette. 'Well, you seem to know what you're doing.'

'Course I do. Anyway, it's no different to having men watching you dance nearly naked on the stage.'

Kath was startled by Ruby's tone. 'Yes, but I won't be going out with any of the men.'

'You never know. You might.'

'We aren't allowed to fraternize with the customers.'

'But you can have boyfriends?'

Kath nodded.

'Well then,' said Ruby defiantly and, checking her watch once more, added abruptly, 'I really will have to go.'

The silence that followed was unnerving. Kath knew Ruby wanted to end this conversation. 'Watch out for yourself,' Kath said as Ruby stood up. 'Don't lose touch. I'm always here for you. Bernie is too. We're your family. The ones who love you the most. All you've got to do is give us the nudge, right?'

But Ruby only smiled in that way she had when she wasn't letting anyone into her true thoughts.

Ruby was nervous. She was waiting in the stylish art deco lobby of the Strand Palace Hotel where Anna had told her she was to meet her client. Anna had said he was a wealthy Texan and was coming to England for a month's holiday.

It was the middle of April and the hotel was busy with tourists, Ruby noticed. All the porters dashing here and there, carrying expensive-looking luggage. Though the hotel wasn't as large or famous as the Dorchester, where she and Paula had lunched, Ruby found this smaller hotel appealing. The lights and furnishings were all original features, she guessed, as she sat on one of the lobby chairs, studying the decor. The Strand Palace, so Anna had told her, had been a favourite haunt of the Americans during the war. The only American she had met before, she reflected, was Taylor. When she thought of him, she remembered Charles and shuddered.

Ruby glanced at the big rectangular clock on the wall above the reception desk. It was twenty past seven. She'd asked the taxi driver to hurry, as Anna had told her not to keep her Mr Marlon waiting. She'd arrived early, just to be sure.

But the looks the reception staff were giving her were embarrassing. She had put on a black cocktail gown with a low neckline, pearl necklace and matching earrings especially for this occasion. But now she felt conspicuous sitting there all alone.

Just then, a tall, middle-aged man wearing boots under a loud blue suit with fringed sleeves, and a huge white hat, came hurrying from the lounge bar.

Ruby froze. She knew immediately it was the man she was to meet. 'Ma'am?' he shouted across the lobby and, as Ruby was the only one sitting there, she smiled. She stood up, her legs shaky under her black gown. Being an escort wasn't what she had expected. Why was she doing this? Because Anna said her girls had to have 'all-round' experience. Ruby knew she had to try her best.

'Jesse Marlon,' the man boomed as he approached and grabbed her hand. 'Pleased to make your acquaintance.'

Ruby's smile faltered. 'I'm pleased to meet you.'

'Say, you're real cute. Anna said you was blonde and beautiful. You come from these parts?'

'Yes, I'm a Londoner.'

'Aw, look at me, no goddam manners.' Ruby was startled as he pulled off his hat and revealed an entirely bald brown head. Before she could answer, he was propelling her across the lobby to the lounge bar where almost every face in the room turned to stare at them.

★    ★    ★

'Cheers,' Jesse said, knocking his tall glass against Ruby's. 'Here's to us, little gal.' He spread his long legs wide as he sat beside her at the marble-and-chrome table. Ruby thought he wasn't bad-looking in a coarse kind of way. But he spoke so loudly, she wanted to say she wasn't deaf, even though he seemed to think she was.

Ruby frowned at the long glass with a sugar coating around its rim. He hadn't even asked her what she would like to drink.

'Cheers again,' Jesse repeated, gulping from his glass as his gaze went over her. 'You can't beat a rum daiquiri.'

'I've never had one before.' Ruby sipped cautiously. She liked the sugar, which had a flavour of lime, but the rum was sour.

'Are you on business in London?' Ruby asked, trying not to sound as if she was offended as his eyes lingered on her breasts.

'Heck, no. I'm here to find me good breeding stock.'

Ruby assumed he was talking about his ranch. 'I don't think you'll find many cows in London.'

He threw back his head and laughed. 'You gotta swell sense of humour, honey,' he boomed while ordering more daiquiris from the waiter. 'And you're mighty pretty. My pa wasn't wrong. He told me if ever I wanted a good woman, I was to come to England. And just look at what I found first try,' he added, his eyes sliding down to her breasts again. 'Good stock, that's what I'm after. A neat little lady like you would fit just right on the ranch.'

Ruby shook her head at the misunderstanding. 'I wouldn't know anything about ranches, Mr Marlon. I'm a model, you see, and I've worked in some of London's most fashionable stores.'

'Call me Jesse, honey. I gotta oil well too,' Jesse Marlon continued as if he hadn't heard what she'd just told him. 'A gusher found by my pappy before the war. My pa, Jesse Marlon the first, he was the roughest, toughest cowboy in Texas and made a dirt pile in the '30s. Did his bit for his country and met my ma while he was in London. Took her back Stateside and reared a whole pride of Marlons.'

'Your mother is English?'

'Right on,' Jesse replied enthusiastically. 'See where I'm coming from, honey?'

'Not really, as I—'

'Let me tell you 'bout my family,' Jesse interrupted and Ruby's heart sank. She listened patiently, wondering how long it would be before he stopped talking and decided to take her to dinner. She hadn't eaten since breakfast. And the rum wasn't helping to settle her stomach either.

But then suddenly Jesse's hand was on her knee and feeling under her skirt. She moved quickly away. 'How 'bout we get acquainted?' he asked with a sly grin. 'I'll send for room service and we can get ourselves comfortable.'

Ruby felt angry and frightened too. 'I thought we were going to dinner.'

'We are. In my room.'

Ruby stood up. 'I have a headache.'

'You what?' Jessie said, looking puzzled. 'I paid for the night.'

'You'll have to ask Anna about that.'

'Hey, just you come back here!' he roared after her. But Ruby was already out in the lobby and hurrying onto the street before she dared to glance back.

How dare he think she was his for the night? It was shades of Charles all over again. If this was what being an escort was, she didn't like it.

'Mr Marlon telephoned. He was very upset,' Anna said abruptly, as later that evening they stood in the lemon room at 10 Dower Street. 'Fortunately Paula was at home and has taken your place. Otherwise I would have been forced to refund his money, which was quite considerable.'

'He put his hand up my leg,' Ruby protested once more, 'and said we should go to his room.' She had explained everything to Anna and had expected a very different outcome.

Anna sighed as if she was addressing a child. 'Then you should have sat a reasonable distance away from him.'

'He didn't even ask what I wanted to drink.'

'My dear, this man is a stranger in London. He doesn't know our customs.'

'I don't think what he did can be an American custom either. If it is, the Americans are very rude.'

'And very wealthy,' Anna corrected her sharply. 'Mr Marlon is a cowboy. Unused to the way the English do things.'

'I think he thought I was just a good–time girl.'

'I'm sure you're confused, Ruby.'

'He even compared me to a cow.'

Anna laughed then, shaking her head as though she'd just been told a joke.

Ruby felt as though she was laying the blame on her and excusing Jesse Marlon. 'Besides, he shouted at me,' she continued indignantly, 'in the middle of a crowded bar.'

'He wouldn't have shouted if you had taken the conversation in another direction,' Anna said, the smile disappearing from her lips. She lit a cigarette and sat down, crossing one leg over the other. 'Escorting is a skill. Learning discretion. Reading the signs and being confident enough to guide your client through a successful first meeting.'

'It'll be me last as well,' Ruby insisted, forgetting her grammar. 'I told you I wasn't cut out for the job. I just want to do modelling.'

'Ruby, sit down.' Anna's stern command made Ruby jump. She hesitated, with half a mind to flounce out, but Anna's eyes were boring into her.

She sat on the edge of the sofa, pulling her dress over her knees.

'Don't sulk, it doesn't become you.'

Ruby looked away. Why was Anna displeased with her, when none of this was her fault?

'Remember,' Anna said quietly, 'the day you first came here? I pointed out to you that the agency required complete discretion. And so, too, its clients. The contract you signed was completely transparent.'

Ruby went to answer but Anna shook her head. 'You must agree you have had your fair share of modelling. I have personally recommended you to Steadman's. And look how successful you've been! Now it's time to gain more experience and honour our agreement. Quite frankly, Ruby, you could have handled this client easily if only you hadn't taken his remarks personally. It should have been your firm but polite response that you had dressed for dinner and would be disappointed not to be able to get to know more about his life while enjoying some of London's finest cuisine.' Anna raised her eyebrows. 'You see? He wouldn't have been able to refuse. And said with charm, it could have persuaded the man to take you anywhere you wished. Certainly the evening would have passed without incident. Had he made any improper suggestions at the end, you could have reasonably taken your leave. With, I am sure, a chaste kiss on the cheek.'

'You mean string him along?' Ruby said on a gasp.

'I would call it tact.'

'But what if he turned nasty?'

Anna shook her head. 'A skilled escort would never allow herself to be vulnerable. What could he do to you in the presence of so many others?'

'The same as Charles,' Ruby retorted. 'I don't want to be attacked again.'

'You won't be if you keep a level head.'

Ruby felt her cheeks burn. The Texan rancher might have paid for an escort for the evening, but that didn't mean he could treat her with disrespect. Or did it? As Ruby considered this question, she suddenly felt cheap and dirty, just as she had with Charles.

'It's late,' Anna said, standing up. 'You acted so professionally in your modelling role, I automatically assumed you would rise to the challenge of the other.' She reached out and tipped up Ruby's lowered chin. 'I'm not forcing you to stay with the agency. If you wish to terminate your contract, I should be very sorry, but I would let you go, if that's what you want.'

Ruby looked into Anna's green eyes. They were warm and kind again and her smile was engaging. 'It's just that Charles frightened me,' she mumbled as Anna led her to the door. 'I suppose I lost my nerve.'

'I understand,' Anna nodded. 'But I'm sure you'll see things a lot more clearly in the morning.'

Ruby made her way miserably up the stairs. Was it her? Was this her fault? If she'd used her common sense, could it all have been so different?

Ruby bathed, relaxing at last in the warm and soapy water. Afterwards she lay in the luxury of her soft sheets and sweet-smelling pillows. She was so happy at Dower Street. What kind of life was there to return to if she left the agency?

The thought was depressing.

She hoped Anna was right and in the morning, after a good rest, she would see everything clearly.

\*   \*   \*

Early the next day, there was a knock on her door. Ruby stumbled out of bed to answer it.

'How are we this morning?' Paula asked, looking glamorous as usual.

Ruby blinked the sleep from her eyes. She had spent a very restless night. 'Come in.'

'I can't stop. Jesse is taking me to Harrods.'

'What?'

'Shopping first, lunch after.' Paula was wearing her black silk robe and her red hair was combed over her shoulders. She walked in and sank down on the sofa in a cloud of expensive perfume. 'I gather you had an interesting encounter with my Texan.'

'*Your* Texan?' Ruby repeated as she pulled on her blue cotton wrap-over.

'He is now,' Paula said smugly. 'I hear you ditched him rather unceremoniously.'

Ruby went to the window and pulled down the sash. She needed some fresh air. She thought Paula would have received the same treatment from Jesse. 'What did he say about me?'

Paula laughed. 'Sweetie, he was most uncomplimentary.'

'His eyes and hands went everywhere.'

'Only to be expected.' Paula yawned and stretched. 'You have to – gently – put them in their place.'

'Did he want you to go to his room?'

'He suggested it, yes.'

'Did you go?'

Paula laughed. 'Of course not. I could see at once he needed schooling.'

'Schooling? Is that what you call it?' Ruby asked disparagingly, folding her arms. 'He's just a dirty old man.'

'Whatever you might think of him, dear, he took me to the Savoy for dinner, then on to the Atlas.'

'The Atlas? But that's very expensive there.' Nick had told Ruby about the Atlas Club, where he was trying to get a membership.

'Not if you're a Texan with an oil well.'

'Well, I hope you'll be happy with your extras,' Ruby said severely.

Paula stood up and joined her at the window. 'You're new at this. But I've had some experience. Men like Taylor, and even Charles, they are fun but just fly-by-nights. Now Jesse is vulgar and loud-mouthed. But he has potential. I'm older than you. I've been in the business a long time. When a man takes you out on a second date to buy a mink stole, and shows you photographs of his oil well and tells you how his pappy is insistent his son find himself an English bride, I think you can say with confidence he's seriously interested.'

'Is that what you want? To be married to an animal like Jesse Marlon?'

'I can think of worse fates.'

'Well, I can't.'

'That's because you're young and naive.'

Ruby felt the hot colour pour into her cheeks. First Anna had lectured her and now Paula. Christmas might have come early for Paula in the form of Jesse Marlon, but Ruby didn't regret what she'd done. Not when she had someone like Nick to be with. A man who respected her, supported her career and hadn't tried to get her into bed within the first few minutes of knowing her.

She pulled back her shoulders and shrugged. 'Good luck, is all I can say.'

'Don't need luck, sweetie, I've got Jesse Marlon.'

When Paula had gone, Ruby sat on the bed. A warm tear fell on her cheek. Anna and Paula had made her feel as though she'd acted immaturely. But she wasn't going to be thrust into Jesse Marlon's lecherous arms. She was a model and was at the start of her career. She had a man in her life to share her success with. Quickly she dried her eyes.

Today she was meeting Nick for lunch at the Jester. And she would ask him to take her to Larry's party. She wanted to show him off. To let her old friends know that she was moving up in the world. And with Nick at her side, she knew she could.

# Chapter Seventeen

It was a beautiful May evening, not yet dark, but dusky. Ruby thought Soho looked magical. There was music playing in the distance, the smell of food in the air, combined with the scent of summer. The streets were as busy as they always were and people were sitting outside the pubs at small tables and on benches. Street walkers in all their finery were touting for custom. The strip clubs were open to all who cared to visit.

The evening held promise and Ruby was eager to show Nick off. He'd worn casual clothes tonight as Ruby had told him how informal Larry's parties were. The smoky-grey roll-neck sweater reminded her of when they first met at Fortuno's, eight months ago. She gave a little shiver. So much had changed in her life since then. His brown hair was a little longer now, but it suited him. As always, he smelled wonderful.

If only Paula could see us, she thought as they approached the small door next to the strip club. Paula might have spent weeks in Jesse's company and been showered with gifts, but she was still no nearer to being presented with the diamond engagement ring she craved. What would Paula say when she saw the dazzling bright red MG sports car that Nick was teaching Ruby to drive?

'The flat doesn't look much from the outside,' Ruby said as they stood at the weathered green door. 'But upstairs is amazing.'

Nick slipped his hand around her waist. 'It will have to be, to get my attention,' he said ruefully. 'You're looking so beautiful tonight, I can't take my eyes off you.'

Ruby felt elated. And when they went in, Larry was hurrying down the stairs. He opened his arms and drew her against his round stomach. 'Darling, I've missed you.' He didn't wait for her to reply and stared straight at Nick. 'So am I to be introduced?' he asked coyly.

'Larry, this is Nick. Nick, Larry.'

Larry took Nick's hand, batting his short eyelashes under his glasses. 'So very pleased to meet you.'

Ruby wanted to giggle as Larry adjusted the knotted light blue scarf around his neck. 'Larry, you've become one of those bo – what did you call the arty types?'

'Bohemians, darling.' He pressed his short, stubby fingers over his loose, flowered shirt. 'Now, are you two ready for an outrageous night?'

Ruby was glad to see that Nick was smiling as Larry crooked a finger and they followed him up the stairs.

The music was very loud. Couples were dancing, or rather moving together, in the small space. Larry gently pushed his way through. Ruby held tight to Nick's hand. Every time she looked at him, he met her gaze, as though telling her how proud he was of her. And when Larry poured them cocktails at the small bar, the gin and sins reminded her pleasantly of the time she'd been here before.

'You finally made it,' Debbie said, appearing with Rog at her side. She looked up at Nick and her blue eyes sparkled. After introductions were made Ruby was surprised to see that Nick soon fell into conversation with Rog.

'So, you don't mind about age?' Debbie asked out of earshot of the men. 'He must be a lot older than you.'

'Doesn't matter to me.'

'You have got it bad, kid.'

'Rog seems to get on with him.'

'My Rog gets on with everyone.'

Ruby listened to Debbie talking about her wedding plans. How the gown Rog had bought from Steadman's had set her fiancé back a fortune. Her parents were paying for the reception to be held at Paradise Row, she boasted. And she wanted a honeymoon in Switzerland, no less. Ruby knew there was only one thing on Debbie's mind. To be Mrs Roger Stacey.

'Ladies, may I interrupt?' Stuart said, joining them. 'You both look gorgeous.' He gazed admiringly at Ruby's rose-pink silk-satin blouse, discreetly buttoned under a string of pearls that Nick had recently given her. Ruby knew Debbie was staring at the pearls too, wondering if they were real.

Just then, Marianne and Bruno joined them, together with some of Stuart's aspiring actor friends. As the laughter and conversation grew louder, Ruby decided she had better not drink too many cocktails. She wanted to have a clear head when she left with Nick.

Ten minutes later she slipped, unnoticed, to the kitchen. Just as before, the tiny space was crammed with wine bottles, glasses and food. She exchanged her cocktail glass for a tumbler and was about to fill it with water when a hand touched her shoulder.

'Hello.'

She looked up to see a tall man smiling down at her. 'Oh, it's you,' she blurted, the heat rushing to her cheeks as she recognized Johnnie Dyer. He was even more handsome up close.

'I see we both have the same idea.' He nodded to her abandoned cocktail glass. Placing his beside hers, he grinned, showing very white, even teeth under his dark skin. 'Larry's cocktails are innocent enough, until the next day.'

Ruby laughed. 'I drank too many last time.'

He stared at her. 'You were at the last party. Yes, I saw you as Margot and I arrived.'

Ruby was flattered he'd remembered. 'Margot? Is that your—'

'Yes, yes,' he nodded, 'but she's not here tonight. So as you can see, the retinue has disappeared.' He smiled, his dark eyes, so large and fringed with long black lashes, sparkled with amusement. 'I'm Johnnie Dyer.'

'And I'm Ruby Payne.' She decided not to say she knew already. 'Would you like some water too?'

'Thanks.'

Ruby filled two tumblers. 'How do you know Larry and Stuart?'

'Through Margot. She's very popular.' He quirked an eyebrow.

Ruby wanted to ask if Johnnie was one of the bohemians that Larry had talked about. But before she could, he said, 'So what do you do?'

'I worked for Larry.' She smiled. 'It was Stuart who taught me how to shampoo and cut poodles.'

Johnnie laughed. 'Did you enjoy shampooing poodles?'

Ruby smiled. 'It helped me through a bad time.'

'Oh dear. I didn't mean to pry.'

Ruby felt obliged to add, 'It was after my brother died. He was only twenty-one.'

He frowned. 'I'm very sorry.'

'I still find it difficult to talk about.'

'Of course.'

She looked into his large, dark eyes. 'Have you lost someone too?'

He nodded. 'Yes, it's devastating.'

She wanted to ask who, but decided she didn't know him well enough. Instead, she said softly, 'I still miss Pete so much.'

'Did you say Pete?'

'Yes, why?'

'Oh, no reason.'

Suddenly Debbie appeared, empty glass in hand. 'I need a refill,' she giggled, looking up at Johnnie. 'Oh, pardon me, I hope I'm not interrupting.'

Johnnie smiled politely, looking uncomfortable as Debbie tried to keep her balance, leaning heavily against him.

Ruby said, a little embarrassed, 'Johnnie, this is Debbie. We worked together at the poodle parlour.'

'Delighted.' Johnnie offered his hand.

'Are you another actor?' Debbie asked, grasping it for much too long.

'No. Not at all.'

'I remember now. I saw you at Larry's last party.' Debbie narrowed her eyes. 'You were with that older woman, weren't you? Lady something-or-other?'

Johnnie nodded and Ruby cringed as Debbie, who was very tipsy, began to pour herself another drink.

'I like your friends,' Nick said as they drove away from the party in the early hours.

'Even Rog?' Ruby asked in surprise. 'He's crazy about insurance.'

'Yes, but knowledgeable.'

Ruby glanced at Nick's profile. He was so easy to get along with and always found something interesting in people. She sank back on the comfortable leather seat of the Buick. 'It's been such a lovely evening I don't want to go home,' she sighed restlessly.

'We could park near the Embankment. Take a stroll.'

'If you like.' A faint light was creeping up in the night sky, Ruby noticed. In a couple of hours it would be dawn. For all the luxury of Dower Street, her room was losing its appeal. She didn't often go downstairs now. Not since Jesse Marlon. Though Anna hadn't asked her to escort a client again, Ruby knew it wouldn't be long before she did. One of the newer models, a pretty young brunette called Cindy, had been given the evening-wear assignment at Steadman's. Ruby had been sent to an underwear shop in Maida Vale instead. The clumsy, boned corsets for the older women customers to view were uncomfortable to wear. The other shop had been near Covent Garden. The modern, mass-produced clothes were all cheap quality, and with no assistant to help her dress.

The noise of the Buick's windscreen wipers brought her back to the present. 'Is it raining?'

'We could always go back to the flat for a nightcap.'

She smiled, meeting his eyes. 'I'd like that.'

He nodded, changing gear as he headed the car in the opposite direction.

Nick made coffee and served it in the lounge. He sat down on the settee and watched Ruby as she moved around the flat, swaying her hips to the strains of Frankie Laine's 'Answer Me' coming from the record player.

He wondered if, at last, he was beginning to enjoy the diversion she had provided these past few months. Had he been on his own too long? Was he ready to settle down?

Perhaps. He enjoyed indulging her, trawling the shops for vases, pictures, rugs. Additions he wouldn't have bothered with before. But Ruby had good taste, and she intrigued him.

She was young, lovely, affectionate, bright. And she could be brighter, he'd realized. He could make something of her, and the only obstacle so far was Anna.

He reached into his pocket for a Gauloise, felt the familiar shape of the packet, and lit up. His eyes slid back to Ruby's petite, womanly figure. Her blonde hair lay across her shoulders in the latest style that many women, he noticed, tried and failed to carry off. She was wearing a soft blouse and the string of Hatton Garden pearls he'd given her. An impulsive investment, but why not?

His thoughts turned to Anna. Her tall, statuesque body and shrewd green eyes. Eyes that might tear a man apart and put him back together again, if the fancy so took her.

Ruby came to sit by his side. Evening in Paris. He liked the perfume. It suited her.

He offered her a cigarette and she shook her head as he knew she would.

'I've been thinking,' she said as she slipped off her shoes and tucked her feet under her.

He raised a quizzical eyebrow.

She leaned her head on his shoulder. 'Anna told me to meet a rich American who would take me to dinner. Only it wasn't dinner he had in mind. Instead he wanted me to go to his room. Of course, I left.'

'What did Anna have to say to this?'

'She was angry and said she could have lost money if Paula hadn't been available to replace me.'

He drew her closer. 'You did the right thing. In this life, you don't have to do anything you don't want to.'

'That's easy for you to say,' she replied with a frown. 'But men seem to treat women very badly sometimes.'

'Yes,' he agreed, trailing a finger across her cheek. 'But I'm not one of them. And very rightly, you turned him down.'

'But Anna said I was at fault,' she continued to complain. 'Even suggesting I should have somehow persuaded him to take me to dinner. Then afterwards given him an innocent kiss. That way, he couldn't have telephoned her to complain he'd been let down.'

'Darling, you are involved with a very astute businesswoman,' he answered with a wry smile. 'Your first mistake was believing Anna was your friend, when in reality she has one thing only on her mind. Her agency and making big bucks.'

'Why didn't you warn me?' Ruby complained, wondering why he hadn't.

He crushed out the Gauloise cigarette. 'Would you have listened? I think not. I realized I had to let you find out for yourself. It's true in this life, experience is the best teacher.' He kissed her mouth, running his fingers through her hair. 'Anna intrigued you. She played her cards very well. You wouldn't have heard a word against her. But I've known her for a long time. And she has earned her reputation as a hard woman.'

'You sound as if you know her well.'

'Well enough. As they say, all's fair in love and war. And the war was very fiercely fought between us.'

Ruby snuggled against him. 'But what shall I do if she asks me to be an escort again?'

'Only you can decide that.'

'I want to be a model, not an escort. But my contract says I have to do both.'

'It's called business.'

'Yes, I know that. But even so, I don't like it.'

He took her face in his hands and whispered, 'You're young, beautiful and determined. But often what we want we can't have. Unless we sacrifice something for it.'

'So, do you think I should?'

'What?'

'Do what Anna wants me to do.'

He laughed softly, looking into her eyes. 'Ruby, you don't need my advice. And as I said before, you probably wouldn't take it if I offered it. Now, can we forget Anna and enjoy this moment?' He drew her against him and decided that tonight he was going to make love to her.

# Chapter Eighteen

'You're even more beautiful naked,' he told her as they lay in bed.

Ruby shivered when he touched her. She wanted to make love but was afraid after what Paula had told her.

'What is it?' he asked softly. 'What's wrong?'

'I don't want a baby,' she blurted.

'Neither do I,' he said, kissing her parted lips. 'Just trust me and I'll make sure you're safe.'

She began to give in to the sensations he aroused in her. His fingers gently teased her, driving away the concerns as her body arched and shuddered; a fire burned inside her belly. She knew there was no other man on earth for her. This was what she wanted.

'You're something else,' Nick whispered. 'Relax, my darling, I won't come inside you.'

Ruby barely heard. But she knew at the height of her passion she would be safe. And after, as they lay exhausted, he drew her against him.

'You see, there was nothing to worry about,' he whispered, kissing the top of her head.

Ruby had no way to express her feelings. Nick had kept his word and she had been made love to in the most perfect way possible without having to consider the advice that Paula had given her.

'Hi,' Nick greeted her, casually strolling into the bedroom, a wide smile on his face. He was carrying a tray and wearing a deep blue bathrobe. It was the first time she had ever seen him unshaven. 'Did you sleep well?'

She sat up in bed, pulling the sheet over her. 'You should know the answer to that.'

Sinking down beside her, he said, 'Breakfast, but I'm afraid to say it's just coffee and toast. I had no idea a special guest was coming to stay.'

'Last time I stayed overnight you gave me soup to drink and cream for my grazed knees,' she said, sipping the coffee. 'I was feeling very sorry for myself after Charles.'

He chuckled. 'You did look like some waif or stray.'

'I felt very silly.'

He took a slice of toast and fed her. 'Eat up, pretty silly, open those cupid bow lips.'

She was so happy. Nick was so caring and considerate. Suddenly she was curious about his past. 'Have you ever been married?'

He smiled wryly and reached over to pour the tea. 'Once, a long, long time ago.'

'What happened?'

'What always happens. People fall out of love.'

'I don't ever want that to happen to me.'

He smiled ruefully. 'Is that why you've chosen an older man to make love to you?'

'I've never thought about age.'

'I'm thirty-five and was sixteen when you were born.' He finished the toast and licked his lips. 'So what do you say to that?'

'Only that I don't care.' She only knew that today everything had changed. Was she in love? She could be. But did she know what love was? Could it be this feeling she had for Nick?

'And who are the men in your life?' he asked, arching an eyebrow. 'What competition have I got? Could it be that young Romeo I first saw you with at Fortuno's?'

Ruby blushed. 'Bernie's just a friend.'

'Are you sure?'

'Of course I am!'

'I would prefer to know where we stood. If we're going to be a couple, that is.'

Ruby felt a shiver go over her. He wanted them to be together! He wasn't disappointed in her. Last night was important to him too.

'You're the only man in my life,' she assured him, leaning across to kiss his waiting lips. 'I haven't any secrets. You know everything about me.'

He grinned, taking the tray. Then he slipped off his robe and climbed back into bed. 'I was going to suggest we went for lunch at the Jester. But now, for some reason, I've gone off the idea.'

Ruby held her breath as he pulled her down beside him.

She loved his strong hands on her, making her feel safe and protected. She would never get used to the way his body felt; strong and muscular. But unlike other men in her life, he didn't use his sex or strength to coax or intimidate her. She was fascinated, aware that as an older man he was experienced. Could she satisfy him as he had satisfied her?

Other than Bernie, she'd never let anyone go the whole way. She had sworn, after such a disastrous experience, never to take sex lightly again. And after Paula's advice . . . she shuddered.

Nick had made her feel confident. And confidence was something no one could take away from her.

Early on Monday, Nick drove her back to Dower Street. 'Have you decided what you're going to do?' he asked as he stopped the car.

'I'm going to be as businesslike as Anna,' Ruby replied. 'I'd be useless as an escort. But I'm a good model. It's in her interests to find me the right work. After all, she doesn't want another telephone complaint.'

'That's a tough line to take.'

'I can be tough when I want something.'

Nick whistled through his teeth. 'My brave little warrior.' He pulled her to him and kissed her. 'Telephone me. We'll do something special next weekend. Perhaps stay a night or two in the country.'

'I'd like that.'

He kissed her once more and Ruby climbed out of the car. She watched the Buick join the early morning traffic, then hurried up the steps. She wanted to think about Nick and the most romantic night of her life. But first, she had to face Anna, and try to keep a business head on her shoulders.

Ruby went into the lemon room where she expected to find Anna at her desk. But it was Paula who sat there instead.

'You look pleased with yourself,' Paula said, touching her long red hair that was drawn up to the back of her head in a pleat. She was wearing her silk wrap-over, but her make-up was perfectly in place.

'I might be,' Ruby agreed with a smile. 'Where's Anna?'

'She's away for the day and left this job for you.' She held out a piece of paper.

Ruby looked at the address. 'Steadman's? I thought Anna was sending Cindy, not me.'

'The rumour is that Cindy flopped.'

Ruby felt even more determined now to call Anna's bluff. Steadman's held high standards and sending some-one as inexperienced as Cindy just hadn't worked out.

'You must have redeemed yourself,' Paula said, reading her mind. 'Look, I'd like to talk more, but I have some news of my own. Jesse is taking me out for lunch and I want to wear something special. He said we're going to celebrate.' She tossed her head, raising her eyebrows. 'I want to look glam when he names the day.'

'So he's going to propose?' Ruby asked as they walked upstairs together.

'On Saturday we looked in the jewellery shops. He bought me a pair of real gold earrings. I would have preferred a ring, but realize the diamonds will come next. As an oil man as well as a cowboy, he does things the Texan way.'

'Diamonds will cost him a fortune.'

'A few thousand pounds are a drop in the ocean to a man like Jesse Marlon. And if he wants to take me to bed, he'll have to marry me first.'

'But what will life be like in America?' Ruby wondered. 'What if you're stuck on a ranch all day? With no company except for the horses and cows?'

Paula laughed. 'I'm sure I'll have a car or two to drive anywhere I want.'

'I hope that'll be enough. You do like living the high life.'

Paula shrugged. 'It's an exchange I'm quite willing to make.'

'Well, I hope you'll be happy.'

'It looks like you've won your battle with Anna.'

'I hope so.'

'She knows when she's on to a good thing. And you are very much that. It's all about money with Anna. And she won't want to lose you.'

Ruby frowned. 'What will she say when you tell her you're leaving for America?'

They stopped outside Ruby's room. 'I'm not looking forward to the showdown,' Paula whispered, glancing over Ruby's shoulder to make certain they were alone. 'She'll be losing an income. And to her, such a loss is unacceptable. I expect her to kick up rough.'

'But isn't Anna an old friend of yours?'

'My dear, you have no friends in this business. There's far too much competition. It's dog eat dog, I'm afraid.'

This truth was beginning to dawn on Ruby. If she wanted to be a model, she would have to fight her corner. Was it really so difficult to be businesslike? She had hoped she was Anna's friend. But she realized this couldn't be.

'Enjoy your day,' Paula said as she took her leave. 'I'm sure Elsie will be pleased to see her favourite model. As for me, next time we meet, I'll be engaged to be married to one of the richest men in all of Texas.'

As Ruby bathed in the luxury of a bath full of soapy, fragranced hot water, using the soaps and creams in the bathroom that were always replenished as if by some magic hand, she allowed her thoughts to go to Nick and the nights they had spent together. He was a wonderful lover, kind and considerate, but also very passionate. She had never felt like this before. He was everything she had dreamed of in a man. There was a chemistry between them and she couldn't wait to be with him again.

As she dressed in a smart, peach-coloured two-piece costume, tan gloves and high heels, a combination she knew would impress Elsie, she was still thinking of Nick and the way he had made love to her. And of their one last kiss and his whispered words that assured her they were now a couple.

Her mind was still occupied with the thought of next weekend and sharing his bed again, when, as she hurried downstairs, she saw Cindy.

'I hear you've been given the job at Steadman's,' Cindy said, looking upset. Ruby thought although very pretty how immature Cindy was. She tended to slouch and look sullen. A smile was worth a million dollars, so it was said in the modelling world.

'Yes, that's right, I have,' Ruby responded with a smile of her own.

'You know, don't you, that I was given the job last time?'

'Yes, I do.'

'Elsie promised she would be seeing me today.'

Ruby frowned. 'Anna makes those decisions, not Elsie. And as you'll learn, nothing is guaranteed in this line of work.'

Cindy pouted. 'I don't need you to tell me that.' She turned on her high heels and ran up the stairs.

Ruby watched the tall, slim figure dressed in a dark blue sheath dress disappear from view. From the top floor of the house there was a bang as a door slammed shut. It was clear Cindy had a mind of her own, Ruby decided, and a temper too. But a tantrum wouldn't be appreciated by Anna, as Cindy would soon find out.

Elsie was nowhere to be found when Ruby walked into the fashion department. The little woman dressed in black with a pincushion tied to her wrist always accompanied her to the dressing rooms. But where was she this morning?

'Good morning, Miss Payne,' a voice said and Ruby saw Mr Steadman junior's assistant striding towards her.

'Good morning, Mr Kent.' Ruby smiled her winning smile although she had hardly spoken to Mr Steadman's secretary, a grey-haired older man wearing a formal pinstripe suit. He was rarely seen on the shop floor.

'You are to go downstairs and wait at the rear exit.'

Ruby was startled. This had never happened before. 'Why?' she asked in surprise.

'On Mr Steadman's orders you'll be going elsewhere today.'

'Do you know where?'

'No. Please hurry along.'

Ruby shrugged. She was disappointed as she liked the store and would miss having Elsie to help her.

Mr Kent nodded to the double doors marked *STAIRS*. He quickly walked off, back to his office. Ruby made her way down the back stairs to the rear exit. It was very gloomy down here and led onto the side road behind the building where all the rubbish bins were kept and the lorries came into their loading bays.

She waited a few minutes until a large black limousine drew up beside her and a chauffeur in uniform got out. He opened the back door, gesturing Ruby to enter.

Ruby looked in. Mr Steadman junior was sitting there. 'Please have a seat, Miss Payne.'

'Thank you.'

The chauffeur touched Ruby's elbow. She climbed in and smiled at her employer, who didn't return her greeting but told the chauffeur to drive on instead.

Ruby sat in silence, the only noise in the car the soft purr of the engine. Mr Steadman was staring straight in front of him, through the glass partition that separated them from the driver. Ruby wanted to ask where they were going.

And what sort of fashions he wanted her to model. She assumed that wherever it was they ended up her clothes would be waiting for her. However, it felt highly unusual to be sitting in Mr Steadman's own car.

Discreetly she studied his profile. He always looked a little pompous when he walked through the department with his nose in the air. A small man with a square moustache, thin lips and receding hairline, he looked more like a bank manager.

Ruby felt flattered. He could have chosen any of Anna's models. Yet here she was, sitting next to him, on their way to what must be a very select event.

She looked out of the window and saw they were in the part of the city full of stately apartment blocks and luxury hotels. Was she to model in one of these?

The car turned off the road and into a small lane. At the end of it was a garage where other cars like this were parked. She was very excited when she saw one or two women, dressed very fashionably, climbing out of them.

So that was it! Ruby decided, her heart thudding. This was to be a private display, where Mr Steadman's wealthier customers would view the latest creations. She had learned from Elsie that sometimes hundreds, even thousands of pounds of clothing could be sold to just one customer at a private showing. Ruby couldn't believe her luck!

The car stopped and the chauffeur climbed out, first opening Mr Steadman's door. Ruby watched as Mr Steadman scuttled off to a side door, and was soon gone from view.

She sat mystified. Where was he? And what was she supposed to do? After a few seconds she found out.

'Mr Steadman has asked me to show you the way,' the chauffeur said, opening her door.

Ruby got out, arranging her clothes and looking around. 'Where are we going?'

'Up to the third floor.' He gave her a puzzled look. 'Can I carry anything for you?'

'No, thank you. I've only got my bag.' She smiled. It was wonderful to be treated so royally. 'Has Mr Steadman gone ahead to meet his customer?' she said to the chauffeur as they took the lift, a very old-fashioned ornate metal cage that clanked and grumbled its way upwards.

'Er, yes, perhaps,' the chauffeur replied. He looked straight ahead of him, his hands behind his back.

Eventually the lift stopped with a heavy thud.

They walked out and along a rather gloomy hall. The carpet was well-trodden but thick and muffled their footsteps. Ruby glanced around for the women she had seen. But the hall was deserted. They must have taken their seats, she thought, beginning to feel a little nervous. Would she have enough time to get ready?

Each door they passed was made of dark, polished wood. The decor looked old but expensive.

'Will there be many here?' Ruby asked as they came to a halt and the chauffeur knocked on one of the doors.

'I've no idea, miss,' the driver said, looking surprised.

Ruby felt anxious, sensing something was wrong.

# Chapter Nineteen

'This way,' said the maid, and Ruby followed. The long hall reminded her of all the old black-and-white films she had seen at the cinema. Leafy green plants stood on glossy marble tables. Large gilt mirrors were hung on the walls. The wooden tiles on the floor were highly polished. At the end of the hall there was a glass door. The maid pushed it open.

Ruby looked out over London. From St Paul's to the River Thames, the spires of many churches and the flat roofs of the city's historic buildings. The room she walked into was filled with tasteful furniture, although this too looked rather old-fashioned. She knew nothing about antiques. But when Nick had taken her shopping, they'd strolled through the capital's many arcades and seen the price tags on this kind of furniture. Whoever owned this must be very rich.

'Come along,' said the maid, turning through a set of Venetian doors. Every window in this room was decorated with heavy brocade curtains tied back with knotted tassels.

Ruby's gaze went to the pair of chandeliers overhead. If she had thought the ones at Dower Street were breathtaking, then these were out of this world. Studded with crystals, tier upon tier, they reflected the daylight flooding in through the windows. Beneath was a sumptuous plum-coloured settee. Every chair in the room was covered in the same rich shade. The smell of a thick, almost sickly perfume drifted in the air.

Ruby thought whoever lived here might be foreign; there were cross-legged, bejewelled Oriental statues and rugs thrown across the floor in exotic reds, ambers and deep greens. In the background, a mystical sort of chant was playing.

'Well?' said a voice, and Ruby swung round to find Mr Steadman standing behind her. He wore a long silk belted jacket with an Oriental design of black, gold and deep blue. On his feet was an embroidered pair of slippers. On his head a black fez like she had seen in the film *Casablanca* with Humphrey Bogart and Ingrid Bergman.

Ruby wanted to giggle. He looked ridiculous.

'Follow me,' he said.

Even before she reached the sickly-smelling room with a monster bed in the middle of the floor swamped by silk pillows, she knew this was a mistake.

The heavy door banged behind her.

'Where are your clothes?' he demanded suddenly.

'What clothes?'

He walked slowly around her, looking her up and down. 'The ones you were told to bring.'

'I wasn't told to bring any. I thought I was going to model at the store.'

'I gave Miss Charnwood-Smythe explicit instructions.'

'I haven't seen Anna,' Ruby said with a shrug. 'She just left me a note.'

'This is outrageous.' Mr Steadman sounded annoyed. His square moustache and his squinting small dark eyes gave him a mean look. 'I was given an assurance you were prepared to wear the costumes I asked for.'

'Costumes?' Ruby repeated, alarmed, glancing around again at the peculiar decor. 'What kind of costumes?'

'Of the torso-articulation type.'

Ruby laughed. 'What?'

'To someone like you, the common term would be belly dancer.'

Ruby's mouth fell open. 'I ain't a bloody belly dancer!'

'I wasn't expecting you to dance,' Mr Steadman replied crisply. 'You just happen to have the well-rounded proportions that interest me. Now take off your clothes and put on those behind the screen over there. They will have to do.'

Ruby's eyes darted to the lacquered screen. It was beside the bed. Mr Steadman was sliding off his jacket. To her amazement he had nothing on underneath. His skinny, naked and repulsive body seemed to twitch as he spoke. 'Well, hurry up!'

Ruby wanted to tell him that he was a disgraceful old man. Instead she turned on her heel and fled.

★   ★   ★

Ruby stood outside the apartment block. She hadn't bothered to take the slow, grumbling lift. She'd run all the way downstairs.

How could she have been so daft? It was common knowledge Mr Steadman lived in a big house with his wife and family. She should have realized something was amiss from the start.

She gazed up at the impressive, respectable-looking old building. Anna must have known. This was her revenge.

Ruby got a taxi back to Dower Street. As she sat on the back seat, she thought of her last words to the maid. 'Tell your employer to look out for his name in the news-papers. I'd like to know what his wife and customers will say when they know what he gets up to!'

The girl had quickly opened the door.

Her threat was idle of course. But she hoped it would give the old lecher an uncomfortable hour or two. Was he proud of his bony chest and what hung limply beneath? If so, no one had ever told him how foolish he looked, standing naked but for a black hat.

Then she thought again of Anna and what she had done. She didn't have an excuse this time.

But when Ruby arrived back at Dower Street, the house was empty. She went up to her room and sat on the bed. The tears brimmed on her eyelids. What was it Nick had said? Anna was a forceful businesswoman. But did she always have to have her way?

Hugging herself, Ruby paced the floor. She had been deliberately misled. Not just today, but from the start, when Anna first engaged her. Perhaps even from the moment she had first sat with Anna in the Powder Room at the Manor.

Ruby gazed about her at the luxurious trappings she had enjoyed for the past few months. Salty tears filled her eyes.

She couldn't let Anna win!

An hour later, Ruby had packed her case. There was nothing much in it; the clothes she had arrived in, Pete's diary and Nick's gift of the pearls. She would go downstairs and tell Anna she was leaving. Anna wouldn't expect that. Paula had said Anna hated to lose an income. She would probably try to say that it was all a mistake. But Ruby wasn't going to listen this time.

She was going to call Anna's bluff.

A noise downstairs made her start. Someone had come in!

Was it Anna?

Ruby walked sedately into the lemon room, her case in hand. Anna was seated at her desk and slowly turned round.

Ruby lifted her chin. Anna's green eyes held no expression at all. 'So, you're back,' she said, crossing her long stockinged legs and reaching for her cigarette case. 'What? No tears of self-pity?'

'Why should I cry?' Ruby said defiantly.

Anna's eyebrows rose. 'Did you really think you were indispensable to me?'

Ruby fought back her tears. 'Is dressing up for a dirty old man what you call business?'

Anna stood up, drawing the smoke into her lungs and folding an arm across her chest. She narrowed her eyes, studying Ruby as if she was a lifeless mannequin in a shop window. 'As a matter of fact, it's very good business.'

'You knew what he wanted, didn't you?'

'I had an idea.'

'You deliberately tricked me.'

Her sharp laugh echoed around the room. 'You should be flattered. He wanted you and no one else.'

'To dress up as a belly dancer?'

'I suppose you'd rather be sashaying down the catwalk?' Anna said with a sneer.

Ruby nodded. 'Yes, why not?'

'Then you'll have to look elsewhere for your fairy godmother, my dear. This one has had enough of your unreasonable demands.'

Ruby sucked in a breath. 'What do you mean by that?'

'Have you looked in the mirror recently?'

Ruby felt sick and faint.

'Obviously not. When next you do, ask yourself who you see. In fact, I'll save you the trouble.' Anna walked slowly towards her, pointing with her lit cigarette. 'You are a self-absorbed, unrealistic and deluded little prude. After all I've shown you and tried to explain, you still think you are in with a chance at becoming a top model, for which, I must add, a totally different body image is required. Because I gave you fabulous clothes to wear and encouraged you to learn something of London's high life, you weren't even bright enough to understand that professions like this all demand a trade-off. No one is exempt. No one escapes playing the game. That is, if you are in it to win it.'

As Ruby's tears formed again on her lids at the cruel honesty of Anna's words, Anna stepped closer. Her beautiful skin, flawless make-up and fragrant scent still had the power to hypnotize Ruby. She felt the sobs trapped in her chest bursting to be free, but somehow she stifled them.

'I trusted you,' Ruby bleated, knowing how pathetic she sounded.

'I didn't ask you for your trust. I asked you to honour your contract.'

'I . . . I didn't know what I'd have to do—'

At this, Anna seemed to swell, her pale cheeks flushing a deep angry red. 'Of course you knew! It was all there in black and white. Any idiot would understand.'

'I'm not an idiot! You conned me!' was all Ruby could think to shout. 'You and everyone here, the lot of you, making out you are what you're not! Mutton done up as lamb, that's what you are. And I pity the poor cow you next take on, giving her what she's not used to. And telling her she can be London's top model if only she'll sleep with a few randy old geezers.'

Anna's green eyes filled with contempt as though revolted by what she saw. Her full and expressive lips parted, her finely pencilled eyebrows rose. 'So that's who you really are, Ruby Payne! A miserable little whinger.

You have, at no cost to yourself, lived off my generosity here in the heart of one of the world's most fabulous cities. You are not only ill-bred and ignorant but very foolish too. You have all the personal traits of a first-class failure and I'm relieved to wash my hands of you.'

It was then the tears really fell, like piercing splinters down Ruby's hot face. They burned her skin, just as effectively as if Anna had thrown acid over her. They trickled into her mouth and fell sourly onto her tongue, causing it to burn and swell. The same tongue that had let her down so badly as her anger and self-righteousness had poured out in retaliation for what Anna had done to her.

'The door's open,' Anna said, turning away. 'You are released from your contract.'

Ruby stared miserably at Anna's straight back under her expensive black costume. An unrelenting, frozen back that shouted the life that Ruby had lived at Dower Street was now over.

Ruby's knees buckled, a faint, swimmy feeling washing over her, causing her to blink hard. This is the end, a voice shrieked in her head. It's over. All that you've ever wanted. Over.

She barely had enough strength to put one foot in front of her. But it was not the excited, adventurous young woman who had entered 10 Dower Street's front door over three months ago. But the lost and lonely child who stood on the pavement outside with her battered suitcase.

# Chapter Twenty

'Here, drink this.'

Ruby took a sip of the brandy. 'Oh Kath, I've been such a fool.'

'Tell me all about it.'

'There's a lot to tell.' Ruby knew she had to explain everything, back to the very start when she had first met Anna at the Manor. 'I have a confession to make. I never went home on your birthday. Instead I went to a club called the Manor.' Slowly she told her friend her woeful story. 'It was one small lie that grew into lots of others.'

'You've fallen foul of some very nasty people,' Kath replied, her expression disappointed.

'Oh Kath, I'm sorry. I deceived you.'

Kath hesitated, then sighed softly. 'I'm glad you had the courage to tell me everything in the end. But you can't go back to Dower Street.'

'I've left my whole life behind me in that room. And it was such a lovely room.'

'Yes, but you paid a heavy price.'

Ruby nodded. She touched her friend's long shining dark hair and sighed. 'Just look at you. The ugly duckling is now a beautiful swan.'

Kath chuckled. 'I won't have all me feathers till I go on stage.'

Ruby laughed too. Even though she was humiliated, shocked and embarrassed at being called common and uncouth, not to mention well-rounded, ignorant and ill-bred, the humour that she and Kath had always shared was comforting.

'Fancy him thinking I was a bloody belly dancer!' Ruby spluttered. 'And I didn't even know what he meant when he called me some fancy name.'

'Belly dancers are very respected in the East.'

'Yes, but I'm in England. And "well-rounded"! What does that mean?'

Kath giggled again. 'It means you've got a womanly figure. Now, cheer up, Anna's isn't the only agency in London.'

'But what do I do in the meantime?'

'Penny's away until Wednesday at her parents'. You can use her bed till then.'

Ruby sniffed back her tears. 'You're such a good friend.'

'Don't have regrets,' Kath said gently. 'Life's too short.'

Ruby nodded, but how could she have believed she was a match for Anna? She had even boasted to Nick that she was. How could she ever face him again?

'Now, I'll find you a nightie to wear. Then run a bath,' Kath said, jumping to her feet. 'I have to be up early in the morning for practice, but you can have a lie-in. In the afternoon we'll visit the agencies.'

When Kath was gone, Ruby looked down at her case. All her lovely clothes were at Dower Street. Her make-up and creams, shoes and bags – the list was endless. She had never imagined Anna would insult her so viciously and cut her off without a second's thought.

What was she to do for money? She hadn't been given any wages. How long would the £5 in her purse last?

The next day Ruby felt a little better as she and Kath made the rounds. But one by one she was turned down. Some agencies had closed doors, others said they were full. One said she was not the right height for inclusion on their books. By tea-time they had exhausted all avenues.

'Cheer up, we'll try again tomorrow,' Kath said as they ate beans on toast that night.

'I don't think so,' Ruby said as she thought of Janet's home-cooked steak and kidney pies.

'But why not?' Kath said in surprise.

'I've decided to go home.'

Kath put down her knife and fork. 'You're welcome here, Ruby.'

'Yes, but you've got to get on with your life.'

Kath frowned. 'Remember, your mum ain't the easiest to live with.'

'I know. But I can't stay in the city centre. It's too expensive.'

'You could always go back to work for Larry.'

'I'd rather not.' Ruby dropped her chin in her hands. 'And listen to Debbie in me ear every day? Don't think so.'

'No, I wouldn't like that either,' Kath agreed.

They fell into thoughtful silence until suddenly there was a knock at the door.

'It's probably Bernie.'

Ruby sighed. No doubt he, too, would think she only had herself to blame when he heard her news.

Bernie sat in the armchair, feeling awkward. He didn't dislike the flat she shared with Penny Webber, but it wasn't very homely. More like a place to practise dancing with its scrubbed bare boards and rail screwed on the wall.

To see Ruby sitting on the couch was a bit of a belter. He hadn't expected to bump into her again. Not with that charmer from Fortuno's hanging around. He had taken an instant dislike to the creep and from what he'd heard lately from Kath, he now liked him even less.

One thing was clear, the geezer could spin a good line. The birds seemed to fall for it an' all. Even Kath was taken in, him saying how much he genuinely thought of Ruby. But why should I give a damn? Bernie thought to himself. I'm doing all right with little Tina Shutler from the works canteen. I haven't looked at anyone else in months!

Bernie tried to bring Tina's sweet face to mind, but the bugger of it was, he could barely remember her smile. Or the colour of her eyes. Or even her voice. Pulling back his shoulders, he tried to ignore the powerlessness he felt when it came to his own emotions.

At last, he said awkwardly, 'Fancy meeting you here, then.'

Ruby just stared at him. Her eyes were red-rimmed and her hair a mess. She was wearing his sister's pyjamas with little ballerina figures all over them. And Kath was fussing round her like an old mother hen.

He wanted to tell Kath to sit down. Relax. She was giving him the heebie-jeebies. But instead he plastered a smile on his face. 'What's up then, Doc?' he mimicked, trying to draw a laugh from the two girls, but none was forthcoming.

'Behave yourself now. Ruby's not in the mood for your daft jokes,' Kath scolded him, and putting her hands on her hips asked, 'Do you want a brew?'

'Wouldn't say no.' He looked around the flat. 'Where's Margot Fonteyn tonight then?'

Kath tutted. 'Penny's away. Now try and say something nice to Ruby while I'm in the kitchen.'

'Give me ten minutes. I'll have her rolling off the settee,' he joked to his sister's back.

When alone with Ruby he fell silent. Until finally he said pointedly, 'I'm fine, thanks for asking.'

Ruby pursed her lips and mumbled, 'I can see that.'

'Glad you noticed I just had me hair done.' He smoothed his hand over the glossy wave that the barber had coaxed into the latest fashion. 'It's called a DA. All the rage in America.'

At this, Ruby's eyes filled with tears. 'Don't talk to me about America!'

'Pardon me! Have they just dropped another bomb somewhere?'

Ruby just stared at him. The tears began to roll slowly down her cheeks.

'Christ, Ruby, what's wrong?'

She leaned forward and cupped her face in her hands. Her shoulders shook and Bernie could hear her gasped breaths. He sat still, wondering if he should call Kath. Then decided against it. Instead he got up and sat beside her.

'Blimey, if we had a quid for every one of them tears we'd be rich,' he said, laughing mirthlessly.

Before he knew it, she had thrown herself into his arms. Soon he was stroking her hair and patting her back trying to console her. And all the old feelings came rushing back.

Just as if it was yesterday.

A clock somewhere struck midnight and Ruby heaved a deep breath as she finished telling Bernie her long tale of woe. She had repeated everything she'd told Kath, who had gone to bed an hour ago, as she had to be up at the crack of dawn.

'So now you know,' she said as Bernie, his tie undone and his new hairstyle flopping forward over his face, got up to walk around the flat.

'This Anna is a bloke done up in a dress if you ask me,' Bernie commented, sitting down again. 'Wouldn't put it past her selling off her old mother if the price was right.'

'What makes you say that?'

'She's got that look in her eye.'

Ruby shrugged. 'I always thought she had beautiful eyes.'

'Yeah, like them big hungry tigers at the zoo.'

Ruby smiled weakly. 'You always exaggerate.'

Bernie sat forward and taking a breath said in a low voice, 'Look, do you want me to go over and sort her out? And while I'm at it, I'll find the Yank too. Give him a bit of his own medicine.'

Ruby was touched as she knew Bernie meant what he said. But the damage had been done and now she had lost all her confidence. 'No, I don't want anything from Anna now,' she lied, trying to ignore the nagging voice inside her head, reminding her that, if she had wanted to live the Dower Street lifestyle, she should have swallowed her pride.

'Then if that's the case,' Bernie said, 'put it all behind you and start again. You're a good-looker, you know that. You could get a job anywhere.'

'Yes, as a barmaid or in a factory.'

'What's wrong with being a barmaid? And me own sister worked in a factory.'

'I don't want men gawping at me over their beers. I couldn't stand the noise and dirt in a factory.'

'Blimey, you don't want much, do you?'

Ruby felt a wave of anger. She had opened her heart to Bernie and he still didn't understand. 'I know what I want. And it's not working in a boozy pub or on a filthy shop floor.'

'So what are you going to do?'

'I don't know.'

'I hope you got your due before you left.'

'Course I did.' She couldn't admit that in her little show of temper to Anna she had walked out without her wages. She stood up. 'I'm tired. I'm going to bed now.'

Bernie stood reluctantly. 'So you really are going back to your mum's?'

'Penny's back tomorrow. I can't stay here.'

'What about this bloke of yours?'

Ruby went scarlet. 'What bloke?'

'This Nick geezer. Kath told me you're seeing him.'

'So what if I am?'

Bernie just stared at her with his big dark eyes. Then, shrugging, he turned and walked to the door. It was half open when he said casually, 'Want a ride home tomorrow?'

'Please yourself.' She wasn't going to let him think he was doing her a favour. 'I can catch the bus.'

'Pick you up in me dinner hour, then.' He walked out into the dimly lit passage. 'By the way, about that diary of Pete's.'

'Have you talked to his mates?' she asked hopefully.

'I asked around, like I said I would. But Pete gave all the lads from the island the cold shoulder after he moved up West. None of 'em knew where he lived much less who Joanie was. Bob Rawlings and Lenny Gooding were the only two to turn up at his funeral if you remember.'

Ruby shivered as she thought of Pete's funeral. The occasion had passed as though she was in a daze. All she could remember was her mum sobbing in her dad's arms and nearly passing out at the graveside. Other faces eluded her, except Bernie and Kath who had been trying to hide their own sorrow.

'So you found out nothing,' Ruby huffed, trying to end the conversation which she knew Bernie was attempting to string out.

'Well, there was something.'

'What?' Ruby said suspiciously.

'I went to the library. Wanted to find out who the WC was who said, "If you're going through hell, keep going."'

'So who was it?'

'Winnie Churchill.'

'Pete was mad about him,' Ruby replied thoughtfully. 'Said he saved our country and defied all the odds. Him and Montgomery Clift the film actor were his two idols.'

Bernie wrinkled his eyebrows as if in deep concentration. 'I'll bet you a bob the ugly mutt you saw in the picture on Pete's wall was one of them bulldogs.'

'How did you know that?'

Bernie wagged a finger. 'Cos Winnie was called the British Bulldog. Got it?'

Ruby nodded. 'You're quite the detective.'

Bernie grinned, stepping closer. 'So there are some things about me you like?'

'Goodnight, Bernie, I'm closing the door now.' She pulled it hard.

As she turned off the lights and made her way into Penny's bedroom, the thought struck her that Bernie could really use his brains when he wanted to. But, he was a lazy devil, and had a one-track mind. He would have rabbited on all night if she had given him half a chance.

It was a long while before sleep came. She was uncomfortable in a strange bed, an unfamiliar room and with Penny's possessions all around her. Another girl's world in which she played no part. Tomorrow she would return to her own world, one she knew – and dreaded. Back to the downtrodden surroundings of the Mallard Road Estate on the Isle of Dogs with the constant clickety-clack of the sewing machine. For all her airs and graces learned in her brief career as a model, she was back to square one.

# Chapter Twenty-One

It was late in the month of August when Ruby sat on the broken wall in the back yard of the prefab, listening to the humdrum sounds of the docks. The gulls were circling overhead, noisy and jostling, hoping for a teatime meal, scraps thrown from a fishing boat or a tug, or the emptying of waste from the many ships' holds. Together with the muted hoots and sirens from the river traffic she could just hear the faint roar of the city's life. Somewhere in those West End streets, Nick was driving the Buick. Would he be missing her as she missed him? What had he been told when he telephoned Anna's to speak to her and arrange their weekend in the country? She had never given him her home address. And yet, if he had gone to Larry's, Debbie would have given it to him.

Ruby sighed heavily, stretching her aching back, unconsciously massaging her work-worn hands as thoughts of Nick seemed to torment her more now than ever. She had resisted the temptation to phone him. Once, a month after coming home, she had walked up to the public phone box and lifted the receiver. But at the last moment replaced it. She was certain he would come to find her. And when he did, it would be easier to sink her pride and admit he was right. Anna had outwitted her.

If only she could go back in time to the encounter with Jesse Marlon. Ruby knew now she could have done as Anna had said. If she had really put her mind to it, she could have kept Jesse Marlon at bay, instead of acting like a spoiled child.

Ruby gazed down at the hard sores on the palms of her hands. Escort work paled into insignificance beside the last three months of drudgery. And the worst of it was, Ruby knew there was more to come. Her mum wasn't getting any better. In fact she was worse. She'd even given up her sewing. It was a relief not to hear the machine whirring away. But the silence left in its place was worse.

Ruby hauled in a deep breath as she thought of the days of her childhood. She and Pete had played in the docks, jumping the barges and mud-larking. They had never fallen in the river as their dad had warned them they would. But Mum would always know where they'd been by the tyre marks left on their legs. They'd tuck in to fish and chips on a Friday night, while Mum and Dad went out for a drink at the pub.

And now she was doing what Mum used to do. The cooking, cleaning, washing, ironing and shopping. She woke each morning wondering if Nick would ever find her. She still had her dreams!

A bright burst of scarlet sun lit the evening sky and a soft breeze lifted the untidy strands of Ruby's hair. August – and harvest time. In Devon, Pete and her had gone scrumping, stealing fruit from the farmers' orchards. Up among the leafy branches they gulped down the over-ripe fruit and swatted away the wasps.

A tall figure came round the side of the house. 'Hello, love, you taking a breather?' her dad said, swiping off his cap and thrusting a filthy hand through his thick, flattened hair.

'Yes, while Mum's asleep.'

He put his arm round her and kissed her cheek. His grubby overalls smelled of Old Holborn. He was forever rolling his own. Even her hair smelled of it now.

'Got a game of billiards tonight. You don't mind, do you?' He put down his battered tin lunch box and sat beside her.

She would be alone again as her mum would either be sleeping or sitting in the chair, her eyes fixed on the window as if in a trance.

'Dad, what can we do about Mum?'

'Dunno, love.' He drew out his tobacco pouch from his trouser pocket. 'I've tried everything in the book. It's like she don't want to live in this world without your brother.'

Ruby thought the same. If only Pete was here. She rubbed her sticky neck, wishing it wasn't so hot. The air was close and the slight breeze didn't blow often enough. Her thin, short-sleeved blouse was damp with sweat and her stockingless knees were red raw. She'd scrubbed the kitchen tiles today, trying not to think about Nick and why he had never tried to find her.

'I won't be late,' her father said as he lit up and blew out a long trail of smoke. 'I'll just have a couple of games, all right?'

Ruby smiled. She knew he was trying to come to terms with Babs's illness. He couldn't even sleep in his own bed now, for fear of disturbing Babs. Instead he slept on the couch.

'Dunno what I'd do without you, gel,' her dad said affectionately. 'I was at me wits' end before you came back. I hope it all ain't too much for you?'

'Course not,' she replied, and seeing the relief on his face she held out her arms. 'Give us a hug, Dad.'

They embraced and she took comfort from his work-manlike strength and familiar smell. He'd been through grief and heartache like her, but they had each other.

And she was grateful for that.

A week later, the first in September, Ruby was at the end of her tether. Babs just wouldn't eat.

'No ta, love. P'raps later,' she said, pushing away the chicken broth Ruby had made. She turned her head on the pillow, looking at the window. As if, Ruby thought, Pete was going to be standing there, a grin on his face, drumming his fingers on the glass pane to draw their attention.

Ruby placed the soup in the pantry under a gauze cloth, a pantry that was now spotlessly clean from the many times she had scoured it. 'I've used so much disinfectant I've turned this place into bloody Boots,' she said and laughed aloud. She was even holding a conversation with herself now!

The hall and the front room were also spotlessly clean. The sewing machine was covered by its wooden case and all her mum's odds and ends of material were folded away in the sideboard. As for all the old boxes, newspapers and moth-eaten clothes that her mum had hoarded, these too had been disposed of. Even her own bedroom was now clear of the junk stored in it. Her single bed and wardrobe were now visible. As for the cockroaches she had discovered climbing the walls, she had swiftly resorted to the Jeyes. The strong disinfectant was lethal to the bugs and killed them stone dead.

A bang at the door made her jump. Maggs Jenkins strode in, without knocking as usual. Her mum's friend had started calling again and Ruby was grateful. While Maggs kept an eye on her mum, she was free to go out for the shopping; Maggs, a tall, angular woman in her fifties with her hair rolled up under a turban, was happy to talk till the cows came home.

'Where are you off to today, love?' Maggs asked, pulling her cross-over apron around her chest.

'Cox Street,' was Ruby's reply, for where else was there for her to go? Market prices were all they could afford on her dad's wages.

'Mum in bed, is she?' Maggs asked, cuffing the drip from her long nose.

Ruby nodded. She lifted the shopping bag from the peg. 'I'll be off then.'

'Don't rush back, love.'

Ruby smiled at Maggs's kind face under the turban. She was a lonely widow and her three children were scattered to every corner of the earth. She had been upset when Babs discouraged her visits but had told Ruby before she left home she was there for Babs if ever she was needed. Ruby knew the value of a good neighbour now, a truth she had never appreciated before.

Ruby left the prefab and at last felt free of her daily confinement. She stood still at the broken gate, breathing in the early September air. Unpolluted by disinfectant or damp, the oxygen swelled inside her. River air, tarry and briny, nature's own medicine. The warmth of the sun played on her back, as if welcoming her to the new day.

As Ruby acknowledged their smiling neighbour across the road and the whistling baker who came round in his van, she felt part of life again. Somewhere inside her a ray of hope flickered that Nick would find her again.

September's chill had set in the following week. The skies were slate grey and the wind that blew off the river had a winter's bite. Ruby decided to light a fire and eat lunch in front of a warm blaze. As she was preparing the soup, she heard a noise from the hall. Thinking it might be Maggs letting herself in, she hurried out.

But the hall was empty. Ruby opened the front door and walked down the path. There was no one in sight on the Mallard Road. Shivering, she went back indoors.

The noise again! Like someone talking. Perhaps Maggs had gone in to see her mum? Ruby hurried in there. The room was empty, the bedclothes pushed to one side. Ruby ran to the bathroom, the kitchen and her own room. A wave of panic flooded her as she hurried out to the yard. All was deserted.

Once again she tried the road. There were a few figures walking up and down, but not her mum. Ruby ran back indoors. She didn't know where else to search. Would her mum have walked down to Maggs's house? But in her nightclothes? Ruby grabbed her coat from the hall stand. Just as she was about to leave, she heard the soft noises again.

'Mum, is that you?' she called.

No reply. Ruby shivered. Who was in the house? She walked slowly forward, her eyes darting around. The sound came from Pete's room.

'Mum?' Ruby slowly opened the door. She hadn't been in here since she'd come home. It still upset her to see all Pete's things just as they were.

'We was just having a chat,' her mother said, looking up with huge, vacant eyes from where she sat on Pete's bed.

'Who was?' Ruby asked, looking round.

Babs smiled in surprise. 'Me and your brother of course.'

Ruby shook her head in bewilderment. 'Mum, Pete ain't here.'

'Course he is, love.'

'Where?'

Babs patted the bed beside her. 'Look, he's smiling at us. Ain't he a handsome bugger?' Babs frowned as she gazed into thin air. 'But I've torn him off a strip. Told him he's got to visit more. That boss of his is working him too bloody hard.'

Ruby's legs went weak. Now her mum was seeing things. She was having hallucinations. 'I've lit a fire,' she coaxed with a shaky smile. 'Let's go in the front room.'

'I've got my boy to keep me warm,' Babs said with a happy expression. 'Look, he's coming to give you a hug.'

Ruby felt a shiver go over her from her head to her toes. What was she to do? Or say?

'There,' Babs sighed, pulling on the buttons of her nightdress. 'He's telling you he wants to talk to you. But you ain't been in here much, have you? You used to come all the time. You and him. Always telling each other your little secrets.' Babs laughed strangely. 'Don't think me and your dad didn't notice. We always knew you two was peas in a pod. And thank God for it.'

The tears filled Ruby's eyes. 'Mum, you mustn't do this.'

'Why?' Babs asked in surprise. 'Don't upset your brother now.'

'There ain't no one to upset!' Ruby burst out. 'You know as well as me that Pete is dead. He took all them pills and we found him that morning. Here where you're sitting. Where he was—' She took hold of her mother's cold hands and shook them. 'Where he was lying. Right? Christ, Mum, losing Pete was bad enough, but we're losing you too. You've got to come back to us. I'm your daughter, after all. I need you. I need you more than Pete does. He's gone. But I'm here, in the flesh, so is Dad. And you've got to realize that.' The bitter tears streamed down her face as she spoke.

Babs pushed her away. 'I'm going back to bed now.'

'Don't leave me,' Ruby called as her mum walked out of the door.

Ruby sank down on the bed.

If only there was someone to tell her what to do.

# Chapter Twenty-Two

Ruby jumped.

She'd fallen asleep on Pete's bed. How long had she been lying here? The mantel clock said half past one. Almost an hour.

She sat up and the conversation she'd had with Babs came back to her. Her mum must be very ill. Nothing was going to bring her back to reality.

Her gaze went to Pete's wardrobe where she'd found his diary. She hadn't read it since coming home. It had been easy to look at it at Dower Street. But here in the room that Pete had occupied, reading his written words made her sad.

What had her mum said? This imaginary Pete had said Ruby hadn't gone in his room to talk to him. This gave her the willies, because this room was indeed where she and Pete had talked together. Though he'd carefully kept hidden the biggest secret, Joanie. Who was this Joanie? Why had he never talked about her?

Ruby stood up and brushed down her crumpled blouse. The tears had dried stiffly on her cheeks. She looked in the mirror to inspect the damage. As she saw her reflection she barely recognized her ashen, puffy face. Where was the person who had spent hours in the bathroom at Dower Street, soaked in scented water? The girl who scoured the magazines for the latest fashions. The model who had paraded so confidently at Steadman's.

How had she come to this?

Ruby's thoughts were disturbed by Maggs calling her name. Quickly Ruby pushed back her hair and took a breath. When she got to the kitchen, Maggs was putting on the kettle.

'Hello, ducks, I reckoned you could do with a cuppa by now.'

'Yes, that'd be nice.'

'How's yer mum today?'

'She was talking to Pete in his bedroom.'

Maggs turned round, a smile on her face. 'Did she say what he said?'

'She said she gave him a ticking off for not coming round more.'

Maggs cackled with laughter. 'Sorry, but I can see the funny side.'

'I wish I could.'

'You'll have to, if this is to be a regular thing.'

Ruby groaned softly. 'Do you think it might be?'

Maggs waved her hand. 'Did she seem happy to see him?'

'Yes, but no one was there,' Ruby repeated. 'There was only us in his room.'

Maggs's thin eyebrows disappeared under her turban. 'No one you could see, at least.' The kettle boiled and began to whistle. Maggs turned off the gas. 'If your mum was happy to talk to this invisible someone, what's the harm?'

While Maggs made the tea, Ruby put out the cups. She sat down and sighed. 'I don't know what to do for the best, Maggs. I feel lost.'

'We're all lost until someone turns on the light in our heads. And believe me, there's lots of lights to turn on before you can see where you're going.'

Ruby laughed.

'That's better. Now drink your brew. And then you can get off to do yer shopping.'

Once, Ruby thought with amusement, she wouldn't have thought shopping at the market would have been the high spot of her week.

Now she couldn't wait to get out of the door.

It was on a cold and crisp Friday later that month when Kath and Bernie called round. 'It's my first day off in weeks,' Kath said, giving Ruby a hug on the doorstep. 'Are you stopping?'

'Bernie's in the car. We thought you might like a ride out. That is, if you can leave your mum.'

Ruby glanced over Kath's shoulder to catch Bernie's wave from the window. 'I could get Maggs to come and sit with her.'

'Who's Maggs?'

'Mum's friend. She lives at the end of the road and calls in most days.'

'Good,' Kath said eagerly. 'Go and put on something nice.'

'Where are we going?' Ruby glanced down at her overalls which were already thin and patched. She had forgotten what nice clothes looked like.

'It's a surprise.'

Ruby didn't know if she was in the mood for surprises. And, in comparison to Kath, who wore a smart herring-bone-patterned coat with a black patent belt and matching high heels, she felt like the dog's dinner.

'Go on,' Kath said, ignoring her hesitation. 'Meanwhile I'll have a chat with your mum.'

'She's in the front room by the fire.'

Kath hustled Ruby towards her bedroom. 'Now, dolly yourself up and prepare for a nice afternoon out.'

Ruby knew Kath wouldn't take no for an answer. Wishing she had washed her hair last night, she looked in her wardrobe. She only had the grey suit with the fur collar that she'd bought from Patterson's. At least it was in good condition. And why shouldn't it be?

She hadn't gone anywhere to wear it!


'Darling girl. Happy birthday!' Ruby found herself folded into Larry's arms. All the smells she remembered from the poodle parlour engulfed her. Doggie hair, talcum powder, shampoo and Debbie's cheap perfume. Debbie and Stuart stared at her over Larry's shoulder, smiles on their faces, and Bernie and Kath stood grinning beside them.

'My birthday?' Ruby repeated, suddenly realizing she had forgotten it was today.

'Happy birthday,' Debbie said. 'Long time no see.'

Ruby blushed. She hadn't even sent Debbie a wedding card. 'Yes, it is. Are you Mrs Stacey now?'

'Yes, and very happy too.' Debbie flashed the diamond engagement ring on her finger by the band of gold.

'I'm sorry I couldn't come to your wedding. I had to look after me mum.'

'So I hear.'

'Have you got a kiss for Uncle Stuart?' Stuart said as he embraced her. 'I'm glad to see you're as beautiful as ever, my dear.'

Ruby was close to tears. She hadn't expected all this.

'Well, let's get the party started,' Larry gushed, taking her hand and dragging her out to the back room. Everyone followed and Ruby was shocked to see a white tablecloth over the bench, complete with a large pink-and-white iced birthday cake and twenty candles. Beside this stood a bottle of champagne and half a dozen glasses.

'Is this for me?' Ruby gasped.

'Who else?'

'What if a customer comes in?'

'We've no appointments for today and there's a *Closed* sign on the door.'

Ruby hadn't noticed. She had been very anxious when Bernie and Kath had appeared. Meeting anyone at the parlour meant giving explanations, and right now she couldn't give them.

'Let's toast the birthday girl,' Stuart said, expertly open-ing the bottle, and everyone screamed as the champagne cork popped out. Soon their glasses were full and Ruby cut the cake with a sharp knife that Debbie handed her.

'You went to all this trouble on my behalf?' Ruby said as she stood with eyes wide.

'You're very special to us, darling. Kath told us about the hell you went through at Dower Street. So this is our way of cheering you up.' Proudly, Larry pushed out his round stomach under his polo-neck sweater. Ruby thought how fashionably dressed he was, in a dark suit and new horn-rimmed spectacles that suited his big eyes. Stuart was wearing a white jacket and Paisley silk scarf that made him look more like an actor than ever. Debbie had chosen a plain brown dress, Ruby noticed. There was a noticeable curve to her stomach. Was she pregnant already? she wondered. Kath and Bernie stood quietly in the background until Larry looped his arm through Kath's.

'This young lady has been very concerned about you,' he said earnestly. 'We all know how hard it has been for you looking after your mother.' His face grew solemn. 'Remember, I had a mother of my own once who I loved dearly, but demanded so much attention I almost forgot who I was.'

'Now, now, Larry, we aren't here to depress Ruby,' interrupted Stuart, waving his hand. 'In fact, we are hoping that, when your problems at home are over, Ruby, you'll come back to the fold.'

She tried to smile. Stuart's offer was a generous one, but the thought of coming back to the parlour and having to deal with customers like Mrs Freeman again wasn't something she wanted. All the same, she said quietly, 'You've all been so kind. Thank you.'

'We're your friends, my sweet,' Larry cooed. 'You can always count on us.'

As everyone was drinking and talking, Ruby looked at Bernie. 'You're very quiet.'

'Don't have much to say, except happy birthday.'

'You managed to keep this a secret.'

'Yeah, well, they told me to keep shtoom.'

'Your sister is such a good friend to me.' Ruby looked down at the sparkling liquid in her glass. Tears were close again. 'So are you, Bernie.'

'Thanks.'

'Don't say it like that.' Ruby saw disappointment in Bernie's face. He still wanted more than friendship.

'Oh, by the way, there's one more guest to arrive,' Larry shouted across the room. 'Should be here any sec.'

Bernie walked away from her to pour himself another drink. Kath looked expectantly through the window and Stuart nodded, adding, 'A very special guest.'

'Who?' Ruby couldn't guess who they meant. But then her heart almost leaped out of her chest as the familiar shape of a large car drew up outside.

Her heart beat so fast she thought she was about to faint. A figure climbed out and walked to the front door. A few seconds later a handsome man wearing a navy camel-haired overcoat entered. Pushing his hand over the immaculate cut of his short brown hair, he smiled.

'N–Nick!' Ruby stammered as he slid his hand around her waist. 'What are you doing here?'

'I've been out of town on business for a while or I would have come sooner.'

'How did you find me?'

He raised his broad shoulders in a shrug. 'Anna told me you'd decided to leave the agency.'

'So you spoke to her? Did she tell you what happened?' Ruby asked anxiously.

'It doesn't matter now, darling. I bumped into Kath in Dean Street a couple of weeks ago. She was on her way to the theatre and I had some business to attend to. It was just the opportunity I needed to ask how you were.'

Ruby looked at Kath. 'You never said.'

'I wanted to give you a birthday surprise,' Kath replied with a grin. 'And when I saw Nick, I realized I could bring you two together again.'

'Welcome back to the real world,' Nick whispered in Ruby's ear as Debbie, Rog, Larry, Stuart and Kath joined them with smiles and laughter.

Everyone, Ruby noticed, except Bernie.

The party was coming to an end and there were tearful goodbyes all round. Ruby promised she would keep in touch and consider Larry's offer of work when her mum was better. She knew that day was a long way off, but her reply seemed to satisfy him.

'Take care of yourself,' Debbie said as she kissed Ruby's cheek. 'Come and see me and Rog when you've got time.'

'Where are you living?'

'We're still at Paradise Row. But we're leaving soon. The twins are driving Rog crackers.'

'I hope you'll both be very happy.' Ruby turned to Larry and Stuart. 'Thank you for today. It was so unexpected.'

'It was meant to be,' cooed Stuart. 'Now, darling, don't leave it too long before we speak again.'

After yet more hugs and kisses, Ruby found herself outside on the pavement with Nick and Kath. She noticed that Bernie had already climbed into his old car parked in front of the Buick.

'Better be off,' Kath said, rolling her eyes. 'And I'm sure you both have a lot of catching up to do.'

Ruby smiled, glancing shyly up at Nick. 'Yes, that's true.'

'Me and Bernie will call at your mum's and tell Maggs you've decided to take a day off and I've persuaded you to stay the night at my place.'

'But will she believe you?'

'I'll make sure she does. Remember, Maggs told you that she'd cook your dad's dinner. And for once your dad will have to stay home and do the honours. Looking after your mum for one evening won't kill him. And Maggs will be on the doorstep to take over early tomorrow. So you two now have no excuse not to be with each other.'

'Yes, darling, Kath's right,' Nick agreed, pulling Ruby close. 'We'll go to Angelo's for dinner, then go back to my place.'

Ruby looked up into his brown eyes as butterflies flew wildly in her tummy. Angelo's. The Italian restaurant that he had introduced her to and which they had made their own. Once again, she felt tearful. She had missed him so much and now there was an explanation as to why he hadn't come after her. So why was she hesitating?

'Hurry up, Kath,' Bernie shouted from the car. 'This motor is guzzling the juice.'

'Bye,' said Kath, pushing Ruby towards the Buick. 'Leave everything to me and Maggs.'

Nick took Ruby's hand. 'Say goodbye to your friends, darling.'

As Ruby waved to the faces gazing out at them, Kath jumped into Bernie's car. With a roar it sped off in a cloud of black smoke.

'What are we waiting for?' Nick said in a husky voice. 'I want to make the most of every minute now that I have you all to myself.' Ruby wanted to say that this was the best surprise she had ever had. Nothing else could compare to seeing Nick again. And to think that now she had him for a whole day and night, thanks to her best friend, Kath.

Nick was pleased to see that, as requested, Angelo had reserved them a secluded table in the corner. He felt truly remiss at the way he had neglected to find Ruby, but his business disputes with Anna had been overtaken by a far more personal issue. Then, two weeks ago, in Soho, he'd bumped into Kath, of all people, a stately, willowy figure he couldn't miss in the crowd. He'd asked after Ruby and taken her for a coffee, there to arrange today's get-together. The meeting was perfect timing. An unforeseen answer to a problem he'd been wrestling with for some time.

Nick gazed across the table at the young woman seated opposite him. Ruby hadn't lost her charm, though he could see that Anna's influence had rather gone by the board. If Anna was nothing else, she could certainly turn out a professional product. The grey suit and fur collar Ruby had chosen to wear didn't do her justice. The light in her lovely blue eyes occasionally sparkled, but then often she would look away from his gaze. He couldn't tell what she was thinking. But he intended to find out.

He smiled, showing his white teeth fleetingly. 'Happy, darling?'

'Yes, very.'

'I hope so. I want tonight to be very special.'

'Oh Nick. So much has happened. I've lots to tell you.'

'Wait until we get home. We'll make ourselves comfortable. And we'll talk over every last detail.'

He grinned again, touching her hand, pleased that so far the day had gone satisfactorily. They'd enjoyed their meal of Angelo's house spaghetti bolognese followed by whipped Italian ice cream sprinkled with nuts and chocolate, which he knew was Ruby's favourite. He'd told Angelo he wanted this occasion to be very special. And he'd been pleased to see that Angelo had reserved them an intimate table in the corner. Complete with a slim lit candle and a vase of tiny red roses that he'd ordered especially, the mood was suitably romantic. He reached across to grasp Ruby's hand. 'You look very lovely.'

Ruby smiled. 'I wish you had warned me to wear something nice.'

'If I had, I would have spoiled Kath's surprise.' He lifted a finger to scoop away the tear that slipped down her cheek. As he did so, the other diners looked round to wonder why the lights had suddenly dimmed. A small group of musicians appeared at their table, two with violins, the other with a guitar. They began to play a love song and he sat back, enjoying the way everyone in the restaurant was gazing at Ruby. She was a natural beauty. If he won her trust, then what was to stop his success?

He plucked one of the tiny red buds from the vase. 'For you, my darling, the most endearingly beautiful of roses.'

He knew that was what she wanted to hear. What any woman would want to hear.

# Chapter Twenty-Three

Bernie stirred his tea thoughtfully, recalling the happy hours he'd spent at this prefab many moons ago. He'd helped Mr Payne in the back yard, in the days when there was a garden of sorts. When spuds had shot up beside the marigolds and wallflowers had spilled over the garden path. In those days, him and Pete had skived a good few days off school as they had in Devon. It had been easier there. The teachers were always pleased to see the backsides of the dirty, smelly East End kids. And if they played truant, well so be it.

Pete was always up the library though, his head in a book. Doing it his own way. Always wanting to learn. He'd liked poetry too, but that was something he kept to himself; Pete had a soft side to him he didn't reveal to many. They had shared a lot as kids, but all that was to stop when Pete got his job with the toffs.

Bernie fidgeted restlessly as he sat with Mrs Payne and his sister. He knew that Kath wouldn't leave her till Mr P got home. And even though Maggs had been reluctant to go, saying she'd cook dinner, Pete knew Kath was

determined to get Mr P's attention. To persuade him back
into caring for his wife and sharing the load with Ruby.
But looking at Mrs P now, Bernie doubted she was ever
going to be the same again. She had that hollow, vacant
look that sick people got and yellowy skin that made the
bags under her eyes look like little purple pillows.

Bernie gulped down his tea. Mrs P hadn't stopped
rabbiting on about Pete. Well, he didn't mind that. But it
was the same thing over and over again. How Pete always
brought home the bacon. How her boy never failed to
bung her a regular few quid. How he'd tell her she was
the best mum in the world and what he was going to do
when he made his mint. He'd pack Mr and Mrs P off on
the holiday of a lifetime. All round the world on a bloody
cruise! Come to think of it, not a murmur of Ruby, who
was doing the hard graft here. Her dad would have been
well and truly shafted if Ruby hadn't come home. And
that was a fact, Bernie thought, trying to dampen his irri-
tation at Babs Payne's whining voice: Pete this. Pete that.
Saint flaming Pete.

'Mind if I use the john, Mrs P?' Bernie asked, suddenly
standing up. 'All this rosie is doing me bladder in.'

Mrs P looked up at him. 'Course, love. And on your
way tell Pete it's teatime. He'll be in his room, playing his
music.'

Bernie glanced at his sister. She gave him an impercep-
tible shrug.

'Yeah, course.' He made his escape, closing the front-
room door softly behind him. He could hear Kath's voice,

then Mrs P's. He thought how he'd soon be round the bend too, if he was here much longer.

He fished for his fags in his pocket. Soon he was gulping back smoke, enjoying the nicotine kick. He'd given up so many times, like Kath had. Penny didn't smoke, insisting it was a killer for the dancing. Now he was even more self-conscious of the habit. Especially round Ruby.

Bernie paced the small hall, thinking of her and trying not to. He'd got a right old headache when he'd seen the way that character had slobbered over her!

Bernie closed his eyes, trying to dismiss the picture of Ruby in the smarmy geezer's arms. He'd seen them in the driving mirror. Standing on the pavement all over each other. What did she see in the charmer? What did Nick bloody Brandon have that he didn't have? The spiel, that was it. The money and the motor. Bernie had to admit the Buick was some runner – even he wouldn't disagree with that.

Just as Bernie was about to turn round, his gaze caught Pete's door. It was open a couple of inches. Inside he could see the wardrobe. He walked slowly towards it.

Nothing had changed in this room. Like Ruby had told him, it was kept as a shrine. There was a stillness here, as though the room was waiting. But waiting for who? Pete?

Bernie shivered. He shouldn't be in here. Mrs P would have forty fits if she knew. But he stood his ground all the same, looking round, inhaling the mouldy, blistering walls, the cold light of day spilling onto the bed. Pete's bed. Where he died. Where Ruby found him. Poor cow.

Bernie sighed again, his gaze taking in the last earthly memories Pete would have had. He'd come home for the weekend, was in good spirits as far as everyone knew. Taken his mum out shopping in the car. Walked Ruby to Island Gardens and gone out for a pint with yours truly. He'd been the usual Pete, a bit more flash than usual, perhaps. Boasting a deal was going down with a right result in the offing. They'd parted on good terms, no questions asked. Bernie had learned to keep his curiosity to himself. He knew Pete liked a bit of brag and why not? His mate was doing well for himself by all accounts.

Then, a day later, Pete was no more. He'd tipped a bottle of pills down his throat together with a bottle of booze. So what had happened in those twenty-four hours to change the course of his life?

Even now, Bernie shook his head. He was mystified. Glancing distractedly at the wardrobe he remembered Ruby had said she found the diary there. Had she put it back again? He went over, looked warily around, before opening the door. He went on his haunches, shuffled Pete's shoes and saw the catch. He lifted it. Nothing there. Ruby must still have the diary. He replaced the shoes and closed the wardrobe.

Then it hit him, like a brick. Pete was hiding his secrets. In his diary. Why else keep one? Why hide it? The clues to his death had to be there. The diary wasn't just some old bit of tat. It was Pete's legacy.

Bernie straightened up. His heart was beating fast. Who the hell was Joanie? She was on every page. She was the one person who knew the most about Pete. The real Pete. The joker Pete, the boaster, the clever bugger. Joanie knew the face under the mask. Past Pete's schmooze and all his verbal.

Bernie studied the picture on the wall. The one beside the wardrobe. The dog in the top hat. Another nod to Pete's worship of old Winnie. *If you're going through hell, keep going.*

So what was Pete's own private hell?

The picture was lopsided and Bernie reached out to square it. Funny, he didn't even like touching it. The frame was good quality but dust-coated. The glass was smudged. Odd that, as according to Ruby, Mrs P liked his room kept spotless.

Then suddenly the picture seemed to fly from its hook. 'You clumsy bugger!' he muttered to himself, reaching down to retrieve it. 'Thank Christ the glass isn't broken.'

Slowly, he turned it over.

He read, then reread the handwritten lines on the back. *For Pete, my love, my world. Forever yours, J. 1951.*

And underneath, a label.

*Cuthbertson Studio. Fine Prints and Photography.*


Ruby didn't want to open her eyes, just in case she woke up in her own bed. Had she dreamed the incredible night of lovemaking? She had never really believed she would find herself back in Nick's arms again. Often, she'd tricked herself into believing that fate would reunite them. Reason enough to propel her through the daylight hours spent caring for her mum, and the dark ones, spent alone. But now it had really happened.

In the dim light, Nick pulled her gently towards him, kissing her eyes, nose and finally her mouth. His hands travelled down to her hips, moving her into the shape of his strong body. She murmured in delight. 'I've wanted this for so long.'

'So have I.'

'What did Anna tell you?' She had said it before she could stop herself. 'I'm sorry, but I have to know.'

'I'd rather we forgot Anna.'

'Yes, but did she tell you about Mr Steadman?' Ruby pressed.

Nick released his hold on her, then, turning on the bedside light, he searched for his cigarettes. 'Young lady, you have just effectively put an end to my romancing. Here, take this.' He held out a Gauloise.

Ruby sat up beside him, covering her naked breasts with the sheet. Obediently she put the cigarette to her lips. A few splutters later, they were both laughing.

'You'll never make a smoker.' Nick slid his arm around her.

'No, but I tried.'

'You're like a little princess, with no vices at all.'

She snuggled against him. 'My biggest vice is being crazy about you.'

'So you'd call that a vice?' He ground the cigarette out in the ashtray.

'Course not. But I keep worrying I'll never see you

again. Or that Anna, like the wicked witch, will cast a spell on us somehow.'

'She'll never do that.' He ran his fingers up and down her arm, making her shiver. Then, playing with her hair, he said in a subdued tone, 'Hey, you're safe here with me now.'

'She played a cruel trick,' Ruby insisted. 'Mr Steadman wanted me to wear a belly-dancing costume.' Ruby looked up at him, at the square shape of his jaw and the smile he was trying to hide. 'It's not funny, Nick.'

'No, but knowing you, I can imagine your reply.'

'I threatened to go to the newspapers. I thought that would give him a fright.'

'I'm sure it did.' He clasped her chin in his fingers. 'Nothing surprises me where Anna's concerned. Sorry, little princess, but I did try to warn you.'

To her shame, Ruby knew she had walked into Anna's trap with her eyes wide open. 'I can see how she earned her reputation.'

'I'm glad that's evident now. I hope you'll never get involved with Anna again.'

Ruby sighed heavily. 'I must admit I miss modelling.'

He pulled her into his arms. 'Most women are content to find a husband, get married, have babies. They don't think about careers.'

Ruby leaned her head on his shoulder. 'I like me fashions and wearing nice clothes. Modelling wasn't like work really. It was doing what I love best. After all, not many girls get the chance to wear the latest styles.' She sighed heavily. 'But I suppose that's all in the past now. I might even have to go back to Larry's.'

Nick was silent for a moment, his brow pleated. 'I don't think there's any call for that.'

Ruby frowned. 'What do you mean?'

'I've just taken on a new warehouse at Chalk Wharf.'

'Chalk Wharf?' Ruby repeated. 'But that's near the Mallard Road Estate.'

'Yes, your turf, my sweet.'

'What are you going to sell in this warehouse?'

'Some very expensive things.' He threaded his fingers through hers and looked into her eyes. 'How would you like to work for me? I'll match Anna's wages and I think I can add some interesting value to the offer.'

Intrigued, Ruby smiled. 'Is this another one of your teases?'

'When it comes to business, I'm always serious. The first rule of the game is never to make an offer you can't back up.'

'But I don't know anything about selling stuff,' Ruby said with a giggle. 'I'd be hopeless.'

'You sold expensive fashions to wealthy people. Besides which, you have the personality, intelligence, charm and good looks to sell anything you so desire.'

He was actually convincing her she could. 'But what about Mum?'

'I'll hire this Maggs on a permanent basis.'

'Would you?'

'Why not?' He smiled, the dimple in his chin

deepening. 'You can repay me in kind,' he whispered as he began to make love to her.

'Just a short way now,' Nick said as they drove through the East India Dock Road towards Chalk Wharf.

Ruby stared out of the Buick window, at the busy roads that were so familiar to her, taking the horse-drawn vehicles and many lorries to and from the docks. Before Nick took her home they were going to the warehouse; he had assured her that what she saw there would convince her to make the changes in her life that would lead to her dreams coming true.

But as the Buick sped them through the dock gates and slowly along the wharfs, she hated what she saw. These very docklands were what she had tried to escape. Mucky, noisy lorries oozing clouds of filth, gangs of stevedores, porters and casuals yelling out in their coarse language, turbaned factory workers milling around the small yards and even those dock dollies with their painted faces brave enough to show up in daylight hours. Cranes, barges, boats and ships thronged the port, causing a non-stop whirlwind of dirt, dust, noise and unpleasant odours. The industrial docklands were a far cry from Dower Street and the glamorous West End.

Ruby's new-found enthusiasm began to ebb away. She loved buying things, not selling them. Modelling hadn't been selling to her. If she was honest, walking the catwalk at Steadman's had been more like showing off! No one had enquired as to what she thought of the fashions. She just wore them. The plain truth was, she had just been a dresser's clothes horse. Not that she had ever thought of complaining. She hadn't had to use her brains. Just her vanity!

'Here we are,' Nick said as Ruby sat forward, surprised to see they were now turning away from the water's edge and driving down one of the lanes containing all kinds of commercial buildings.

'This is it,' Nick said, parking outside a large warehouse. 'Not much from the outside, but wait till you see what's beyond those rather unremarkable doors.'

He helped Ruby climb out and led her to a small, roughly painted metal door, secured by a strong lock. At eye level there was a small square opening.

'What's that?' Ruby asked as they walked in.

'You open it to see who's there,' Nick told her, 'like this. All part of our security as well as the locking system and night watchman.'

'Why do you need so much?' Ruby asked in all innocence. The warehouse seemed just like an ordinary warehouse. One of the many in the industrial areas of the wharfs, just like she and Pete had played around as kids. Sometimes their owners left barking dogs inside to ward off any intruders. But night watchmen were expensive. The market traders who usually rented those sort of premises preferred to take care of petty thieves themselves.

'You'll see why very soon.' He unlocked and pushed open a second door, also made of steel. Ruby walked into the cavernous building with high cathedral ceilings and under them wooden crates piled upon wooden crates.

'What's in all those?' she asked curiously.

'Come along and I'll show you.'

Ruby followed him down the narrow aisle, her spirits at an all-time low. At least when she was home she was free to go to the market. And as much as she loved Nick, her eyes told her this was not an environment she could be happy in. When Nick showed her into a room with blinds at the glass windows, she gave a little shiver. How could anyone ever want to work in a place like this, day in and day out?

If what was in the crates was machinery of some kind, it would be very boring. If it was food, like tins, or perishables, it would be even less interesting. The light suddenly went on. Ruby blinked hard as she looked around. She could hardly believe what she saw. The room was full of the most amazing animal furs, pelts, coats, collars, hats and beautiful textiles.

She looked at Nick who was standing silently, one eyebrow arched. Ruby went over to the nearest white fur coat that was draped over one of the crates. She put down her bag and touched the animal skin.

'Nick, what fur is this?'

'Bear skin, from the Americas. Let me help you.' He slid it on her. Her fingers slipped through the exquisite fur and she buried her face in its luxury. 'Did this come from a real bear?'

'Yes, of course.'

'Poor thing.'

He shrugged. 'The indigenous people of the Americas have to make a living from hunting. They wouldn't survive otherwise.'

'How much does the coat cost?'

'Many, many hundreds of pounds.'

'As much as a car?'

'Perhaps more.'

Ruby pulled the warm skin around her, inhaling its own peculiar, distinctive scent. 'And you want me to sell these?'

'That's the general idea.'

Ruby tried to reply, but she couldn't. She was in fashion heaven. To think that Nick had kept all this a secret, waiting until he found her again to share it with her.

She stepped into his arms and in the warm, white folds of the coat he drew her into a long embrace.

# Chapter Twenty-Four

Two weeks later on a damp and dismal October Friday, Ruby closed her bedroom door. She was dressed in a smart, deep blue, figure-hugging suit, ready for her first working day at the warehouse. On this occasion Nick had asked her to model one of the coats. It would be her first experience of big business.

Glancing in the hall mirror she touched her freshly washed hair that now shone like spun gold, admiring again the expensive suit with velvet collar and cuffs that Nick had taken her up to Selfridges to choose.

Even though she looked her best she felt sick with fear. She still wasn't certain she could carry this off. Taking a deep breath, she walked into the front room where Maggs was on her knees, coaxing the fire into life. Her mother sat watching, wearing her dressing gown and slippers. Ruby had got her up at the crack of dawn and encouraged her to eat some porridge. She had explained where she was going today, hoping Babs wouldn't miss her. But she needn't have worried. Her mother was already in that other world, where nothing but her dead son was of interest.

'Maggs, will you be all right? Ruby asked as she slipped on the mink that Nick had given her to wear. It was a sumptuous coat and Ruby adored it. Even Anna didn't own a coat like this. Though it did seem out of place in the prefab.

'Good gracious,' Maggs said as she grabbed the edge of the couch and hoisted herself to her feet. 'I ain't ever seen a coat like that before.'

'No, neither have I.'

'What sort of fur is it?'

'Mink, so I'm told.'

Maggs chuckled. 'I'm none the wiser.'

'The mink in America has really thick, silky fur, I've learned, which feels like velvet when you touch it.'

'Blimey, you're a hive of information, ducky.'

'I've tried to do my homework.'

'I don't like the idea of wearing animals, meself,' Maggs said, keeping her distance. 'Ever since my old mum got fleas from the fox collar she wore round her neck. She was alive with the perishers and it put me off fur for life.'

Ruby grinned. 'I hope this hasn't got fleas.'

'You'll soon know about it if it has.'

They laughed together and Ruby looked down at her mother. 'What do you think of me new coat, Mum?'

Babs looked up. 'Very nice. Have you said goodbye to your brother?'

'Now, now, Babs,' Maggs cautioned gently. 'Your daughter would like a bit of encouragement. This is her first day at her new job.'

Babs glanced at Ruby and smiled. 'Don't forget to take your sandwiches with you.'

'I won't.' Ruby bent down to kiss her cheek. At least that was a sensible answer.

'I'll see you out,' said Maggs, giving Ruby a wink.

'Cheerio, Mum. See you later.'

Babs nodded, showing no emotion at all.

Ruby stood with Maggs in the hall. If it hadn't been for this kind soul, she wouldn't have been able to leave Babs unattended. Even her dad had acknowledged they'd found a treasure in Maggs.

'I've left corned beef, potatoes and carrots in the larder,' Ruby chattered, trying to calm her nerves. 'There's plenty of milk and tea. I managed to get Mum to top and tail, but she needs a bath—'

'Look, love.' Maggs stopped her in full flow. 'Stop fretting. Leave your mum to me. I'm only too pleased to look after her. I would have done this as a favour. You didn't have to pay me.'

'We all have to live, Maggs. And me mum can be difficult at times. Looking after her ain't an easy job.'

'Are you sure you can afford the fiver?' Maggs asked again. 'To be honest, I've rarely had one of these notes in me purse. I'm almost embarrassed to spend it. In fact, I think I'll take it home and frame it.'

Ruby shook her head. 'Just put it by for a rainy day. Or treat yourself to something up the shops.' She had insisted she repay Nick from her wages. He'd agreed, but added with a rueful smile the £5 would doubtless be covered in her very first commission. Ruby couldn't quite believe that was true. But she intended to stick to her principles.

'Oh, by the way, ducks,' Maggs said as Ruby was about to leave. 'Your friend Bernie called yesterday to see you. I told him you was up the West End shopping with Mr Brandon. I asked him if he wanted to wait till you came back, but he hopped it.'

'Did he say what he wanted?'

'No. Just that he'd call again.'

'Did you tell him I'd got a new job?'

'No,' Maggs said firmly. 'It wasn't up to me to say.'

Ruby didn't want Bernie turning up at the warehouse. But he'd have to know sooner or later where she was working and who she was working for. This was news she had saved to tell Kath. As her best friend Kath was entitled to be the first to know. So yesterday, she'd asked Nick to stop the car outside Kath's flat where she'd left a letter to explain what had happened. There was even a telephone at the warehouse, so Ruby had given her the number to call.

'If he stops by again, Maggs, tell him I'll be in touch.'

'All right, I will.' Maggs held out her dirty hands from the fire she had been making up. 'I'd give yer a kiss goodbye, but I wouldn't like to see that lovely coat of yours get mucky. Good luck today. And, Ruby, if you was my girl, I'd be very proud of yer.'

Ruby smiled, nodding. 'Thanks, Maggs.' She knew that Maggs was trying to make up for the affection Babs wasn't showing. But nothing and no one could replace Pete in her mum's affections.

And that's a fact of life I have to accept, Ruby thought as she closed the front door behind her and saw the Buick appear round the corner.

Nick led his buyer into the small room and gestured to one of the two chairs. The man was Russian and looked it. He wore a small dark fur hat that sat squarely above his swarthy features and heavy jaw barely disguised by the turned-up collar of his overcoat. Nick noted the excellent quality of his clothes and leather shoes. The two heavies accompanying him, however, were not so well attired. They wore boots and duffles and the required aggressive expressions. Neither spoke, only the head man who was now dismissing his men to stand outside.

'Welcome to London,' Nick said, offering a cigar. But the foreigner shook his head.

'No. We do business,' the man growled, a suspicious look in his dark eyes.

Nick hesitated, then gave an indifferent shrug. He might as well try to get on good terms with his customer. No names had been exchanged, at least, no genuine ones. The man had travelled thousands of miles to make contacts in Britain, as currently the fur trade was booming. Which was why he himself had got into the business. But then, Nick thought with satisfaction, his punter would also have to travel thousands of miles home. But not before Nick had put his own proposition on the table.

'So how would you like to do this?' Nick enquired politely. 'Pounds or roubles?'

'You have roubles?' said the man in surprise.

'Roubles, pounds, dollars. Your choice.'

'Money now?'

Nick nodded, congratulating himself for having taken the precaution of equipping himself with major currencies. He had learned that each trade was unique, but number one on the list was to impress. Like him, the man was a merchant. Each deal depended on how the cash was 'lost' in the accounting. The crates of ermine furs that Nick had purchased from him were only a small part of the process Nick had in mind.

'*Da,*' grunted his companion, now fully involved in the conversation. 'We deal.'

Nick nodded, hiding his satisfaction. Greed was so predictable. Greed was one man's edge, the other's blindfold. 'Some refreshment?' Nick enquired. 'And perhaps I have something else you may be interested in?'

Once again the man stared suspiciously at him. Nick rose to his feet and rapped at the interior door. 'Ruby, would you come in, please?'

The door opened. Nick beckoned Ruby. She was wearing a knee-length grey-striped fur coat and looked stunning. 'Wolverine,' Nick said casually, as he took a bottle of vodka and tumblers from the small cupboard. 'Canadian wolverine. A beautiful and rare fur, don't you think?' He glanced at the Russian whose face was now showing lust rather than suspicion.

'Ruby, show us the quality, please.'

Ruby did as she'd practised, walking a few feet and turning, sliding the coat from her shoulders. She turned it inside out to reveal the thick folds of skin and hand-stitched lining before drawing it on again.

'You trade with Canada?' the Russian demanded.

'Canada, the Americas, the East,' Nick replied, offering the tumbler of vodka.

'*Na zdorovie!*' exclaimed the man and threw the generous measure of vodka back in one gulp.

'*Na zdorovie!*' Nick did the same.

'How many?' was the next enquiry.

'Pelts?' Nick filled the glasses again.

'Wolverine,' snapped the Russian. 'No imitation. We trade.'

'Perhaps,' Nick agreed hesitantly. 'At the right price. Or perhaps an amicable exchange. Fur for fur, in this case.'

'You owe me roubles!' the Russian exclaimed thunderously, bunching his fist and bringing it down on the desk.

'Yes, and if you prefer, take your money. I keep my wolverine. I'm happy either way.'

Nick was relieved to see the punter sling back more alcohol as he stared lasciviously at Ruby. He'd probably had days of fasting on the ship that had illegally entered British waters, and hadn't seen a woman so spectacularly beautiful as Ruby for weeks, even months. And dressed as she was, who wouldn't want her? Nick thought as he observed the man's natural hunger for sensual pleasure.

'I see your cash,' the Russian said suddenly. 'Show!'

'Fair enough,' Nick replied easily, lowering his glass and rising to his feet. He turned slowly, smiling at Ruby, and walked to the large metal safe in the corner of the office. He obscured the Russian's view as he dialled the coded numbers.

Once the safe was open, he took out the revolver and surreptitiously slipped it in his pocket. Then he grasped the hefty leather briefcase and, making every movement count, he returned to the desk.

Meeting his customer's gaze, he noted his punter's avid expression and wet, almost drooling lips. With slow precision, Nick unlocked the briefcase with another key from the ring at his waist.

The small lock snapped open. The leather folds of the briefcase parted.

He was delighted to see the Russian's eyes when he revealed the contents.

'My God, Nick, all that money!' Ruby gasped as she sank down in the chair that the Russian had recently vacated. 'Isn't it dangerous to keep it here?' She was freezing even though she was still wearing the wolverine coat. The Russians had frightened her. She had tried not to look into the leader's eyes, but when she did she became chilled to the bone. The man was a giant and very menacing-looking. Nick had warned her not to be anxious. The man was here to do business and business only. Even so, she had been relieved to see the back of him.

'A very satisfactory trade,' Nick told her, pouring himself a shot of vodka from the last of the alcohol left in the bottle. 'My wolverine for rare Soviet Union ermine. Would you like a drink?'

'No thank you.'

'Don't look so frightened, darling. Everything went well. You played your part and earned your first commission.'

'I didn't do much.'

'He changed his tune when he saw you in the coat.'

'Yes, but I thought I'd have to do some selling.' Ruby felt a little disappointed.

'The deal was complicated. I didn't want to throw you in at the deep end.'

Ruby watched Nick sip the clear liquid. 'Will all our customers be as unpleasant as that?'

Nick laughed, throwing back his head. 'My darling, they were just traders after a good deal.'

'They looked like a band of thieves.'

'No, they were just hard characters from a part of the world we don't know very much about. While Western and Eastern governments quarrel between themselves, people like him and me use the opportunity to get rich.'

Ruby sighed. 'Well, I didn't like it when he got angry.'

'That's all part of the game.'

'What does that mean?'

Nick reached across the desk to take her hand and draw her to her feet. 'It means you've just secured your first commission.'

Ruby opened her mouth to ask more, but Nick silenced her with a long, intense kiss. 'You'll like tomorrow's customers,' he whispered. 'They're Irish and far more charming.'

Ruby slid her hands around his neck and grinned. 'At least I'll be able to understand them.'

'I'll tell you what to say.'

'What will I be wearing?'

'Have you heard of ocelot?' he asked, placing his hand under the coat and over her breast.

'No, what is it?' She trembled.

'One of the most sought-after animals in the world. Very similar to a jaguar or leopard. It lives in the South American forests.'

'Does it have spots?' she asked, trying to concentrate on what he was saying and not where his hands were going.

'Many. Their pelts are particularly valuable.' His kisses began again, fierce and demanding as he dragged the fur coat from her body and, pushing aside her blouse and bra, drew a gasp from her throat.

# Chapter Twenty-Five

It was the end of October and Ruby was looking forward to meeting Kath at the El Cabala. She was wearing a fashionable winter's coat as it wasn't yet cold enough to show off one of Nick's furs. Nor, Ruby thought ruefully, was the El Cabala an appropriate place to wear one.

'I'm glad to see you looking more your old self again,' Kath said as they sat with their espressos in the window seat of the Oxford Street café. 'By what you told me in your letter, things are looking up.'

'Yes, they are,' Ruby agreed eagerly. 'As I wrote, Nick offered me a job working for him and I agreed.'

'You said that Maggs is with Babs.'

'Yes, I was a bit doubtful at first, but Mum doesn't seem to mind. Maggs is a good sort.'

'When Bernie called round, this Maggs wouldn't say where you were.'

'I told her not to tell anyone,' Ruby said with a grin. 'I knew Bernie would be round at the warehouse in a flash and that wouldn't have been convenient.'

'My brother can be a bit nosy,' Kath admitted, 'but it's

only because he cares about you.' Ruby watched Kath touch the collar of her dress, which was a pretty, corded design in beige that really suited her slim figure. 'You don't need to worry about being pestered,' Kath added, also with a grin. 'He's going steady.'

'What! Who with?' Ruby asked in surprise.

'A girl called Tina Shutler from his works canteen.'

'Is she pretty?'

'Not as pretty as you. But she is a nice, homely sort of girl who I'm sure will make him happy.'

'Are they serious?' Ruby asked and Kath's dark eyes twinkled.

'Did you know Bernie actually bought a house?'

Ruby was even more surprised. 'No. Where?'

'A place over Chrisp Street. He asked me if I wanted to move in. But I'm happy with Penny now. We seem to rub along all right. Our flat is close to the Windmill and not a long way to walk. Which is handy with our unsocial hours. And I must say, Penny has a sensible head on her and keeps me in line. I ain't ever short of a bob or two now and I pay my way.'

Ruby giggled. 'Not like us, then? Always borrowing from Peter to pay back Paul.'

'Those were the days,' Kath said on a sigh as she pushed back her glossy dark hair. 'I do miss them a bit.'

'Me too,' Ruby admitted, but not wanting to get too sentimental asked quickly, 'I never had your brother down as a house-owner. He's too footloose and fancy free.'

'He's quite the home-owner,' Kath said reflectively.

'He don't go out on the pull much now and he talks more about the cost of paint than he does of a pint. But enough about Bernie. Tell me about Nick.'

Ruby felt her cheeks glow. 'Well, after we left you at the poodle parlour, we went to Angelo's, the Italian restaurant I told you about. Some musicians played us a love song. It was so romantic.'

'Did you stay the night with him?'

Ruby felt the hot colour in her cheeks. 'I think you know the answer to that.'

Kath giggled. 'I do now.'

'We've certainly made up for lost time.'

Kath looked down at her coffee. 'Are you in love?'

She nodded. 'I think so.'

'I know you're swept away, but try to keep your wits about you.'

'You sound like Penny talking.'

'Well, I suppose I might. Dancers tend to live in each other's pockets. They know there are always men who'll put on an act in front of a pretty girl. And as much as I like your Nick, I don't want you ending up down in the dumps again like you were when you left Anna's.'

Ruby shrugged. 'Nick wouldn't hurt me.'

'Do you ever miss modelling?'

'If it wasn't for Anna, I wouldn't be where I am today.'

'That's true.'

'But it was a hard lesson to learn.'

Kath leaned her elbows on the table and with a serious expression asked, 'Do you really enjoy working in a warehouse? I mean, from what I remember when we was kids, those dockside warehouses were cold and draughty.'

'It isn't Dower Street, not by a long shot,' Ruby admitted. 'But I do have a fascination for fur.'

'Who would have thought?' Kath grinned. 'My best friend, an expert in fur coats.'

'Not quite an expert yet.'

'As long as you're having fun.'

'Yes, I am. Now tell me, is there romance on the horizon for you?' Ruby asked inquisitively.

'Well . . .' Kath hesitated. 'Perhaps.'

'What does "perhaps" mean?' Ruby asked, her interest piqued. 'Have you met someone?'

'I might have,' Kath mumbled as she sipped her coffee. 'But Clem is just someone who works at the theatre.'

'Clem?'

'It's Clement really but everyone calls him Clem. We haven't even been out yet. But we talk a lot.'

'About what?' Ruby asked, even more intrigued.

'We do have the theatre in common. The more I know about the world of stage, the more I'm hooked.'

'Has he kissed you yet?'

'Trust you!' Kath exclaimed. 'There's more to seeing a bloke than sex.'

'Well sex certainly helps,' Ruby said, eager to air her new-found knowledge. 'You don't really know you're a woman until you can't stop wanting a man.'

'Hark at the girl,' Kath said, laughing.

'It's true. When he's in your mind day and night—'

Ruby stopped abruptly as she saw a figure in the crowd outside. The hair was certainly the right colour and the height. Could it be?

She jumped to her feet and asked Kath to wait for her. Then she rushed from the café to see if it was really who she thought it was.

Bernie was rubbing his hands together, aware that for the first time in the year his fingers were numb with cold. He was about to operate the oldest hydraulic crane in Tilbury, in service for almost eighty years, and he had a tricky manoeuvre to perform. Since he'd been preoccupied, thinking about Ruby, he hadn't managed to dodge the powerful spurting of water gushing from the worn-out seals of the crane as it powered into action. He had in consequence got his working trousers and donkey jacket soaked. October's sudden chill wind cut fiercely across the river and deepened his discomfort as he scaled the thirty-foot vertical ladder to his cabin.

Once inside, he took a breath, preparing to ascend the next ladder in order to remove the securing pin. Today he was unloading crates of tea from an old lady that had seen years of service from the Port of London to the Far East and Australia. It was a slow job, but he enjoyed every moment. It still gave him a thrill to be part of the old seafaring traditions that really hadn't changed much over the years. He loved the Oriental smells rising from the holds and the sights and sounds of the gangs of porters and foreign seamen, and the challenge of a new day.

As he scaled the next ladder, his damp trousers flapped in the wind. His cheeks hollowed in the air. The view that met his eyes was unmistakable and took away his breath every time he saw it. The city, cloaked by grey cloud, was behind him, the estuary, winding like a ribbon, in front. The jibs of the smaller cranes nodded many feet below and the water-fronts looked busy, despite the recent port depression.

He had a gut feeling he would be one of the last men to operate this antiquated old beast. It was rumoured the port was in decline. Perhaps one day, and quite unbeliev-ably, this stretch of water would be free from shipping. The manufacturing and commercial industries were moving out to the suburbs. There were rumours that permanent jobs were for the chop and only casuals would be taken on. He'd be one of the first to go if that was true.

Buffeted by a sudden squall, Bernie hung on at the top of the ladder, managing to remove the securing pin. Carefully he began to descend the ladder, then stopped where he was. From the corner of his eye he saw a large dark car idling along the wharf.

His breath stood still as he watched Nick Brandon draw up to an old container boat that was new in port. It was a battered old tub and low in the water. Which meant it was carrying a heavy load, not as yet visited and vetted by port authorities.

Bernie narrowed his eyes and watched the figure closely as it boarded the gangplank and disappeared.

What business did Nick Brandon have at Tilbury?

Bernie climbed the rest of the way down and jumped

back in his cabin. From here, he could see nothing. At least nothing other than the winches and derricks set close to midships of the vessel he was working on. If it hadn't been for his foreman glaring up at him and offering a finger, he would have risked climbing up again to wait for Brandon to reappear.

But he'd have to get this job done first. And hope that the Buick was still there later, when he could nose around and find out what was going down.

Ruby hurried after the figure almost lost to sight on busy Oxford Street. Pushing her way through the crowd, Ruby cried, 'Paula? Stop! It's me, Ruby.'

The woman turned slowly. Ruby took a shocked breath. It was Paula, but not the Paula she remembered from Dower Street. Her face was hidden by an unflattering scarf, the collar of her dull grey coat was pulled up to her chin, and a lock of red hair escaped over her forehead.

'Hello, Ruby.'

'Paula, how are you? I thought you'd be in America by now.'

Paula's dark eyes flinched. 'Well, there you are then. As you can see, I'm not.'

Ruby wanted to ask what had happened to Jesse Marlon, but she could see Paula was eager to get away. Quickly she said, 'I'm with my friend drinking coffee in the El Cabala. Would you like to join us?'

'No, I don't think so.'

'It would be lovely to catch up.'

'Another time maybe.' Paula kept the collar of her coat up to her face. Ruby could barely hear her mumbled words.

'Paula, I don't get up to town as much as I used to. Do you have any time free this afternoon? I really would love to talk to you.'

'I . . . I don't know,' Paula said, looking around at the pedestrians passing by. Ruby thought she looked nervous, even frightened.

'Just half an hour,' Ruby coaxed. 'Somewhere less crowded.' She had the feeling Paula wanted to get away from the crowds.

'All right,' Paula agreed, but reluctantly. 'Marble Arch at about three. I'll sit on the bench by Speaker's Corner reading a newspaper. But don't be late. And there is a chance I might not turn up.'

'Why's that?'

'Please don't ask any more. Not here anyway.' She sank even lower into her coat, then without saying goodbye hurried off.

'Who was that you were talking to?' Kath asked when Ruby joined her inside the café again.

'Paula, from Anna's. She was Anna's favourite model. Do you remember, I told you about her and her boyfriend Jesse Marlon?'

'Oh yes, the American who tried it on with you at the Strand Palace.'

'The last I heard he was taking her back to America to marry her.'

'Obviously that didn't happen. I wonder why?'

Ruby shrugged. 'She looked very strange. As if she didn't want to be recognized. In fact I almost missed her. It was a glimpse of the red hair that drew my attention.'

Kath looked at her watch. 'Crikey, I'll be late for practice.' She stood up, hurriedly putting on her coat. 'Sorry. But I have to catch the bus.'

Ruby walked out onto the street with her. 'It was lovely to meet up. Don't leave it too long to call me,' she said, embracing her friend. 'Remember, I'm on the telephone now.'

'Yes. It is all right if I give your number to Bernie?'

'As long as he doesn't pester.'

'He won't, now he has Tina. But I know he just wants to say hello.'

Ruby looked at her pretty, confident friend, who a year ago wouldn't have said boo to a goose. 'Life at the Windmill certainly suits you.'

'Yes, it does,' Kath said, waving her hand at a red bus coming along the road. 'Bye, Ruby, take care of yourself.'

'I will.' Ruby stood watching the tall, elegant figure weave through the crowds to the bus stop and jump up on the bus's platform. From inside, Kath waved from the window as it chugged out of sight.

Ruby smiled to herself. Life had certainly taken on a new meaning for her best friend. But was this entirely due to the Windmill? Or had it something to do with Clem?

Ruby strolled down Oxford Street, thinking of the many luxuries she wanted to buy. She had several hours before she met Paula. *If* she met Paula. And she intended to use those hours frivolously!

# Chapter Twenty-Six

At three o'clock in the afternoon, Hyde Park looked deserted at first sight. But small groups of people emerged from the mist, a ghostly white veil over the landscape, not yet a fog but threatening one. Ruby shivered in her warm coat, put down her bags and sat on the bench near Speaker's Corner and waited. She was grateful for the rest. The two large bags were heavy, one from Selfridges and the other from a Park Lane boutique just around the corner. She had bought clothes, shoes and jewellery and still had more to buy.

Now she was beginning to regret this arrangement. What if Paula failed to appear? She would have wasted valuable shopping time. With her first three commissions she had not only paid Nick back in full for Maggs's money, but had put £20 away in the Post Office, taken out an account at the bank, and had enough left over to generously spend on herself. She had also bought Babs a silk scarf and new slippers. Ruby was thinking of her mother when there was a tap on her shoulder.

'Let's walk,' said Paula without any salutation.

'Where to?' Ruby asked, puzzled. 'I've me bags to carry and they're heavy.'

'Just through the trees there. To the next bench, where we can't be seen.'

Sighing and a little annoyed, Ruby did as Paula asked. 'What's all the cloak and dagger stuff?' she asked as Paula hurried along, head down.

'I'll tell you in a minute.'

Ruby said no more, but she was relieved when finally they came to a park bench and Paula, looking right and left, nodded. 'Here will do.'

They sat together and Ruby looked intently at her friend. 'Why are you so jumpy, Paula? And why—'

Ruby's breath caught in her throat as Paula pulled down her collar. A livid red mark stretched across her cheek and it took all of Ruby's self-control not to recoil. 'My God, Paula, what happened? Were you in an accident or something?'

Paula's dark eyes looked coldly into Ruby's. 'You could say that. An accident on purpose, from our friend Jesse Marlon.'

Ruby felt the blood freeze in her veins. 'But you were going to get married and live in America.'

'He dumped me for Cindy.'

'What!'

Paula cleared her throat with difficulty as her fingers went up to her collar and laid it over the scar. 'The first I knew of it was on the day you left. I waited for him to arrive. He didn't. So I caught a taxi to the Strand Palace

Hotel. I went up to his room and came face to face with Cindy. I don't mind admitting I wanted to scratch her eyes out there and then. But I turned my fury on Jesse instead.'

'Oh Paula, I'm so sorry. Did Anna know he'd been double-dating?'

'Of course she did. She was the one who set it up. She wanted to destroy my chances of leaving the agency.' Paula sighed heavily. 'I should have known of course. I tried to keep my plans under wraps, but she found out. So she fixed Jesse up with a complimentary night out with Cindy, and that was it. Cindy's young and beautiful. What man could resist such a creature?'

'But how did you get that − that mark,' Ruby said, one half of her wanting to know the gory details, the other shrinking from it.

'For the first time in my working life I let my emotions take over. I had a showdown with Jesse. He told me I was a fool to have taken him seriously. He'd never intended to ask me to marry him, he admitted. He just wanted − everything physical he could get. And, darling— ' Paula laughed mirthlessly. 'He got it.' She shifted uneasily, looking over her shoulder and back again. 'I was the one in the wrong. You had every reason to walk out on Jesse. He's an animal and even though Anna made you pay for not pleasing him, you saved yourself a most degrading experience.'

Ruby sat quietly, her stomach going over. Then she thought of the lecture Anna had given her on that night she had walked out on Jesse Marlon. Anna's words went through her mind. *Escorting is a skill. Learning discretion. Reading the signs and being confident enough to guide your client through a successful first meeting.*

It was all a lie. A cover. Anna knew all along the monster that lay under Jesse Marlon's playboy exterior.

'Did he do that to you?' Ruby asked.

'I threatened to take him to court for breach of promise. Of course, I couldn't have. That kind of threat takes money. But we had a flaming row and before I left the Strand Palace I went to the management and informed them their wealthy guest on the third floor had no intention of conducting legitimate business from their grand hotel. Instead, he was using his suite as a brothel. I let my opinion be known, to all who would listen, and left with at least some small satisfaction. That was, until a week later, when Anna arranged an appointment for me in Kensington. The taxi found the place and I paid it off. However, the address wasn't legitimate and I found myself wandering around a dark street, trying to hail another taxi. A hand went across my mouth and I was dragged into an alley. I . . . I was punched and kicked and finally felt something hot on my face. The burning sensation was agony. A man's voice whispered, "With compliments from your American friend." Then he advised me to get out of town before something much worse happened.' Paula lifted tear-filled eyes. 'I was in hospital for several weeks. Anna had my things delivered there. I had nowhere to go. No future with a disfigured face. No money. And I was in pain and terrified for my life.'

Ruby swallowed. 'Oh Paula, how awful.'

'I left the city and went home to my mother's in Surrey.'

'Do you live there now?'

'Yes, Mother lent me the money to have an operation on my face. Hence my visit to Harley Street today. But I hate coming up to town.'

'No wonder you looked so scared.'

'It's an experience I never wish to repeat.'

Ruby reached out for Paula's hand. 'Can I help somehow?'

'Just remember this could be you. Never go near Anna again. Be warned, she is heartless and takes revenge on anyone who opposes her.'

Ruby felt sick to the pit of her stomach. She had known Anna was heartless but was she evil?

Paula gently wiped a tear from under her eye. 'Do you know there was a police raid on Dower Street?'

'No. When was that?'

'A month ago. Gwen told me. She has cut off all ties with Anna after she managed to free herself from Charles. You were extremely fortunate to have escaped his attentions.'

'But I thought Gwen liked Charles.'

'She hated him. She told Anna about his violent behaviour and that was when you appeared on the scene. Anna planned to foist him off on you. But after his attack, you refused to have anything to do with him. So it was then

Anna forced Gwen to cooperate by blackmailing her. Poor Gwen has a fifteen-year-old son. He boards at a very prestigious public school. As Gwen is single, she can only afford this luxury by working for Anna. And if it were to be revealed that the boy was being educated out of the proceeds of prostitution, as Anna threatened, that would be the end of Gwen.'

Ruby gasped. 'Anna would do that to Gwen?'

'Oh yes, in a heartbeat, my dear. We all have our secrets. And Anna discovers them.'

'What happened when the police went to Dower Street?' Ruby enquired, hoping to hear that Anna had been foiled.

'Anna, Cindy and another model were taken into custody. They were released soon after without charge. Gwen believes the whole thing will be dropped as one or two top policemen use Anna's services.'

Ruby shuddered. Anna, it appeared, was beyond the law.

'So you see how lucky you are?' Paula said quietly.

'Yes,' Ruby nodded. 'I do.'

'One other thing,' Paula said as the mist thickened around them. 'I hope you aren't still seeing Nick Brandon.'

'Why?' Ruby asked in alarm.

'He's bad news, Ruby. I don't know for sure but—'

Ruby sat up, at once on the defensive. 'Actually, I work for him. And he's only ever been a true gentleman towards me.'

At this, Paula seemed to stiffen and shaking her head

said, 'I see, it's true love, is it? Then you won't listen, whatever I say.'

'What do you mean?'

A man's figure emerged from the fog, walking very slowly towards them. Paula jumped to her feet. 'I must go.'

'But wait, Paula!'

Ruby tried to grab her bags and follow. But by the time she had her bags in her grasp, both Paula and the man had disappeared.

As Ruby found her way back to Marble Arch, the lights of the cars were barely piercing the thick yellow sheets of fog and even the noise of the traffic seemed distant. Marble Arch itself was hidden from view and though Ruby searched the few shapes she could see, even running up to one tall woman she thought she recognized, none of them turned out to be Paula.

The next day was Sunday and Ruby woke early. She gazed out of her window and onto the back yard, not seeing the tumbledown shed or heaps of junk hidden under the dying autumn weeds. Nor was she seeing the prefabs at the back, all with their semi-flat roofs poking above the fences that, like theirs, were in dire need of repair. What she was seeing was Paula's once beautiful face scored by acid and unsightly. A face that would never be repaired by any surgeon, no matter how skilled he was. The flaming red wound was there to stay and Ruby knew Paula must know it too. Paula was grasping at straws, going to Harley Street, any fool could see that. But it was the straw that kept her going.

Ruby unconsciously touched her own face. She thanked heaven that she hadn't been the one to suffer Jesse Marlon's wrath. But, as Ruby stared sightlessly from the window, it occurred to her that it was Anna who had arranged the meeting in Kensington for Paula's so-called client. Anna must have been fully aware of Jesse's intentions, just as she had been of Charles's deplorable behaviour and Mr Steadman's hidden fetish.

Questions whirled through her mind. Was Anna finished with her yet? And why had Paula warned her against Nick? What had she been going to say about him before that man had walked out of the fog?

If only they'd had more time. Ruby slipped on her dressing gown and went into the icy kitchen. She took a rag from the cupboard and cleaned the condensation from the windows. The smell of mould was strong and would have been worse if Maggs hadn't kept a fire going. Maggs liked the warmth, but she preferred to sit by that warmth, rather than work in it. Ruby still had to do the housework when she came home from the warehouse. There was washing, ironing and cleaning to attend to. At least Maggs was a good cook.

Ruby put on the kettle, blinking the sleep from her eyes. Could Paula be jealous? Envious of the life that Ruby had with Nick?

Since leaving Paula, a dark cloud had followed her. As if Anna was watching, waiting to seize her chance to

extract yet more revenge. As Ruby made tea, she heard
Paula's voice once more, laden with bitterness and fear, in
the creeping fog of Hyde Park.

Ruby liked to walk to work. Nick was always first to
open up the warehouse and insisted she needn't arrive
until nine. Fortunately there was no need for her to cross
the bridge where often pedestrians and traffic alike had to
wait until the ships and barges passed beneath.

Instead, she took the narrow, cobbled lane that wove
between the derelict, uninhabited riverside cottages.
Ruby didn't like walking along it but the short cut took
her straight to the industrial estate. All the cottages had
been condemned many years ago and their windows and
doors were boarded up. But sometimes there were creaks
and groans that sprang from the rotting timbers, eaten
away by the floods and high tides. This morning her
thoughts played tricks on her, making her jump as she
imagined a shadow here, a figure there. And even though
she knew she was safe in broad daylight, she almost
screamed aloud when a hand landed on her shoulder.

'Blimey,' Bernie said, as she jumped back, 'it's only me.'

Ruby put her hand on her chest. 'You scared the life
out of me, Bernie!'

'Sorry. I called out but you didn't hear me.'

'How did you know I was here?'

He stared at her, hunching his shoulders under his navy-
blue donkey jacket. 'I called by your place and Maggs said
you'd already left. Kath told me you were working for

Brandon so I put two and two together, guessing you'd avoid the bridger.'

Ruby shrugged. 'So what do you want?'

'Ruby, for old times' sake, you gotta listen to what I have to say. You can always tell me to get lost after. Meet me up the Bricklayer's tonight at seven, right? I promise not to keep you more than a few minutes.'

'Bernie, if this is a wind-up—'

'And watch out for yourself today.'

'What do you mean by that?'

Giving her a mysterious stare, he stuffed his hands in his pockets. 'Just take care, that's all.'

Ruby watched as he walked away, wishing she had refused to meet him. The knot in her stomach had tightened and she was left with the uncomfortable feeling that Bernie was going to tell her something she would prefer not to hear.

# Chapter Twenty-Seven

'I'll be back later today,' Nick told her, taking the money case from the safe. 'I have a big deal coming up in the West End. So just amuse yourself, darling, while I'm gone.'

'I don't like being on my own,' Ruby complained as she accompanied Nick through the warehouse to the front entrance. 'It's creepy in this big place when you're not around.'

'I won't be long,' Nick assured her. 'Look, we'll go somewhere special this weekend,' he coaxed. 'I'll book tickets for a show and we'll have a meal in town.'

He kissed her but Ruby was left feeling anxious. Was it Bernie who had alarmed her, or Nick's attempt to quickly dismiss her fears?

And when, by the close of day, she was still waiting for his return, the sensation deepened. The warehouse was dark and full of shadows even though she put on all the lights.

At the sound of someone banging at the outer door, she froze. Who could it be at this time?

'Who is it?' she asked through the small opening in the locked outer door.

'Garry McBride,' said the rough voice.

Ruby was immediately afraid. Garry McBride had paid several visits to the warehouse. He was a loud-mouthed trader who had cut up rough once or twice, even though Nick had said he was harmless enough.

'Nick's not here,' she answered. 'Come back tomorrow.'

'I'm off out of the country in the morning,' he shouted impatiently. 'And your boss wants to see the colour of the money I have stuffed in my pocket. Open the door and I'll leave it with you. That way, everyone's happy.'

Ruby didn't know what to do, but she supposed she couldn't refuse him. Reluctantly, she pulled back the lock. To her dismay, McBride barged in, followed by four big men.

'Where's he gone?' McBride demanded.

'I don't know. He had to go up West and see someone on business.'

'When will he be back?'

'It could be any time,' she croaked, aware that his men were rifling through the warehouse. 'If he knew you were coming he would have been here to meet you.'

'This is a little surprise visit,' McBride grunted, 'an off-the-cuff hello.'

'I thought you had cash in your pocket.'

McBride laughed in her face. 'Surprising what the mention of money will do!'

She could smell alcohol on his breath and closed her

eyes; she didn't want to see or smell him! Where was Nick? Why wasn't he here to deal with McBride?

She heard a loud crack and when she turned round one of the men was forcing open a crate. Tossing out the furs packed inside it, he began to open others.

McBride grabbed her arms and shook her. 'Where's the stuff gone?' he demanded.

Ruby shrank away. 'I don't know what you're talking about.'

'We'll see about that. You'd better come clean or else!' He shook her so hard her teeth rattled inside her head.

Ruby gulped, trying to turn her face away as he shook his fist in front of her.

Just then a loud noise came from outside. There was the sound of dogs barking and a high-pitched whistle.

'The law!' McBride pushed her aside. He signalled to his men and they all ran out of the warehouse.

Ruby collapsed against the wall; her arms hurt and she felt sick with fear. When a tall figure approached, she closed her eyes and screamed.

'It's all right, it's only me,' Wally, the night watchman, said, wrestling to restrain two fierce-looking dogs on leads. 'Are you all right?'

Ruby nodded but she was terrified. All around the dogs' jaws was bubbling white froth as they snarled and growled, pawing at the ground and drooling.

'Don't worry, these won't hurt you,' Wally assured her, although she found that hard to believe. 'Who was that rum lot that just ran out of here?'

'G–Garry McBride,' she managed to answer, frightened to move an inch in case the dogs leaped at her.

'I scared them off with my whistle. They thought I was the dock coppers with their dogs, see?'

Ruby thought her legs were going to fold. She had had one terrifying experience after another; how could Nick let this happen?

'Did they rubbish all these crates?' Wally asked, looking at the chaos.

Ruby nodded. She couldn't find her voice.

'I'll go and make certain they've gone. Go to the office, love, have a seat and a tot of brandy if there's a bottle around. I'll be back when I've put me dogs away, all right?'

A few minutes later she was sitting on the chair in the office, feeling dazed and tearful. There was no alcohol but she didn't want any. She had come within a hair's breadth of a beating and perhaps even worse if that thug had had his way. This wasn't at all what she had imagined selling fur coats would be like. Ruby wiped her wet cheeks with a shaky hand. She hated this warehouse. She hated Nick's customers. She even hated the fur coats.

'You sure they didn't rough you up?' Wally asked as he came alone into the office, pushing back his cap and peering into her white face.

'He might have if you hadn't come along.'

'I saw their motor outside and thought it looked suspicious at this time of night. So I got me dogs out.'

'I'm very glad you did.' She sniffed, managing a smile, but she had made up her mind now that when Nick came back she was going to tell him that working in the warehouse just wasn't for her. And after he knew how Garry McBride had threatened her, she was sure he would understand why.

Nick arrived back an hour later and Ruby was still close to tears. She jumped to her feet ready to throw herself into his arms as he walked in the office and tell him how badly she'd been treated. But before she could open her mouth, Nick demanded in an angry voice, 'What the hell's happened here? Wally says you let McBride in.'

Ruby was so shocked she could hardly reply. 'I didn't want to, but he said he had money to give you.'

'And you believed him?'

Ruby choked back a sob. 'You shouldn't have left me alone, Nick.'

'You're a grown woman,' he retorted coldly. 'I pay you to do as I tell you. And that doesn't include inviting in riff-raff like McBride.'

Ruby gasped. 'But you said he was harmless!'

He waved his hand impatiently. 'You should have used your common sense and kept the door locked. Now tell me what he said.'

Ruby stood up, but her legs were shaking so much she sat down again. He didn't seem at all concerned that she was upset and hadn't even asked if she was all right. 'Well, come on, Ruby, what did he say?'

'He asked where the stuff was. He thought I knew.'

'Did you tell him anything?'

'No. What was there to tell him? He didn't want the furs. They seemed to be looking for something else.'

Nick growled under his breath, pushing his hand through his dishevelled hair. 'You do realize he's ruined all my stock because you acted so foolishly?'

Ruby burst into tears. 'It wasn't my fault. You should have been here.'

'Those bastards will pay for ruining my stock!' He went to the safe and knelt down. When it was open, Ruby gasped when she saw what was in it.

He slipped the gun into his pocket and rose to his feet. 'We're leaving,' he snarled, snatching her coat from the chair and throwing it around her shoulders. 'Don't come to work tomorrow. In fact, don't come here until I let you know when it's safe to turn up.'

She had no intention of ever setting foot in this place again, but she was too shocked to say so. 'Take this,' he said, pushing a tightly rolled bundle of pound notes in her hand. 'Go shopping and forget about what you've seen here today.'

She stared at the money. 'But why—'

'Shut up and get in the car. I'll lock the doors behind us.'

Tears stung her eyes as he pushed her roughly from the office. He hadn't even given her the chance to say how McBride had frightened her.

As tears rolled down her cheeks, she knew she had to face the fact that tonight the man she loved had seemed to turn into another person altogether.

# Chapter Twenty-Eight

Bernie was waiting outside the Bricklayer's. He had paced the wet pavement for a good twenty minutes, wondering if Ruby would actually turn up. He consulted his watch under the lamplight. He had told her seven on the dot. What was he going to do if she didn't show?

The drizzle of rain was annoying and he was tempted to pop in the pub for a pint. But if she arrived, he might miss her. Knowing Ruby, she'd hightail it given half the chance.

He ditched the cigarette butt in the gutter and sauntered up the alley beside the pub where he'd parked his car. Then he walked back, turning up the collar of his coat to keep out the rain. Glancing along the street, he saw the tall, flat-fronted buildings where Kath and Ruby had lived. The bedsit hadn't been much to speak of, but at the time he'd not had the resources to rent a better place.

'Bernie?' a voice said at his shoulder.

Coming back to the present, he peered under Ruby's dripping umbrella. 'Didn't think you was coming.'

'I nearly didn't.'

'I'm glad you did. Come on, let's go inside for a drink.'

She shook her head firmly. 'Not tonight, Bernie, I don't fancy it.'

'Nowhere else much to go except for my place.'

'All right,' she agreed hesitantly, 'but will your girl-friend mind?'

He kept a straight face. 'What girlfriend?'

'This Tina Shutler your sister told me about.'

He laughed, wiping the rain from his face. 'Jealous, are we?'

'No, course not.'

'All right, then. At least we'll be in the dry.' Taking her arm and dodging the spokes of her umbrella, he steered her to the car. He could have downed a pint easily to give him Dutch courage; she wasn't going to like what he had to tell her. Not one bit.

'Sorry the old drum is a tip,' Bernie apologized as he swiped a paint-smeared sheet from the only chair in the front room. With a flick of his hand he dusted the cushion and stepped back. 'Didn't know I was going to have visitors or else I'd have tidied up.'

His gaff wasn't up to scratch and there were more pots of paint in the larder than spuds, but he had taken to the house like a duck to water. The upstairs had two good-sized bedrooms and downstairs was a kitchen and scullery. Every wall needed papering but he reckoned that by Christmas he'd have most of the work under his belt.

Ruby sat down, pushing back her wet hair. 'So this is all yours?'

He edged the pile of unsightly rubbish out of view with the tip of his boot. 'An old bloke was selling up, moving in with his daughter over Romford way, and needed to get rid of it on the quick. I asked him how much for cash. He said a grand. I said seven hundred. And the deal was done.'

'Seven hundred *pounds*?'

'Yeah, well it ain't tanners!'

'Seven hundred pounds is a lot of money.'

'I've put in a lot of overtime.'

She glanced at the stepladder propped against the paint-peeling wall. 'You need a nice lampshade in here, one of them modern cone-shaped ones. And you could do with good-quality lined curtains to keep out the cold. And maybe you should consider buying one of them room dividers from G Plan. I've seen them in Selfridge's and they're all the rage. Not to mention a comfortable settee of course. Something that's not heavy but easy to move around.'

'Yeah, I've got my eye on one,' he lied as though he knew what G Plan was. But if he didn't know about furniture, he certainly knew about this do-it-yourself lark. He was learning to turn his hand to all manner of jobs. He got tips from his mates, who, like him, had invested their hard-earned savings in bricks and mortar.

His plan had been to persuade Kath to move in with him; they'd never had a real home together, even the prefab had turned into a slum. Their dad had lived like the drunken pig he was and their mum, Molly, had been a drinker too. What with that and the TB that had killed her, she'd had no interest in homemaking. But now with Kath finding her feet at the Windmill, he was on his tod and enjoying his freedom.

'I'm gonna buy an HMV telly too,' he said with a grin.

She looked impressed. 'A telly?'

'Yeah, and one of them record players hidden in a cabinet like you see on the films.'

'You'll be charging to walk in the door soon.' She gave him a nervous smile. 'So what is it you want to tell me?'

He sat beside her, knowing this wasn't going to be easy. 'Last week, I was up in me cabin,' he began awkwardly, 'and there I was, minding my own business as usual, when I see this motor drive along the wharf. It stopped and a bloke I recognized got out. He walked up to this old rust-bucket and boarded her. But what struck me was that this foreign lump was sitting low in the water, you couldn't even see her Plimsoll line. From where I was sitting it was obvious she was listing.'

'So what's this got to do with me?' Ruby asked with a frown.

'It was Brandon who boarded the vessel.'

She gave a bewildered frown. 'Are you sure?'

'Positive. I had a gander along the wharf. The Buick had gone when along come the dock rozzers. They swarm all over the wharf and board the old girl. My gaffer told me she was heading north when an old Navy mine hit her bows, holed her below the waterline and forced her to limp back to port.'

'So what are you saying?' Ruby said in a whisper.

'There was cargo found aboard, Ruby. Crates of fur pelts. She was a smuggler. Caught in the act in British waters.'

Ruby jumped to her feet. 'Are you accusing Nick of smuggling?'

'Sit down.' He pulled her beside him. 'Listen, I ain't accusing anyone. But the cargo was contraband. In view of the Cold War going on between Britain and the Soviet Union it's a dangerous game someone's playing. Added to which there's always the risk of anthrax. The docks was on red alert after that. But I saw Brandon on board that vessel before the law arrived. He must have gone down to have a butcher's, see if there was anything or anyone that linked the smuggler to him.'

With a choked gasp, she whispered, 'Is Nick in trouble?'

'I'd say there's a good chance.'

She didn't say another word and neither did he. After all, it was as plain as a pimple on a pig's arse.

Brandon was up to his eyeballs.

Ruby sat very still, trying to understand what Bernie had told her. Her thoughts went round and round. Where had Nick been today? He had a gun. Why would he keep one in the safe? After all, he'd hired Wally to patrol the warehouse. And why had he been so angry that she'd let McBride in?

'This could be serious,' Bernie said quietly. 'The coppers will tug someone's collar. You don't want to be involved.'

'I'm not.'

'I know that but they don't.'

'Nick loves me,' she sobbed. 'He wouldn't do that to me!' Ruby felt her head swim. She saw McBride's ugly face with its flat bruiser's nose and thick lips. She felt him shaking her and knew that he was about to strike her. This image floated in front of her eyes as she passed out.

'Ruby!' A hand was patting her cheek.

She opened her eyes and everything flooded back. McBride, his gang, the broken crates and, worst of all, the memory of how, when they had arrived at the prefab, Nick had carelessly bundled her out of his car. He hadn't even given her a kiss goodbye. It felt as if he just wanted to get rid of her.

'Sit up,' Bernie said, easing her gently forward. 'And when you feel up to it, you'd better tell me what's going on.'

Taking a deep breath, she nodded. 'Nick left me all alone today. I told him I didn't like it there without him, but he said I had nothing to worry about. Then, just as it got dark . . .' Ruby shivered at the memory, 'there was a knock at the door. It was a customer who said he had money to give Nick. So I let him in.'

'Oh Christ,' Bernie said beside her.

'I know it was stupid. Nick thought so too. But I wasn't to know that he'd turn nasty and break open the crates.'

'Did they touch you?' Bernie asked in concern.

Ruby swallowed as she remembered McBride's raised fist. 'No, but I think he would have if Wally, the night watchman, hadn't turned up and frightened them off. He blew his whistle which must have made McBride think it was the police.'

'Garry McBride from across the water?' Bernie said in surprise.

'Do you know him?'

'Who doesn't?' Bernie replied shortly. 'He's a notorious villain who's spent as much time in the jug as out. Whoever gets involved with him can only be up to no good.'

Ruby felt sick. The more she was finding out, the deeper Nick seemed to be implicated.

Slowly she told Bernie about the case full of money and the trade with the man from the Soviet Union. But it was when she added that she had seen Nick take a gun from the safe that Bernie's eyebrows shot up.

'A shooter?' Bernie repeated. 'Ruby, that's bad news.'

'I know. Oh Bernie, I can't believe what happened.'

Bernie sighed heavily. 'Look, I know your heart's set on him. But you gotta live in the real world. The more you tell me, the more it turns out he's a wrong 'un. Whichever way you look at it, he's trading dodgy goods with dodgy punters.'

'But why does he need me to do that?'

'Appearances, doll. You're easy on the eye and can put a punter in a good frame of mind while he does them up like a kipper.'

Ruby wanted to scream it wasn't true. There was no proof, only what Bernie had seen at the docks. But that could be coincidence, couldn't it? Even as she thought it, she knew she was lying to herself. She wanted to believe that Nick loved her and would never put her in danger. But events today had proved otherwise.

'Look, I know you think I'm out of order,' Bernie continued. 'But who carries around that kind of money? Only the bank and major villains. The Russian fell into a trap. The money was just window-dressing. Canadian wolverine is a quality skin with a high value. What was found in the hull of the ship looked like wolverine, but was wolf. And wolves are as common as muck.'

Ruby stared at Bernie. 'You mean Nick swindled him too?'

Bernie nodded. 'This old vessel I saw is about as legit as Al Capone's distillery. Brandon gets wind of it being towed into Tilbury, probably a porter or casual on his payroll. He boards it, knowing he's for the high-jump if there's anything to link him to the pelts.'

'Do you think there was?'

'Dunno, but it's likely.'

'So what happens now?'

'In my opinion, Brandon will do a runner.'

Ruby felt her lungs tighten. 'What, leave London, you mean?'

'Leave the bloody country, I should think. You don't mess around with the dock authorities or the Soviets.'

Ruby felt a piercing pain in her chest. She loved Nick.

And he loved her. Or she thought he did. Would he really run away from her?

She fought back the tears. 'But why did Garry McBride rip open those crates? What was he looking for?'

'Dope,' Bernie said without hesitation. 'Drugs are what McBride did his time for. He must have had a deal with Brandon and got short-changed. You was dead lucky the nightshift clocked on when they did.'

For a while they sat in silence, and Ruby tried to think of a reason why all this could be wrong. Perhaps somehow they had miscalculated and put the blame on Nick when in reality there was another explanation. But as the minutes ticked by, she was left with the empty desolate feeling that she knew came with the truth. Nick was a criminal and he had used her. She had been blind to this because she loved him. The truth that he didn't love her was a very hard pill to swallow.

Bernie got out his cigarettes and lit one. Taking in a deep breath, he said softly, 'You remember that day me and Kath stayed with your mum till your dad got home?'

Ruby nodded.

'I went into Pete's room and found a clue to Joanie.'

'What?'

'I saw the picture on the wall. The dog with the black top hat. As I reached out to touch it, it fell into me hands.'

'How did it do that?'

'Dunno.' He grinned. 'P'raps Pete did it.'

'Don't be daft.'

'Anyway, on the back, it says, *For Pete, my love, my world. Forever yours, J. 1951.*'

'1951?' she repeated. 'The year Pete died.'

'There was a label too. *Cuthbertson Studio. Fine Prints and Photography.*'

'Cuthbertson? I know that name.'

'Who is it?'

Ruby sat up. 'I met a couple at Larry's party. Marianne and Bruno Cuthbertson. They own a studio on Wardour Street.'

'Do you reckon they'd remember selling the picture?'

'We could ask.'

Bernie grinned. 'Tomorrow morning, then?'

Ruby nodded. Suddenly she didn't feel so desperate. She would put all thoughts of today behind her. After all, Nick had told her not to go to the warehouse. And, as much as she wanted to confront him over what she now knew, her questions would have to wait.

# Chapter Twenty-Nine

'Have you got the picture?' Bernie asked early the next day as he drove them towards Piccadilly.

'Yes, it's safe in my bag.' Ruby was as nervous as Bernie sounded. Added to her concerns about Nick, which she had tried to put to one side, she was hoping they would discover who Joanie was. This girl was the one in whom Pete had confided his true feelings.

It was a mild October day and the sun trickled through the white clouds above Wardour Street as they walked past the famous Pathé Building and the smells from the Italian restaurant reminded Ruby of Angelo's. Her heart gave a sudden jerk. They had shared so much together. She needed to hear the truth. He owed her that much, at least.

On the other side of the road was a block of small shops with striped awnings, a butcher's, a barber's and an old-fashioned-looking tavern with a small group of men standing outside.

The delivery boys on their bicycles swerved in and out and music drifted from the small windows, framed by grubby curtains, above.

Bernie pointed to a sign next to a cabaret club. Her tummy tightened as she read the gold-and-black lettering. *Cuthbertson Studio. Fine Prints and Photography*.

'Looks like we've found it,' Bernie said and Ruby's heart lifted. Perhaps now they would solve the mystery of Joanie.

Marianne Cuthbertson slipped from behind the counter of the shop. 'Why, it's Larry friend, Ruby!'

Ruby was surprised to be recognized. 'Yes. This is my friend, Bernie Rigler.'

'Charmed.' Marianne said coolly.

'Is Bruno here?'

'Unfortunately not. He's working on a particularly difficult commission. Twins of aristocrats. Babies can be most unhelpful. The photos he took yesterday were useless, I'm afraid. But there we are! Spilt milk and all that. Now tell me, what are you doing in these parts? Have you come to call on Larry?'

'No, we came to see you. It's about a picture you framed.'

'Really? Which artist?'

Ruby felt embarrassed. All around them were glamorous photos of people and places. The walls were lined with black-and-white portraits, and looked very sophisticated. The long, narrow studio had two heavy drapes crossed over one another at one end, with a modern, black-leather bucket chair underneath.

'We want to know if you recognize this,' Bernie said, jogging Ruby's arm.

She opened her shoulder bag and took out the picture. 'We was hoping you'd remember it.'

Marianne took the picture and frowned. 'As it happens, I do recall this picture. It isn't one of ours of course, and I remember it because we were asked to frame it, not a task we would usually perform on cheap cartoons. But—' Marianne stopped and frowning suspiciously said, 'Before I provide any more information, may I ask what this is all about?'

'The picture belongs to my late brother, Pete.'

'I see. So this is a personal enquiry?' Marianne pressed.

'Yes. You see, Pete took his own life.' Ruby paused, composing herself as she spoke. 'No one can guess why. He was happy and had everything to live for. The only clue we have is this "J" who was his girlfriend Joanie. We're hoping she's the one who came here and that you can remember her.'

Marianne smiled wistfully. 'How sad. Clearly a matter of the heart. But I'm sorry to disappoint you. The person who brought this in wasn't your Joanie. It was a man. A tall, very good-looking young man, dressed impeccably in an expensively tailored suit.'

'Pete!' Ruby said excitedly. 'He was always the height of fashion.'

'Yes, he was quite memorable,' Marianne agreed. 'And so was this cheap picture, as I identified it immediately as a piece of cheap wartime propaganda. I wouldn't have thought it was his style at all. A rather vulgar pastiche of the country's leader Winston Churchill. Two a penny in their day.'

'That fits perfectly,' Ruby agreed excitedly. 'Pete hero-worshipped Winnie.'

'You're lucky,' Marianne added with a click of her tongue. 'At first, Bruno turned down the commission. Look around you. We don't deal in cartoons or frame any photograph or picture that won't add to our hard-won reputation.'

'So what changed his mind?' Bernie said in an offended tone.

Marianne stared coolly at him. 'I did.' With a slow, intimate smile she handed the picture back to Ruby. 'This young man, your brother, was a very appealing personality. I enjoyed and responded to his flirtation. He knew exactly how to conduct himself in the presence of an older lady. But Bruno, dear that he is, can be a little pompous at times about the work he takes on.'

'And Pete was the one who collected the picture?' Ruby asked.

'He returned a week later to approve the framing. He liked it, of course. And settled the account directly. Which added to his credibility and to my opportunity to flirt outrageously once more.' Marianne laughed girlishly.

'Then you'd have a copy of the receipt?' Bernie said.

'Yes, of course,' Marianne answered disdainfully, looking down her nose. 'Our books are all in good order.'

'Could you look it up for us?' Ruby asked. 'You see, Pete and Joanie, the girl who gave him this, were very much in love. Perhaps we can find her and she will have something to tell us that no one else can.'

Marianne nodded. 'One would have preferred to frame something a little more sensitive to their romance,' she mused. 'But there you are, the image obviously meant something to them.'

'Yes, it did,' Ruby said quietly, wondering if she would ever find out just what that something was.

Bernie waited for Ruby by the shop's front door. Though this Marianne lived on another planet to him, she clearly had a soft spot for Ruby. She'd disappeared downstairs to search the record books. A couple of window shoppers passed and some posh geezer was making an enquiry. While the place had all the trappings of success, Bernie reckoned they were short on business.

His mind drifted to Pete. Had he kept Joanie a secret for a reason? Was she a working girl? Could she already be shacked up with another geezer? Ruby hadn't given any thought to that one of course. Pete was lily-white in her eyes. But if Pete's romancing was as dodgy as his punters, then Ruby might be in for a shock.

Bernie heaved a long sigh, watching Ruby turn towards him, a look of excitement on her face. She was holding a piece of paper and Bernie's heart did a flip.

'Marianne's given me this,' Ruby said as Bernie read aloud the address. 'Soho Square. It ain't much, is it?'

'It's all we've got.'

'No number?'

'No.'

'Well, I hope the house jumps out and bites us. Cos I reckon we're on a fool's errand. Pete didn't give a number cos there wasn't one.'

'Stop beefing, Bernie. Go home if you want. I'll manage on my own.'

'You know I wouldn't do that.'

'Then come on. We'll walk there. It ain't far off.'

She took his arm and together they made their way through the warren of Soho streets. Past the poky shops, cafés and restaurants, the dingy strip joints and through the milling tourists and eccentric-looking locals.

When they entered Greek Street, Ruby stopped. 'There's something familiar here.'

'Like what?'

'Pete told me all these stories about Soho. Its history. How all these foreigners came to London to live and work.'

'Yeah, and this is called Greek Street, ain't it?' he said impatiently. 'There's Greeks, obviously, Italians, French—'

'Shut up, Bernie, I'm trying to remember.'

'Remember what?'

'See those trees at the end of the road there?'

'That's Soho Square.'

'Bernie, I do remember this place! It's where Pete took me that Sunday.'

'Are you sure?'

'I think so.' She gazed up at him with her big shimmering eyes.

'Come on then.'

When they got to the small green park, Ruby gave a choked gasp. 'Look, that shop used to sell books. It was very pretty once.'

'It ain't now. It's all boarded up.' Pete studied the small, abandoned and smoke-stained façade. 'Don't look like it's been used in a while.'

'The door next to it,' Ruby replied. 'That's Mr Raymond's house.'

'You're certain?'

'Yes. Pete must have given this as his address.'

They walked slowly across the road and Bernie went up to the weathered, neglected door. 'There's no handle, no way of getting in. No bell even.'

'It was a shiny black door once,' Ruby whispered. 'Oh Bernie, it was so beautiful.'

'So this was Pete's boss's place?'

'Pete called it Mr R's bolt hole.'

Bernie rubbed his chin thoughtfully. 'He's certainly not here now. The place is empty and boarded.'

They stepped back on the pavement. Bernie could see that once the gaff had been quite elegant in its own way. London was full of these tall, once imposing buildings, and this place had certainly seen better days.

'Visiting here was the best day of my life,' Ruby told him in a dreamy voice. 'Pete served me scones and jam with a silver spoon. I felt like a princess.'

'Did you see Mr Raymond?'

'No. But I felt like – well, there could have been someone else there.'

'Why?'

'Don't really know. It was just a feeling. If it was Joanie, then why didn't Pete introduce us?'

'Christ, Ruby,' Bernie objected, 'he was showing you a good time. Wasn't that enough?'

Ruby stared up him. 'Yes, but if he had a girlfriend wasn't it only natural for him to show her off?'

'S'pose so,' he admitted. 'But I reckon we're drawing a blank now. At least you know where it was that Pete took you to. If Joanie was ever here, she ain't now.'

'Yet, I still feel something and don't know what.'

'I told you, it's memories, gel. They pop up and do your head in sometimes. But look at it. Empty. Deserted. Abandoned. There's nothing more to find out.' As Bernie slid his arm around her waist, intending to leave, he saw an old man waving at them from the bench across the road. He was tempted to ignore the torn filthy mitten exposing the nicotine-stained fingertips that waggled in the air, and the long straggly beard and old raincoat tied at the waist with string. But something made him pause, as the old gent threw his dog-end to the ground to join the many others littering the rough grass.

'You wanna know about that place?' shouted the man as he pushed his ancient bicycle towards them, staggering under the weight of the many bags attached to its handlebars.

Bernie and Ruby nodded together.

★    ★    ★

'Give us a shilling,' demanded the tramp from under his tousled bush of matted grey hair. His long nose poked out from hairy eyebrows and his toothless grin made Ruby squirm. She could smell his body odour and the alcohol on his breath.

'Why should we do that?' Bernie said in a warning voice, pushing Ruby out of the way of the fumes.

'Cos you'd like a bob's worth of information, that's why.'

Ruby was surprised at his clear speech and twinkling eyes just visible under the woolly fringe.

'What sort of information?' Bernie demanded.

'About that gaff.' The head nodded to the door they had stood outside.

'What do you know about it?' Ruby asked eagerly.

'A shilling first, missus.'

Bernie dug into his pocket and pressed a coin into the grubby hand. 'Now, spill the beans,' he said as the tramp inspected the money, then pushed it into one of his bags.

'It's not been used since before last Christmas,' the old man told them.

'That could be a year ago,' Ruby said disappointedly.

'And how would you know anyway?' said Bernie suspiciously.

'I live here, don't I? Under that tree over there. That gaff is locked up good and tight now. I've tried to get in meself.'

'Do you remember when the bookshop was open?' Ruby asked.

'Before the fire, you mean?'

'What fire?' Bernie said in surprise.

'The fire someone started. Dunno who. Them books went up like a bonfire. I tell you, it was the warmest I'd been that winter.'

'Was anyone in the house at the time?' Bernie asked.

'That'll cost you a quid.'

'Your rates are going up fast,' Bernie complained.

'I'll be on me way then.'

'No!' Ruby put up her hand. 'Bernie, please pay him.'

The tramp took the pound note and spat on it. 'Yer, they took the corpse out. I saw it all with me own eyes.'

'Who was it?' Bernie asked suspiciously.

'Don't yer read the papers?'

'No, so who was it?' Ruby demanded.

A toothless grin appeared on the man's face. 'Ronnie Raymond, a loan shark who was too mean to toss me a sixpence when I asked for one. He deserved what he got, I reckon. Loaded, he was. But he wouldn't give you the time of day without charging, the mean sod.'

Ruby held her breath as the small, piercing eyes narrowed into slits. 'Good riddance to bad rubbish, that's what I say.'

'Is there anything else you can tell us?' Ruby said desperately.

'For a quid we deserve more than that,' Bernie grumbled.

'What do you want to know?' the old man replied tersely. 'The bleeder's shoe size? Go on, bugger off, the pair of you.'

Ruby stared at him as he began to push off his bike. She felt the tears very close as Bernie put his arm around her shoulders. 'This really is the end of the line, Ruby.'

'If Mr Raymond had been alive he could have told us all about Pete. And maybe Joanie.'

'P'raps it's better this way,' Bernie replied as he urged her back towards Greek Street. 'He don't sound a very nice bloke. Come on, we'll go for an espresso.'

Ruby's thoughts were once again in turmoil. Mr Raymond was dead, the last person in London who could have led them to Joanie.

# Chapter Thirty

Bernie arrived at Tilbury early on Wednesday morning. After giving his boss some spiel about yesterday and his self-appointed day off, he was on his way to have a gander at the old tug; see if he could suss out anything more, now that the quarantine men had given it the once-over.

But when he arrived at the wharf he was startled to see an empty berth where the ship had been. His gaffer had said nothing about it being removed and he didn't like to go back and enquire. Just then, as he was staring down into the murky waters as they lapped hungrily at the mossy wharf stone, he heard a group of men talking about how the work was drying up and how standing on the stones waiting for a job to come up was reminiscent of the old days before the war. So Bernie moved towards them, hands in pockets, trying to earwig on the conversation.

He was in luck. One of the port labourers had been there all day yesterday, touting for work. 'Nothing but that sick foreigner,' said one man. 'And it would have taken more than a day's pay to persuade me to work on her.'

The others all agreed. 'Someone had to do it,' another said. 'So Shorty Evans volunteered and a couple of his mates.'

'Shorty's up for most things,' was the reply. 'With a habit like he's got, he might as well grow four legs his bleeding self.'

'Yeah, lives at the track. If he had a wife, she'd be keeping him in a kennel.' They all laughed at they stamped their booted feet to keep themselves warm.

'So what happened to the ship?' Bernie enquired as he surreptitiously joined the group.

'PLA condemned it. Took it off to the knacker's yard.'

'Anthrax?' Bernie asked.

'You could smell the rot a mile off,' said the man. 'I wouldn't like to be the patsy who tried to pull one over on the authorities.'

'And the crew?' Bernie said.

'Bloody Soviets! But they say the finger is pointed at someone local and, whoever that punter is, they'll slaughter him for giving Her Majesty's men the hag.'

Bernie couldn't have agreed more.

Especially as he knew who the culprit was.

Unable to wait any longer, Ruby made her way to the Bayswater Road. She was going to confront Nick and ask for the truth, even if it was what she didn't want to hear. Better knowing than not, she had decided.

The big block of flats was easy to recognize and she entered the glass front door and studied the bell plates.

She searched for the name Brandon, but couldn't see it, though there were one or two unmarked bells.

Well, she would just go up and knock on the door. Glancing in the large, brass-framed mirror, she studied her reflection: an attractive blonde in a navy-blue coat with blonde hair styled down to her shoulders. Navy-and-white button earrings – discreetly visible, a light coating of powder on her nose and a pale apricot lipstick. Confident of what she saw, she entered the lift and felt her heart leap. She knew she had to be strong and not let her emotions get the better of her.

She exited the lift and walked along the cold, cheerless passage. Nick had been so kind and attentive, taking care of her that night Charles attacked her at the Manor. But on Monday she had seen a different side to him. Which one was real? she wondered.

Ruby stopped at the plain, unvarnished door. She stood still, trying to compose herself. There was no noise of traffic as the small, square-paned window at the end of the passage was securely shut.

She raised her hand to press the bell. Then she noticed the door was slightly open. Her heart missed a beat. Pushing the door with her fingertips, Ruby peered in. The small hall was deserted. 'Nick, are you there?' she called uncertainly.

There was no answer.

Closing the door softly behind her, she walked into the lounge. 'Nick?' she called again. Only silence greeted her.

In the kitchen she saw an empty wine bottle and several

glasses on the drainer. She touched the glasses lightly, remembering the nights they had spent together in each other's arms.

Pushing the memory aside she returned to the lounge. The pictures on the wall – *her* pictures – and the cushions, those they'd bought together, were all still there, and the radiogram and stack of records.

Retracing her steps, she went to the small bedroom. The bed was bare. There were no pillows or covers. Her legs felt weak as she hurried into Nick's bedroom. The bed was unmade. The door swung open on the wardrobe.

It was empty.

All his suits, shirts, socks, shoes – everything – gone! For several minutes she stared at the vacant shelves. His smell was still there, as if only a short while ago he had been standing where she was standing.

Ruby went to the drawers beside the bed. They, too, were empty. A crushed Gauloise was lying in the ashtray. She stared at it, breathing in all that she could of the man who had made love to her so passionately in this bed.

Her final search was in the bathroom. No razor, soaps or personal effects. A half-used tube of toothpaste stood on the hand basin.

Ruby went back to the lounge. The silence was almost painful. The flat was just an empty shell.

'His clothes were all gone,' she told Kath, who had been surprised to see Ruby turn up at the Windmill and had taken her into the dressing room that, so early in the morning, was deserted. Kath had pushed away the costumes and Ruby sat down on a stool in front of the long mirrors, refusing to let the tears fall.

'Did you knock on his neighbour's door?' Kath asked, passing Ruby a cup of strong tea.

'No. What would be the use?'

'So where do you think he is?'

Ruby shrugged. 'Bernie said he'd probably leave London.'

'Is Bernie certain it was him at the docks?'

'Yes. And anyway, as I've explained, after what happened at the warehouse, there's no reason not to think he's in a lot of trouble.'

'Just thank your lucky stars he didn't implicate you too.'

Ruby put down her tea with a gasp. 'What if he's been arrested?'

'It's sure to be in the newspaper.'

'Hello? Can I come in?' A young man poked his head round the door.

Kath sprang up. 'Clem, I want you to meet Ruby.'

Ruby smiled and held out her hand. 'I've heard a lot about you.'

'Vice versa.' Clem grinned shyly. Ruby liked this gangling young man who seemed to be very fond of Kath. And with a slight stab at her own heart, she knew by the way they smiled at each other they were in love. Kath looked radiant. This could have been her, if only Nick had been genuine.

'Come and have coffee with us,' Kath said, sliding an arm through Clem's. 'We'll cheer you up.'

But Ruby declined. She knew they wanted to be alone together. Kath had found someone to love and her whole life was changing. Ruby knew Kath didn't need her any more. Well, not as she had before, anyway.

'Call round to Penny's and we can chat,' Kath told her as she saw Ruby out. 'Clem has a very nice brother if you're interested.'

Ruby just smiled.

There had only been one man for her. But it seemed that man was now gone – though she was beginning to think he had never really existed!

# Chapter Thirty-One

Bernie gripped the stone-filled sock secured tightly by string that was in his pocket. The weapon wasn't much of a defence, but it had proven effective when he was younger. Pete and him had landed up in one or two skirmishes. Sometimes they'd had the stuffing knocked out of them, but they'd always come up smiling. Well, not smiling exactly, but with their teeth intact.

The wartime youths had been a far cry from the louts of today. There had seemed a reason for defending your turf in the early 1940s, as there was so little of it. The *Luftwaffe* hadn't left much to fight over, so knocking seven bells out of a rival camp was the norm. There was no hard feeling because the foreign buggers had been the enemy. Not the kids from other parts of the East End, or even over the water. But now it was different. There was a harder class of criminal, like McBride.

Bernie could even stomach the Soviet as he wasn't British, but McBride was a disgrace to the country, a thug. He'd no values, no standards and certainly no scruples. Given half the chance he would have hurt Ruby to get the information he wanted. And the irony of it was, she didn't have anything to tell him. She was a kid and saw what she wanted to see. And for the past year, she'd had eyes for no one except the man Bernie was planning to have a serious word with tonight.

Cautiously, he made his way to the warehouse; the night wasn't pitch enough to obstruct his view. The moon reflected an even path along the broken stones and up to the warehouse. The front door was closed and he gently leaned a shoulder against it.

'Bugger,' he cursed when it refused to give. He knew by the glass skylights reflecting light that someone was inside. And that had to be Brandon. Perhaps there was a back entrance?

Careful where he trod, Bernie made his way to the rear. The soft noises of the night surrounded him; the docks at rest, the gulls still picking at the water as it rolled into high tide. A hoot or two from the boatmen, the faint hum of the city.

He listened for voices. None that he could hear. No night watchman on the prowl, as he'd expected. If he could only get his hands on Brandon!

Then something moved behind him. He made to turn but he was too late. An arm went round his neck, a knee buckling his back and the cold tip of a knife at his neck.

He was helpless, trapped, unable to move as the point of the knife trailed round to his Adam's apple. He knew that one clumsy movement and he'd be spurting blood from his jugular faster than a leaking water main.

'Where's yer dogs?' a rough voice demanded in his ear.

'What dogs?' he coughed, pulling at the arm so he could breathe. But it was clamped like a vice around his neck.

'You got just one chance, son. And this is it. You and your animals had the better of us on Monday. Answer up now and you might not live to regret it.'

'Monday?' Bernie repeated. 'I wasn't here Monday.'

'Cobblers. Those animals are vermin. It's them or you, chum.'

'You've got the wrong bloke,' Bernie rasped, realizing he'd been mistaken for the night watchman. 'I ain't particular about dogs meself.'

'A comedian, eh?' snarled his captor and Bernie knew the end was in sight if he didn't act quickly.

'All right, all right,' he agreed quickly. 'I'll show you where I keep 'em.'

'No clever moves, or the blade goes straight to your ticker,' the man threatened and Bernie took a quick breath. The arm relaxed, and he was pushed forward. A silver moon spun out of the clouds at that moment and he felt in his pocket for the sock. As he trod slowly over the rubble, the knife followed him.

'Get along there, you bugger. And you'd better not be wasting my time.'

Bernie went a little faster and, stumbling, he realized the ground was even rougher round this side of the warehouse. It was fly-tipping paradise and he spotted two piles of rubbish in front of him. He took a long stride, praying the man behind wouldn't notice. All he needed was a split second to unbalance the sod. Bernie slid the sock and its weighted stones furtively from his pocket. He sidestepped the obstacle and the man behind cursed as his boot rammed into the waste.

Bernie's first blow took the wind from the man's lungs, the second scored a notch in his forehead. Bernie watched as the big ox stumbled and fell. There was a satisfying groan and Bernie was on him, throwing his hardest punches. He heard the crack of bone and the splatter of tearing flesh. And he punched and kicked, breathless and sweating, until at last he rose unsteadily to his feet.

He looked down at the concussed man, saw the knife beside him and went to pick it up. But even before his fingers touched the handle, a hand gripped his shoulder from behind and he was hauled backwards, feet splayed out in front of him and his hands clawing at the air. Then something large and heavy sliced his scalp in two and he was lying on his back looking up at the stars.

The last he remembered was the blow to his balls and the jeering voices around him. His last thought was, as he squirmed in torturous agony, that he could hear hell's own hounds dragging him down into the fire.

'Are you all right, Mum?'

Babs sniffed as Ruby helped her to her chair in the front room. 'Just a bit of a cold.'

'Maggs said you didn't eat your dinner.'

Babs smiled wearily as Ruby tucked the blanket over her. 'Didn't fancy stew.'

Ruby knew Maggs was a good cook. But even Maggs was concerned that Babs wasn't eating. When she'd arrived home yesterday from the West End, Maggie had said that Babs had been off-colour. And now, studying her mother's pale face – paler than usual – Ruby could see Maggs was right.

'I'll cook your favourite,' Ruby said as she knelt at the hearth and slipped the poker between the scarlet flames. 'Sausages and mash. And we'll eat together in here, in front of the fire. Pity Dad's at work, it would have been nice, just the three of us.'

Babs turned up the collar of her dressing gown. 'Ain't Maggs coming in?'

'No, I'm having a day off from work.' Ruby stood up, smothering a yawn. She hadn't slept a wink. She scoured the newspaper before bed, but found nothing. Even though she knew the truth about Nick, the questions kept tumbling over in her mind. Had he deliberately led her on? Had he just used her without even liking her!

'You're a good girl, do you know that?' Babs said, giving Ruby a start. 'You always was, but you had your brother to look after you.'

Ruby felt a stab of pain. She missed Pete so much. He would have helped her through the heartache. 'Yes,' she agreed softly, 'he always did.'

'When I'm better, we'll go down the market, shall we? Like the old days when you was a little girl?'

Ruby sat down. 'Would you really like that?'

'I used to take you all the time.'

'I know. I remember.'

'You was such a pretty little thing. Golden curls and those big hazel eyes of yours.'

'They're your eyes, ain't they, Mum? People said we was alike.'

'It upset me when you went away to Devon.'

Ruby felt sad. Her mum hadn't talked about Devon for ages. What was she thinking? What was going on in her mind? It was as if the real Babs was trapped somewhere in that body, the mum that Ruby remembered, always laughing and mucking about with their dad. 'I missed you and Dad too.'

'Everyone had to send the kids away, you know. It was the Blitz and then there was the doodlebugs and rockets. Seemed it was always raining bombs. And one day one of them could have fallen on us.'

'Yes, it must have been very frightening.'

'Not as frightening as the thought that we might not see you again.'

Ruby took her mum's hand. 'You've never said that before.'

'I should have said, then.'

Ruby sniffed. 'Me and Pete missed home. It was like we did something wrong being sent away. That's why we found it so hard.'

'You never did nothing wrong. You was perfect kids and we was so proud of you. But the war crushed us. And me and your dad was terrified, not knowing what to do for the best. Your dad wasn't called up as he had a reserved job in the docks, and there was lots of women on their own, without their husbands. I should have been grateful I had him home. And I was. But my heart ached all the time for my babies.'

'That's a lovely thing to say.' Ruby brushed away a tear.

'I wish I'd told your brother too.' Babs let out a long sigh. 'I should have. And that's why I wouldn't let him go. There was so many things left unsaid. Still, he came last night and everything's all right now.'

'Last night?' Ruby repeated. She felt scared. Was her mum delirious?

'He stood by the bed,' Babs said with a smile on her face. 'And kissed me. I'm happy now I've seen him.'

'Mum . . . ?' Ruby sniffed again.

'Don't worry, love, I'm happy now. And I want you to be.'

Ruby sat in silence until her mum fell asleep. She listened to her soft breathing and slowly drew a tuft of grey-blonde hair behind Babs's ear. Ruby sat, quietly holding her mum's hand and thinking over what she had said. Did Pete come in a dream? If he had it must have been very real to Babs.

'Thanks, Pete,' she murmured to herself. 'You put a smile on Mum's face today.'

A calm stillness surrounded them. Ruby felt an invisible weight lift from her shoulders. Babs's face was serene as she slept, the lines of grief disappeared.

Ruby suddenly remembered the happy family her mum had described. It was the war that had changed everything.

After it, she and Pete were grown-up. Her parents had lost the kids they'd said goodbye to. Just as she had lost sight of the mum she had known, due to Babs's sickness.

She hadn't thought of it in that way before. She stood up and smiled. Her mum looked at peace again.

Wally Wagman lifted his hand and silenced the three starving dogs at his side. They watched his every move, waiting for the next command, knowing they wouldn't be fed until he was satisfied.

Wally stood still in the darkness of the wharf, listening to every small movement. As much as he wanted payment – and Brandon had dodged him so far – no way was he going anywhere near the warehouse. Not until he knew the score. Those ruffians he'd chased off earlier in the week had dispatched his fourth dog, the oldest and least savage, but still his favourite. They'd slit her throat and she'd been gone even before he found her. But not before she'd done some damage, as still in her teeth were shreds of clothing. That young miss of Brandon's had had a close shave. And she had his dogs to thank for her escape. Not that he'd get any thanks. The place tonight looked deserted.

Stepping slowly forward, he folded his fists, protected by the brass knuckles, and beckoned the dogs to follow. Their ears were bolt upright. They stole beside him, the hackles on their backs as stiff as yard brooms. One signal from him and they'd fly at any movement. But if those boys were tooled up, shooters at the ready, the iron bar under his overcoat and his dogs would count for nothing.

'Steady,' he whispered to his hounds, and they stood, motionless, sniffing the air. He watched them. No indicator to them of human presence. They were hungry and alert, but undisturbed. Wally walked forward. Again he listened, and not a whisper. This late at night, there was only the river lapping down at the wharfs. A dock dolly or two falling out of the pubs. The whistle of the wind through the derelict buildings. Not even the cry of a last hopeful gull. Just the night sky above him and a deserted feel.

As the moon threw more shadows over his path, he moved stealthily towards the entrance. The breeze was cutting up rough and his dogs shivered with its energy.

Once more he tightened his fists. The brass knuckles were heavy and cumbersome around his fingers, but he was taking no chances this time. Inside his overcoat were his tools of the trade, buckled to the lining. The steel baton, a sheath knife and a set of razors sewed into the cloth to match those in the peak of his cap.

As he neared the small door, he saw the crack of light and froze. It was open an inch. The locks and bars were wrenched away. There were gaping holes in the wood. He turned swiftly, looking behind him to the left and right. Not a movement. Wally slipped out his steel weapon and his animals growled, eager to enter. But he instructed them to wait and they did, bristling and seething, impatient to be freed.

'Not yet, boys,' he muttered, moving close to the open door. He tucked the tip of the weapon inside and pulled gently. No sound. Not a pin dropping. Just the pale light.

He entered and took a sharp breath. Whoever had been here had been no friend of Brandon's. And they had left their calling card. The crates that had lined the warehouse had been shattered and piled up, glued together with furs. From the centre came a curl of smoke telling Wally the bonfire had recently been lit. He searched the deserted building, watching for movement, then signalled his dogs. They leaped away, eager to find a quarry, sniffing every inch with the tip of their noses.

Wally hurried to the smouldering heap and knew that in minutes where he was standing would be ashes. Whoever had done this had been planning on a speedy escape. He'd missed them by inches.

A dart of alarm went through him as the snarling and growling of the dogs pierced the silent night. He guessed they'd found satisfaction in the office. Hurrying to join them, Wally tempered his curiosity. It could be a trap, but if it was, his dogs weren't sensing it.

Pushing at the office door, where he had first met Brandon who had hired him with a convincing promise of payment, he knew at once this was no trick. The body on the floor, now being enjoyed by his dogs as they licked and sniffed, was clearly stone-cold dead. It lay face down, blood congealing on the floor in a pool. He knelt beside it and pushed. There was a hole through the forehead, and another dividing what was once the bald hairline.

Someone was a fair shot. And this unlucky bugger had come a cropper.

Wally stood up, watching his dogs paw and froth at the damaged remains. He glanced swiftly around the small room, then opened the drawers in the desk. Nothing of value, just papers and a woman's scarf. His eyes travelled to the safe close by. The heavy door swung open. Was it Brandon who emptied it? Or thieves? Either way, Wally knew he wasn't waiting to find out.

Calling his dogs, he pulled a rag from his pocket and made his way through the smoke-filled air. He gave a wide berth to the simmering fire, but not before he had scooped up a pelt. Out in the night, he examined it. So this was Brandon's treasure! More fool those who had ever bothered to burn it!

An explosion sent Wally stumbling. He cast the fur aside, eager now to be away before the blaze was noticed. But then he realized his dogs were gone. With a punch of alarm to his stomach he listened again. He could hear them snarling. Wally levelled his steel bar, followed the sounds to the rear of the warehouse and stopped when he saw the man. Bundled up against the warming wood, he was shielding his face with his arm. The dogs were all about him, investigating, snapping and biting.

Wally yelled at them and they stopped. He moved closer slowly, step by step. Eventually he peered into the bloody and battered face. The eyes stared up at him. But he could see no expression. Was it Brandon? No. Was it one of them other clowns? Somehow, he didn't think so.

The story didn't add up. They wouldn't have left one of their own here.

'Who are you, pal?' he shouted.

An arm was raised, but then the body toppled forward.

# Chapter Thirty-Two

It was Saturday morning and Ruby was late up. She rubbed her eyes and looked out of the window. At last the rain had stopped and a bright new day had dawned. The clock on the small table beside her bed said almost nine. She'd overslept. Her mum must have slept late too and her dad gone to work. Pulling on her dressing gown, she went quietly into the kitchen. To her surprise, her dad's battered tin sandwich box and thermos was on the table. Had he forgotten to take them to work?

The door to the front room was open. His bedclothes were still on the settee. Last night he'd been very tired and hadn't even bothered to go to the club. Had he too slept late? Ruby went to her mother's room. Her dad, wearing his dressing gown, sat beside the bed where her mum was still asleep. Her chin was resting on the bedcover, as if her dad had pulled up the cover.

'Dad?' she whispered. 'Did you oversleep too?'

He looked up at her and said nothing.

'Why ain't you at work?'

He took her hand. 'Ruby, sit down.'

She pulled up the small stool. 'I'd better make Mum's tea.'

'She won't want none this morning.'

'But she likes her first cuppa.'

'Yes, but not today.'

Ruby followed his gaze. It was then she saw the grey-blue tinge of her mother's skin and the peaceful expression which she had at first taken to be sleep.

'I'm sorry, love.'

Ruby gave a choked gasp. 'She ain't – is she?'

'I came in this morning to kiss her goodbye,' her dad said in a choked voice. 'She looked so beautiful, like she was a girl again. I didn't realize till I bent down and felt her coldness that—'

Ruby gave a whimper. She jumped to her feet and shook the silent figure under the bedclothes. 'Mum, it's time to wake up.'

'It's no use, gel, she's gone.'

'She can't be,' Ruby said, flopping down on the stool. 'It was only a cold.'

'Don't think it was the cold that took her.'

Ruby stared at the lifeless face. She wouldn't ever see those eyes open again. She and her mum had only been saying the other day how alike their eyes were.

Ruby wanted to cry but she couldn't. I can turn on the waterworks over things that don't matter, she thought guiltily. Things or people that I can't have that I think I want. And now, when I have good reason, I can't.

'Ruby, I loved your mother,' her dad mumbled. 'She

wasn't the woman I married, but she still meant the world to me. P'raps if I'd stayed in more, taken more notice, she would still be alive.'

Ruby stared at her dad. He looked old and grey as if he'd aged overnight. 'Dad, don't blame yourself.'

'Who else is there to blame?'

'Me,' Ruby said huskily. 'I left home because I couldn't stand Mum going on about Pete. I just wanted to get away.'

'She couldn't help herself,' Dave Payne murmured, staring at his wife. 'And neither could we help her. But it don't stop me feeling guilty.'

'I always thought she loved Pete the most.'

'That ain't true, love. But he was her boy. And when you have kids one day, you'll know what it feels like to love a son.'

'I know that now,' Ruby said as she held tightly to her dad's hand. 'Mum told me the other day how much you missed us when we was sent to Devon.'

'We was heartbroken.'

'You never wanted to send us away, but you had to.'

Her dad blinked back his tears. 'It was cruel,' he croaked. 'Being separated from your kids. The government said we'd be responsible for your deaths if a bomb dropped on the house. So we had to go along with it. Like thousands of others. But at least you were evacuated with Kath and Bernie. Knowing you two were with mates gave us some comfort. We knew you'd look after one another and you did.' He reached for Ruby and she put her arms around him.

'Don't cry, Dad. You did all you could for us and for Mum.'

'It don't feel like it. I drowned all my sorrows up the club like a coward and left the poor cow to grieve. I didn't want to go under, see? I still wanted a life. And now it's too late to tell her she was the best wife a man could have. All those hours she spent working that blessed sewing machine! She never did have any customers, you know. It was just a way of keeping herself going.'

'You did the best you could,' Ruby whispered, kissing her dad's forehead. 'Mum didn't really have the heart to go on after Pete. We both wanted to start afresh, but Mum didn't. I think she was ready to go with him.'

'What makes you say that?'

'We was talking yesterday,' Ruby said with a hitch in her voice as she stared at her mother's still form. 'Mum told me she'd seen Pete the other night. He stood by her bed and kissed her.'

'She didn't know what she was saying,' her dad replied, wiping the tears from his cheeks with his hanky. 'People don't come back from the dead.'

Ruby held her father close again as sobs racked his body. She had to be strong for him. What harm was there in believing that Pete had come for her mum? The picture she had in her mind of them together helped a little. After all, who was to say that just because you couldn't see someone they weren't really there?

★    ★    ★

'Bernie! Bernie! Open up. It's me, Kath.'

Bernie carefully rose from the chair as he heard the banging on his front door. His fingers tightened over the strapping that the nurse had applied to his painful ribs. He took a shallow breath; every movement was jarring. But at least he could just about see through his left eye now. And the hospital nurse had done a fair job with the stitching on his scalp. But he certainly wasn't going to win any prizes for his charm and good looks.

He hauled himself slowly to the front door. Kath was standing there. Unfortunately the split on his lip wasn't healed. His smile was more of a grimace than a welcome.

'My God!' Kath exclaimed, her eyes wide in alarm. 'What's happened to you?'

'This is me new look,' he muttered. 'All the blokes are going for it.'

'Oh Bernie!' Kath exclaimed and was about to launch herself at him when he put up his hand.

'Better not, Kath. I'm still pretty sore.'

She stood still, staring at him. 'Have you had an accident?'

'Come in, make yourself at home.'

Bernie slowly led the way to the front room. 'Sorry there's nothing much in here.'

'You sit down on the armchair. I'll find myself something.'

Kath hurried out and was soon back with a grubby wooden chair. She fussed over him, making him comfortable with the cushions. 'Now, what sort of trouble are you in?' Kath said, seating herself beside him. 'I thought you'd left those days behind you.'

'I have, or thought I had,' Bernie said grimly. 'How much do you know about Ruby's boyfriend?'

'Nick? Not much really. Other than he's done a runner from his flat.'

'How do you know that?'

'Ruby went there. She's so blindly in love with him, she'd do anything to keep him.'

'He's in deep trouble, Kath.'

'I guessed that.'

Bernie took another slight breath, trying not to flinch as he did so. 'The bastard never intended to be straight with her. He was using her to put up a front for his business. He was fiddling some big crooks like Garry McBride.'

'Is that who did this to you?'

'Could be. I went over to the warehouse to sort out Brandon. When I get there, this geezer jumps me. He thinks I'm the night watchman so I gave him a bit of aggro, then his mate turns up. Sounded like it was McBride, because someone yelled "Garry". Together they put the boot in. It was Wally the night watchman that eventually turned up and found me. Took me to the hospital and they stitched me up. He told me he'd gone to sort out Brandon, same as me. But all him and his dogs found was a body.'

'A dead one?'

'Well, it certainly wasn't sitting there telling gags. He had two holes in his head. And I know for a fact that Brandon kept a shooter in his safe. Whatever went on there that night, the safe was left empty and a fire was lit. We only just got away in time before the whole place went up.'

'My God, Bernie, you shouldn't have gone there alone.'

'I wanted to get my hands on him.'

'Instead someone got their hands on you. How bad is it?' Kath leaned forward to open his shirt.

'Just a few cracked ribs and cuts.'

'And a black eye and a gash on the top of your head where your hair used to be,' Kath added ruefully. 'Did you or the night watchman inform the police?'

'That's a daft question. No one but a fool wants to be involved in arson or murder. And there's another scam he had going. Crates full of fur, all cheap wolf. Wally found them on the fire. So his intention was to fiddle others like he did the Russian.'

'Do you think Garry McBride found Nick?'

'No, I reckon McBride sent in his man, the big bald bloke, and Brandon blew him away. Then made his escape. He's got more lives, that geezer, than Houdini.'

Kath sighed. 'Poor Ruby. She never knew the half. Bernie, you don't think he'll come after her, do you?'

'Don't think so. He's got McBride after him. Not just the coppers.'

'I've something to tell you,' Kath said after a few minutes. 'Prepare yourself for a shock.'

Bernie gripped the arms of the chair. 'Is it Ruby?'

'She telephoned me this morning to tell me her mum had died.'

'What, Mrs Payne?' Bernie stared at his sister. 'When?'

'Yesterday morning. Mr Payne found her. She died in her sleep. Although she did have a cold, it wasn't enough to kill her.'

Bernie sat without speaking. Eventually he said, 'How's Ruby?'

'Don't really know. Her money ran out in the telephone box. So I jumped on the bus to come over to you.'

'I'll drive us over there now.'

'You can hardly move, let alone drive,' Kath protested. 'And what will Ruby say when she sees your face? You can't tell her about the warehouse. Not with her mum dying.'

'Don't worry, I'll think of something.' He pushed himself up from the chair. 'Just get my jacket from the hall stand, will you?'

Bernie watched his sister hurry out. He'd have to keep all he'd found out to himself. This wasn't the time to tell Ruby she was mixed up with a number one shyster. And maybe – just maybe – if McBride got to Nick Brandon first, the south London face would save him and the coppers the trouble.

# Chapter Thirty-Three

Ruby stared at the empty bed as Maggs tucked over the clean cover, a dark blue candlewick fitting for the occasion. 'We'll leave the window open, but draw the curtains together as a mark of respect,' she said softly to Ruby. 'Now, is there anything else I can do for you or your dad?'

Ruby shook her head. 'No, nothing, thank you.'

'Have you thought about the funeral?'

'The undertaker said yesterday it would probably be the Monday after next. She's being buried in East London Cemetery. There is a plot next to where Pete is.' Ruby swallowed.

Maggs put her arm around Ruby's shoulders. 'It will be very fitting, I'm sure.'

'Can you come?'

'Yes, course. Would you like me to make dinner for you and your dad before I go?'

'No thanks. Neither of us feels like eating.'

'You've got to keep your spirits up.' Maggs patted her hand. 'I'm only down the road if you want me.' She paused, looking into Ruby's pale face. 'Your mum was a lovely lady. I'll miss her.' Maggs sniffed and Ruby nodded.

'You was a good friend to her, Maggs. Stuck with her when she got ill.'

Maggs sighed and taking her handkerchief from her pocket she wiped a tear from her eye. 'Look after yourself now. And your dad. I'll call by in the week.'

'Thanks.'

Ruby waited until she was alone. She wanted to think about her mum. She said softly, 'I know you're with Pete, Mum. I know you're safe now. But I miss you.' She held back the tears. 'I know you're there and always will be. But Dad don't. So look out for him, won't you?'

It was a while later when Ruby heard a knock on the door and went to open it. 'Kath, Bernie, what are you doing here?' she said as she embraced them.

'I was worried when your money ran out,' Kath said.

'I wanted to let you know what happened.'

'Sorry to hear about your mum,' Bernie said as they stepped in.

When they were all seated, Ruby looked at her two friends and remembered what her dad had said that morning. The four of them had been evacuated together, had looked out for each other and eventually come home together. She hadn't realized before just how much she valued Kath and Bernie. Even if Bernie drove her to distraction and Kath had been so clingy, they were still here for her, and she loved them for it.

'Have they taken your mum away?' Kath asked, tears brimming in her eyes.

'Yes. The funeral will be on Monday week.'

'Is she going to be buried with Pete?'

'Dad and me didn't want him disturbed. So we asked for a place close by.'

'Did the doctor say what was wrong with her?' Bernie asked.

'She did have a cold and she hadn't been eating. It was as if she just drifted away.'

'Is there anything we can do?'

Ruby shrugged. 'Don't think so. But you could go out and have a word with Dad, Bernie. He's in the yard, clearing up the mess.'

'What's he doing that for?' said Kath.

'To keep busy,' Ruby replied. 'He was very upset and tearful, so I told him to go out in the fresh air. It is, after all, a fine day.'

'I'll see if he wants a smoke,' Bernie said, getting to his feet.

'What happened to your face?' Ruby asked.

'Cut meself shaving.' Bernie was gone before she could ask more.

'Now tell me what happened,' Kath said, reaching out to touch Ruby's hand. The small gesture brought tears to Ruby's eyes. She held them back.

'Mum just went in her sleep.' The flames of the fire sparkled and crackled, the only noise in the room. 'There was no time to say goodbye. That's what hurts the most.'

'There's never a good time to say goodbye, not when you love someone.'

'Mum told me she'd seen Pete by her bed.'

'Did she have a fever?'

'Don't think so.' Ruby suddenly gave a sob. 'I don't want to start crying. I might never stop.'

Kath took her in her arms. 'There, there. There's nothing wrong in shedding tears,' she whispered, sniffing back her own. 'We've shed enough between us, ain't we?'

Ruby nodded, holding tightly to her friend.

It was much later when Bernie and her dad came in. Ruby had dried her tears and felt better. She and Kath had made tea and cheese and pickle sandwiches. They all sat round the fire to enjoy them.

Everyone talked about the old days and Ruby smiled when she heard Bernie grumble about the many times his dad had fallen over blind drunk in the road. It was always Dave Payne who had picked him up. 'Though, as soon as he could stumble one foot in front of the other, he'd be down the boozer again,' Bernie said with a gruff laugh.

Kath recalled the clothes that Babs made for her on the sewing machine as her own mother didn't know one end of a needle from the other. 'Do you remember, Ruby? She could knock us up a dress in an afternoon? She was so clever with her fingers.'

Ruby nodded. 'She was always sat at the Singer.'

'That bloody racket,' Dave said fondly. 'It drove us all crackers.'

'Yes,' Ruby admitted. 'But I miss it now.'

'Thanks for the help this afternoon, mate,' her dad said to Bernie. 'We got rid of a lot of rubbish.'

'You're welcome.'

Ruby looked at Bernie as she handed him his cup of tea. 'You've been in the wars,' she said with a sad smile. 'And it don't look like a shaving brush that did that to you.'

Bernie went scarlet, noisily slurping his tea. 'They put these bloody lamp posts everywhere these days.'

They all managed to laugh. Ruby knew her mum wouldn't want them to be sad for long. Sitting here with her dad and Kath and Bernie felt right. They were paying their respects in their own way. Remembering the life they had lived with those who had once shared that happy life with them.

A brief service was held at the Congregational church in Poplar. It was where, three years ago, they had said goodbye to Pete. Ruby watched as Kath and Bernie arrived, along with Maggs. They stood at the coffin with bowed heads then took the pew opposite to listen to the minister.

The coffin was decorated with flowers, white and red roses from her and her dad. White chrysanthemums from Maggs and a spray of beautiful mixed flowers from Kath and Bernie. Ruby was dressed in a black suit for the occasion and was grateful for the delicate half-veil that was attached to her pill-box hat. It hid the grief in her eyes and the tears that had escaped during the last hymn, 'Abide With Me'.

She held fast to her father's arm as they walked out to the hearse and watched the pall-bearers slide in the coffin. Then they all climbed into the black limousine to follow the hearse to the cemetery. No one spoke, but she was grateful for the money Nick had given her. If Nick had done nothing else for her, his money had provided a dignified funeral. One that befitted her mother: a solid oak casket with little brass handles and fragrant roses that Babs would have approved of. Her mind had wandered during the service, as she had sat by her father on the polished pew and listened to the minister's carefully prepared words. But he was new to the parish and didn't remember the last time they had visited the church. Ruby had found it difficult to speak about Pete. After all, none of them had expected to return after three short years.

The small cortège drew up in the cemetery and Ruby and her father walked slowly to Pete's grave a few feet away from where Babs was to be buried. Ruby left at his headstone a heart-shaped posy of violets, pausing to remember her brother. Then, joining the others, they listened in silence to the minister's committal.

'"Forasmuch as it has pleased Almighty God of his great mercy to take unto himself the soul of our beloved Barbara Anne Payne here departed: we therefore commit her body to the ground; earth to earth, ashes to ashes, dust to dust . . ."'

Ruby took one of the roses. As the casket was lowered, she kissed the rose's petals before throwing it down. Her father sprinkled earth. They stood silently gathered, each with their own thoughts.

Ruby knew that Pete would be there, smiling his lovely smile and waiting for Babs. And they would walk off together into the sunset, just like they did on the films.

'Dad, you should go to the club tonight,' Ruby said. It was now December, the beginning of a very cold month. Ruby had just finished preparing her dad's lunch box.

'Don't think I'll bother, not till the better weather,' her father replied as he tucked the battered tin and flask of tea into his workbag. He usually walked to work, but had taken to cycling lately. Ruby knew he cycled to the cemetery to have a word with Babs. He said he found consolation that way.

Ruby kissed him on the cheek before he went out of the back door. Since the funeral, her dad hadn't gone to his club, but spent all his free time painting, repairing and doing up the prefab, just as he had in the old days.

Sometimes Bernie called round and helped with the decorating. There had been no word of Nick and Bernie would have heard from the dock authorities if there had. The only clue to the mystery was an article in the newspaper describing the fire at Nick's warehouse and the charred remains found within.

Ruby shuddered when she thought of that night McBride had threatened her. She had come so close to disaster. And Nick hadn't even cared!

As the days passed, Nick's money slowly ran out. Ruby considered going back to the parlour. Larry and Stuart had sent a beautiful card of condolence. Enclosed with it was a short letter, assuring her that, if ever she wanted to return, her old job was waiting for her. Debbie had sent a card too asking Ruby to visit her and Rog at their new house in Streatham.

Everyone had been very thoughtful. But she didn't want people's pity. She had to get on with her life.

# Chapter Thirty-Four

On the first Monday of December, Ruby found two letters on the mat. She took them to the kitchen and studied them.

One was from the stonemason; Babs's headstone would not be erected until the spring when the ground would be firm. And although Ruby had settled the fees for the black marble stone and the gold inscription, the churchyard fees were outstanding.

Ruby sighed, putting the invoice aside. The other letter, a white envelope, was addressed to Ruby Payne. The handwriting was unfamiliar. Perhaps it was from someone sending their condolences?

'Dear Ruby,' she read, suddenly sitting up in the chair.

'We've met once, at Larry and Stuart's party. I was with a companion at the time, Lady Granger.' Ruby read the two lines again, then continued:

*I apologize sincerely for bothering you. However, as I am leaving the country very soon, I must take a risk and ask if you would meet me. I have something to tell you which I think you*

*should know. Please be at the statue of Eros, Piccadilly this*
*Sunday, where I shall meet you at eleven o'clock. Regards,*
*Johnnie Dyer*

Ruby read the letter again. There was no address. What
could Johnnie Dyer have to tell her? He must have got
her address from Larry.

Should she go?

Of course. Her curiosity wouldn't let her do otherwise.

On Sunday morning Ruby took the tube to Piccadilly
Circus. She had put on her warmest coat, since the weather
was on the turn. All week it had been wet and windy and
very unlike Christmas. But this morning they had woken
to a frost, and she had suddenly become excited. Christmas
in London was something she had always loved. The
lights, the stores, the atmosphere. And today she had
promised herself all these after meeting Johnnie. Perhaps
she'd even call on Kath and tell her about whatever it was
Johnnie had to tell her.

As Ruby walked the short distance from the tube station
to Piccadilly Circus, her heart lifted. It seemed like an
eternity since she was up here. As she stood waiting by
the statue of Eros, watching the morning traffic circulate,
she thought of the glamorous life she'd once led in
London's West End. When living at 10 Dower Street,
wearing beautiful clothes and modelling them for the
fashionable stores had become the norm. And then she
thought of Anna and the night at the Manor when they

first met. And the long journey of discovery she had taken since.

A redhead walked by and Ruby thought of Paula. She wondered if she had ever recovered from her disfigurement. There was Gwen too, and Charles and Mr Steadman; their faces passed fleetingly through her mind. So much had happened in such a small space of time.

Ruby watched the couples, holding hands or with arms linked. They laughed as they fed the pigeons and stared in wonder at the figure of Eros. London at Christmas was spectacular. In the distance, the clock face of Big Ben shone clearly from the Palace of Westminster. This was the London she knew and loved, but without someone to love, what did it all mean?

'Miss Ruby Payne?' A tall, dark-haired figure stood in front of her. Johnnie Dyer was dressed in a short camel coat and dark suit, the epitome of fashion. His black hair was swept back, showing off his fine-featured face. His dark eyes were smiling and, as he leaned forward to kiss her cheeks, she smelled his subtle aftershave. 'I'm so very glad you came,' he said, looking about them. 'Are you alone?'

'Yes,' Ruby said curiously. 'Did Larry give you my address?'

'Actually, no.'

'Who did?'

'My car is parked not far away,' he said, taking her arm. 'I'd like to show you something before I answer your questions.'

'I . . . I'm not sure,' Ruby said, pulling away. 'Why can't you tell me now?'

'Because here is not the place.' He looked anxious. 'Please trust me. I promise to make everything clear.'

Ruby hesitated. She was more confused than ever now. Why all this secrecy? What could he possibly want to tell her that was so important he couldn't tell her now?

'I understand your reluctance,' he said quietly. 'But this is very important. And, if my plans work out, I may not be back in England for a very long time.'

'Where are we going?' Ruby asked, curiosity getting the better of her.

'Not far.' Johnnie took her to his car parked a few streets away.

Where, she wondered, was he taking her?

Johnnie drove them to Greek Street and parked the car. They walked to the end and stopped at the little green park. 'Why have we come here?' Ruby asked in surprise.

Johnnie guided her to the bench that Ruby remembered the old tramp had sat on. The wooden seat was newly painted and the grass had been cut around it.

'They're trying to smarten up this area,' Johnnie told her as they sat down. 'But for me, they'll never succeed whatever they do.' Ruby shivered in the cold air and lifted her eyes to the house and bookshop across the road. The boards had been removed from the windows and scaffolding had been erected around the buildings.

'Those properties have been sold to a developer,' Johnnie continued as he followed her gaze.

'How do you know all this?' Ruby asked with a suspicious frown.

'Do you remember that house?' Johnnie asked, once again avoiding her question. 'I have a reason for asking.'

Ruby couldn't imagine how Johnnie would know about Pete. But why else would he bring her here? 'I came here with my friend in October,' she said warily. 'We were looking for someone.'

'Someone special?'

'Yes, a girl who might have known my brother before he died three years ago.'

Johnnie stared at her solemnly. 'Did you find her?'

'Why do you want to know?' Ruby asked. 'Why all these questions?'

'Please Ruby, just tell me how you came to be here.'

Ruby relaxed a little. He seemed very genuine. Could he have known of Pete? 'My brother had a picture framed at the Cuthbertson Studio. His girl-friend wrote on the back. She signed herself as J, but we know from Pete's diary she was Joanie. I thought, well, no I hoped, she could shed some light on why he took his own life.'

Johnnie stared at the house. 'Yes, I think Joanie could.'

Ruby sat bolt upright. 'Do you know her? Did you know Pete?'

'Bear with me a little longer. Did you recognize the house over there?'

Ruby took a sharp breath. 'Yes, I went there once when I was—'

'When you were almost fifteen.' Johnnie gazed at her steadily with his sad, intense expression. 'It was a Sunday and Pete made a big fuss of his little sister. You shared tea and scones and Pete showed you round the house.'

Ruby took a startled breath. 'How do you know that?'

'I was there too.'

'You were? But why didn't Pete introduce us? Did you live here with him? Did you know him well?' Ruby asked, more confused than ever.

'Yes, I knew him,' Johnnie said quietly. 'I recognized you at Larry's party. You see, Pete often spoke about you. He told me you were beautiful and he certainly didn't exaggerate. When you told me that your brother's name was Pete, I knew there was only one Ruby – you.'

'But why didn't you say at Larry's party?' Ruby demanded.

'Your friend came along. She was quite drunk and so I decided it wasn't the right time.'

'So what made you decide on now?'

'I'm going away, Ruby. I wanted to tell you before I went.'

'Tell me what?' She was angry but she was also excited. At last she had found someone who knew Pete and had even been in this house when she'd visited.

'Ruby, please don't be upset. You see, I'm the Joanie you've been looking for.'

Ruby felt a punch to her stomach. 'What kind of joke is that?'

'It's no joke.' He gently put out his hand. 'It was me who wrote on the back of that picture. *For Pete, my love, my world. Forever yours, J. 1951.*' His dark eyes didn't flinch as Ruby drew in a breath. 'Pete's idol was Winston Churchill as I'm sure you know,' he continued. 'The dog and hat was a private joke between us. I loved your brother very much. And he loved me. But we were always scared about being found out. I'm sure you're aware that a relationship like ours is illegal.'

Ruby sat in shocked silence. She looked at this handsome man beside her and knew instinctively he was telling her the truth. He couldn't guess at the wording on the back of the picture either. Nor that Pete's hero was Winston Churchill.

'We knew each other for five years,' Johnnie explained in a subdued voice. 'We met through Ronnie Raymond, our mutual boss.' He looked down at his well-manicured hands. 'Ronnie encouraged us to be ourselves, as if he sympathized with and approved of our relationship. We were fooled of course and went on our merry way, until the day dawned when we both realized that he knew everything about us. From dates and times, to photos and personal information. He told us that he had enough evidence to send us to prison for many years. That was how he blackmailed us into his dirty work.'

'W–what sort of work?' she stammered.

'We looked after Mr Raymond's clients.'

'What does that mean?'

He looked up, his eyes full of unshed tears. 'I think you can guess.'

'Pete drove Mr Raymond around,' she insisted.

Johnnie smiled sadly. 'Yes, but that was a very small part of his work.'

Ruby felt like hitting him. How dare he insult Pete like this? Tears filled her eyes. She was so angry she could scream.

'I'm sorry, Ruby. I really am. But the reason we never told anyone was because of the way you're feeling now. And yet we were just two people who had fallen in love. We couldn't help being the same sex. I thought you might understand. After seeing you so friendly with Larry and Stuart, I was hoping you would.'

'You're talking about my brother.'

'Yes, and I loved him and miss him too. More than you could ever imagine. You can't imagine what it feels like to be in love and never be able to express it in public.'

Ruby felt so many conflicting emotions she couldn't reply. Pete had loved this man? Her Pete? Her beautiful, perfect brother?

'Pete and I were forced to work for Ronnie Raymond,' Johnnie said after a while. 'He would fix us up with people, often wealthy ones like Lady Granger who you saw me with at the party.'

Ruby swallowed. 'So you're still seeing her?'

'Not like that, no. She is a genuinely nice lady and has become a friend, perhaps the only one left from those days who doesn't expect anything from me, other than my company. She knew Pete and liked him very much. She kept our secret.' Johnnie took a deep breath. 'You see, Ronnie was an opportunist. He got people to like him and trust him and found out their grubby little secrets. Then he'd make you do what he wanted or vengeance would be his.'

Suddenly Ruby thought of Anna. She had done exactly the same, humiliating and controlling people in any way she could. Pete had fallen into the same trap as Anna had set for her.

'Ronnie extorted sums of money that would make your hair curl,' Johnnie said bitterly. 'He deliberately gave us the use of this house, allowing us to think we had a modicum of privacy. But the house was not only wired, it had secret cameras too. He didn't leave anything to chance. That was how he made his millions.'

'Did you know this when Pete brought me here?'

'No, not at that time. Pete was so happy, he wanted to share our secret with you. He was convinced that, even though you were very young, you would understand.' Johnnie sighed and looked away. 'But when it came to the time, he got cold feet. I was waiting in a room at the top of the house. Waiting with my heart in my mouth for Pete to explain the facts to you. But he just couldn't do it. You were so young and innocent. And he was ashamed. And so you left that day, never knowing that I had been standing only a floor above you.'

Ruby cleared her throat. 'I knew there was someone else there. I felt it.'

'I only wish I had known that. Perhaps if I'd come forward first? But Pete always reminded me that we were criminals in the eyes of the law. I didn't want to lose him and so I just waited – and hoped he would call me down to meet you.'

Ruby sat trying to put all the pieces together. Her adored brother, who she had thought was a ladies' man, was nothing of the sort. But why hadn't she guessed before? He never had any permanent girlfriends. He was always telling them about his work, but never any real details. He spoke of Mr R as though he was just his wealthy boss. Described all the glamorous parts that he knew would impress her. And then her mouth opened slightly. 'Your name,' she whispered, 'Johnnie. It is like Joanie.'

'Take out the letters "h" and "n",' he agreed, 'and replace them with an "a". Another of our little secrets. And although I never read Pete's diary, he said it was safer for him to refer to me as Joanie.'

'You knew he wrote a diary?'

Johnnie nodded. 'Pete was very eloquent. I admired him so much.'

Ruby felt more confusion, followed quickly by an overwhelming dismay. This man had known Pete intimately. He'd loved him. Just like Larry and Stuart were in love. And she'd accepted their relationship. So why was it so difficult to accept Pete and Johnnie's?

'Do you know the reason why Pete died?' Ruby could hardly bring herself to ask that question.

Johnnie pulled up the collar of his camel coat. 'I believe it was that monster Ronnie Raymond. He wasn't satisfied with prostituting us, he intended to make us his prisoners forever. It was all about money with Ronnie. We weren't people to him. We were animals. To be trained to do as he wished.' Johnnie looked into the distance. 'One day, Pete told me he'd had enough. He was braver than me. I was always the coward.' Johnnie sniffed back his tears. 'So Pete went to Ronnie and said it was the end of the road. He could do his worst. We were in love. And we were going away together, out of his reach.' Johnnie's handsome face crumpled. 'It was, of course, a bluff. Ronnie didn't fall for it. After all, he had photographs, information, ugly, plenty of despicable evidence at his disposal. The dirt would follow us wherever we went. Why should he let us go? And so he threatened to go first to your parents.'

'Oh God,' Ruby whispered. 'Poor Pete.'

'He took it very badly. That was his worst nightmare. He loved his family so much. So Pete became a beaten man. He knew we'd never escape Ronnie's clutches. I – I blame myself for not guessing he might do something terrible. But he hid his emotions. Just like he hid everything else. He was a professional. And so he took the only way out.' Suddenly Johnnie's shoulders sagged and he cupped his face in his hands. His sobs rocked his body and Ruby felt like crying too.

Now the truth was dawning on her. Pete had been living a lie and was too ashamed to confide in her. But the knowledge that he almost had, that he had wanted to, was in a way liberating. For the past three years she had lived with a question mark in her life. That question had now been answered. And for all its implications, she at last knew the reason for Pete's tragic passing.

# Chapter Thirty-Five

Ruby looked at the distressed young man sitting beside her. He said he had loved Pete and that Pete had loved him and they had shared the guilt and heartache together. Ruby felt that pain too as she thought of a criminal like Ronnie Raymond and the untold evil he had done. 'Thank you,' she said softly. 'For having the courage to tell me.'

'P-Pete would have wanted you to know,' Johnnie stammered. 'And though we were forced into an intolerable situation, our love remained strong right up to the end.'

It was some while before either of them spoke as they sat on the bench under the leafless trees of the square.

Finally Johnnie composed himself. 'What can you think of me?' he said quietly. 'I wasn't even at Pete's funeral. I was so afraid.'

'You loved him and that's what counts.'

'Do you really mean that?'

Ruby nodded. 'But I wish Pete had told me on that day at the house. I would have been shocked. But I would have understood – eventually.' Ruby added with a husky sob, 'And perhaps I might even have stopped him from taking his life.'

'No, Ruby. Ours was a forbidden love. It was destined to end badly. And both Pete and I knew it.'

Ruby dried her eyes on a handkerchief, then passed it to Johnnie. 'What are you going to do now?'

'I'm leaving the country. Pete and I were planning to go to Spain on the money we made for that bastard. We intended to buy a villa. He hoped that one day you would join us.' Johnnie dabbed at his eyes. 'We had so many dreams. I think of Pete everywhere I go in London. You can't choose who you fall in love with,' Johnnie said bleakly. 'Now I have to find a way to live without him.'

'I hope you find happiness.'

'Pete was the only one. Always will be.' He sniffed, returning her hanky. He looked over to the house. 'I hope Ronnie Raymond burns in hell, just as his house has.'

'You know Ronnie Raymond died in the fire?' she asked.

For a long moment he said nothing, then looked into her eyes. 'Oh yes, Ruby. I know. Ronnie couldn't be allowed to live, you see. He had to pay for Pete's death. Someone had to put a stop to all his evil.'

She shuddered, feeling a coldness go over her. Had Johnnie had a hand in Ronnie Raymond's death? Had he deliberately set the fire? Is that what he was saying? She couldn't bring herself to ask. The expression in Johnnie's eyes was now pure hatred. She was glad when he stood up.

'Thank you for meeting me today, Ruby. I'll give you a lift back to the East End.'

But Ruby shook her head. 'No thanks, I'll make my own way.'

'If that's what you want.'

'Good luck, Johnnie.'

'Good luck, little kitten.' He smiled. 'Yes, your brother always called you that. But I can see that the little kitten has now grown into a beautiful cat.'

Again tears were close as Johnnie Dyer walked away. She watched his tall, upright figure disappear into Greek Street. And then she sat down again on the bench.

She wanted to think about Pete, about how much he had wanted to share his secret with her. This knowledge was bitter-sweet. For she wished he had. She knew that she would have loved him all the more for sharing with her and tried to help him solve the problems that had eventually led him to take his life.

It was late afternoon before Ruby left the square. Thinking over all she now knew, she, too, saw that Johnnie and Pete's love had been doomed. If it wasn't for her dear friends Larry and Stuart she would never have met Johnnie and the true story of Pete's life would never have been revealed. Pete had lived in a shadowy, sordid world and Ronnie Raymond was the reason Pete had taken his own life. There had been no satisfaction for Raymond though, as Johnnie had taken it into his own hands to meet out justice. The punishment, it seemed to Ruby, had been fitting for the likes of an evil man like Ronnie Raymond.

She found herself looking up at the historic monument of Marble Arch. She had walked miles, her feet taking her towards the shops of Oxford Street and their sparkling lights. The dusky afternoon made them seem even brighter. Over her head the decorations were illuminated. People were rushing here and there for their last-minute shopping.

This was where she had come so often, buying anything she desired, spending money like water. Anna had encouraged her. Just like Ronnie Raymond had encouraged Pete.

It wasn't long before Ruby had turned towards the Edgware Road. She knew she had to see Dower Street one last time. With each step, she remembered the life of luxury she had enjoyed at Anna's – and had chosen to give up.

As she turned the corner, she saw number 10, standing elegantly in the gloom. Ruby shivered in the cold, grey evening. Hidden in the shadows, she paused on the other side of the road. The lights of number 10 were switched on and there was movement inside the house.

Then the front door opened.

Ruby moved down onto the steps of a basement. As she peered through the iron railings, her tummy tightened. Who would come out of that door?

It was Janet who appeared on the doorstep. The housekeeper hurried down the white steps, carrying two small suitcases. She waited on the pavement looking left and right. The lights in the house went out.

Ruby's heart pounded. Who was Janet waiting for?

A car came slowly along and stopped. Ruby fell back, catching a painful breath when she saw it was the Buick. Her stomach twisted as Nick climbed out and greeted Janet. He quickly took the suitcases and stowed them in the boot of the car.

Janet disappeared into the house again. Ruby blinked rapidly as, a few seconds later, Anna stepped out and hurried down to Nick. She was dressed in the same pale fur coat that Nick had given Ruby to model. Bitter tears stung Ruby's eyes. Her body seemed ice cold as Nick took Anna in his arms and kissed her.

Ruby held tightly to the railings. This was the man she thought she had loved. The man who she thought had loved her. He wasn't hurt, or lying injured somewhere, or waiting cold and alone in a prison cell.

He was here with Anna.

Their kiss was long and passionate. If only she could make her legs move, Ruby thought in a daze, she would run across and confront them. But all she could do was stare helplessly as Nick assisted Anna into the car.

The roar of the Buick's engine rumbled into the night.

And the car disappeared.

When Janet came out of the house again she took a key from her purse and locked the door.

Slowly Ruby climbed up the steps and crossed the road.

'What are you doing here?' Janet asked, looking surprised.

'Is Anna going away?'

'I don't know.' Janet tried to pass by, but Ruby grabbed her.

'I'm sure you can tell me,' she said, suddenly filled with anger. 'Would you rather I call the police?'

Janet shook her hand away. 'What do you want to know?'

'Everything.'

The housekeeper stared ahead coldly. 'The agency has closed. It's over, Ruby. Whatever you've come back for, it's too late.'

Ruby remembered what Paula had told her that day in Hyde Park. 'Was Anna raided by the police?'

'How do you know that?'

'Never mind. Just tell me where Anna and Nick are going.'

The small woman gave a long, uncaring sigh. 'Have it your own way, much good it'll do you. They're leaving the country.'

Ruby felt her legs buckle. 'Do you know where?'

Janet shrugged. 'Europe, America, Australia – the choice is yours.'

'But what about the agency girls?'

'What about them? Anna and Nick don't care. They're off to pastures new.'

She laughed coldly at Ruby's shocked expression. 'You surely couldn't have thought a man like Nick Brandon had eyes for a silly, greedy little upstart like you?'

Ruby gulped back the tears as Janet watched her.

'Wake up, you little fool,' Janet continued. 'He used you, just as Mrs Brandon did.'

Ruby's mouth fell open. '*Mrs* Brandon?'

'Oh yes, she is his wife and between them they have a good thing going. He with his warehouses and she with her girls. They juggled you between them. You were a pawn in their game. Not that you were the first. There were others before you and will be again. Wherever they go, they will attract more gullible victims. Girls falling over themselves to snatch what the Brandons tell them is a glamorous new career.'

Ruby sank back against the railings. 'Did Paula know they were married?'

'Everyone did, it seems, except you.'

'Why didn't she tell me? I thought Paula was my friend.'

'You have no friends here. They all did what Anna told them and kept their mouths shut. And when they didn't, well, you know for yourself what could happen to someone who crossed her.'

Ruby stared at this unremarkable woman who had just delivered a blow equal to the impact of a bus and was now staring at her with undisguised pity.

'Go home to the East End, Ruby, where you belong.' She pushed past, shoulders squared as she marched off along the pavement.

Ruby stared up at 10 Dower Street and the memories crowded back. She was both ashamed and angry. How could she have been so blind?

Well, she was blind no longer. Good riddance to bad rubbish, as they used to say as kids. With her chin held high, she made her way back to Marble Arch, leaving Dower Street behind her forever.

# Chapter Thirty-Six

'Merry Christmas, one and all!' It was Kath who opened Bernie's newly painted red front door on Christmas Day. 'Hello, Ruby, Mr Payne – Maggs! Welcome everyone!' She kissed them on their cold cheeks as they stepped in. 'Let me take your coats.'

Ruby thought how lovely Kath looked in her red dress, with sparkly festive twine wound carefully in her long dark hair. Since knowing Clem she had certainly blossomed.

'Thank you for inviting me,' Maggs said, touching her newly permed hair as she slid off her coat. 'Now, how can I help you, ducks? I'd like to make myself useful.'

'This is your day off, Maggs,' Kath replied with a grin. 'But if you like, you could give Clem some help in the kitchen. I left him with the carving knife and instructions to slice the turkey breast first, but I'd feel happier if you could keep an eye on things.' Kath hung the coats on the hall stand. 'Mr Payne, why don't you go through too and get Bernie to pour you a beer?'

'Don't mind if I do,' Ruby's dad said, swiftly disappearing down the hall.

'Let's have a chat before the party gets started,' Kath whispered, pushing Ruby into the front room.

'Oh, this is lovely,' Ruby gasped as she gazed at the freshly decorated walls glowing in the light of a modern cone-shaped lampshade. In front of the window was a small Christmas tree, complete with coloured balls and tinsel. 'Last time I saw this room, there was just a stepladder and a pot of paint.'

'Bernie's worked hard to finish the house,' Kath nodded. 'He wanted to have it ready for today.'

Ruby looked around once more. She walked over to the heavy, patterned drapes that hung each side of the window. 'These curtains are very good quality.' She ran her fingers over their softness and smiled ruefully. 'I can see Tina had a say in choosing these.'

'That's where you're wrong,' Kath said with a grin as she stuck a poker in the fire and the scarlet flames roared up the chimney. 'Bernie has surprisingly good taste. And anyway, the two lovebirds have split up.'

'They have?' Ruby frowned at this news. 'But I thought Tina and Bernie were going strong.'

'He didn't have his heart in it.'

'Why was that?'

'He said he wasn't ready to settle down. Tina, of course, was mad keen to start a family.'

'Well, Bernie's not getting any younger.' Ruby sat on the comfortable new settee. 'All he really needs now is someone to share this house with him.' She recalled how empty and desolate this room had once seemed, but now it felt like a real home, except perhaps for the finer details of a woman's touch.

'I'm so happy you agreed to come to us for Christmas,' Kath said eagerly. 'I've been dying to introduce Clem to friends and family.'

'Do I hear wedding bells?' Ruby asked, raising a curious eyebrow.

'It's early days yet,' Kath declared but Ruby noticed she was blushing deeply. 'We've both got our careers to consider. And for now, we are having the time of our lives at the Windmill.'

'Who would have thought last year,' Ruby said on a long, wistful sigh, 'that I would be sitting here this Christmas, talking to a real-live Windmill girl, the star turn of the chorus line?'

Kath blushed again. 'Not quite yet, Ruby.'

'You were made to be a dancer with those long legs of yours. Just look at you, all glammed-up and a real head-turner. As for me, well, it's obvious, ain't it? I've got big boobs and a wiggle but I've no talent and I'm broke.' Ruby half-laughed, trying to hide the cheap and tacky blue sheath dress that she had found on the market stall.

'Ruby, you are gorgeous, you know that.'

'Thanks, but I miss all me nice clothes.'

Kath chuckled. 'Cheer up, you'll soon get a job again. And be back down the shops spending all that money you ain't got.'

Ruby smiled. She had learned a very big lesson, that money and the life it bought wasn't everything. It had hurt deeply to know that she had been a willing victim to Nick and Anna. But after careful consideration, she had taken steps to redress the balance; a thought that now gave her some comfort.

Kath knelt on the furry brown rug by the fire and looked into Ruby's eyes. 'So, from what you told me on the telephone last week, I take it that Nick and Anna are long gone?'

'Yes. And I wish them the worst of luck.'

'That doesn't sound like you.'

'I've grown up a bit, Kath, and got to thinking. What they did was unforgivable, to me and to the other girls. In fact it was fraud.'

'Who told you that?'

'I went to the police and told them everything.'

Kath sat back on her heels in alarm. 'You did what?'

'I thought about what Janet said,' Ruby replied, folding her fingers together on her lap. 'There would be other girls like me. If not in England then abroad. Some would believe their lies and end up with broken hearts if not broken morals. Or perhaps both. Like I nearly did. So, I decided to tell the law.'

'What did they say?'

'I had to write a statement about Anna and the agency that was really a high-class brothel and Nick with his warehouse of furs, and of course McBride and the man from the Soviet Union.'

'Crikey, Ruby, that took some nerve.'

'The detective told me that Interpol would be informed as Nick was already on their wanted list for other scams in this country. I got a ticking off for not reporting him and Anna immediately. They said I was withholding evidence.'

'What did you say to that?'

'I said better late than never. What could they do to me that hadn't been done already?'

Kath giggled. 'My God, Ruby, talk about a woman scorned!'

'I just hope there's justice in all this. And most of all, no one else gets caught up as I did. I was such a fool.'

'You were in love.'

'With a dream,' Ruby corrected quietly as she met Kath's gaze.

'We all have those.'

'Yes, but yours came true with Clem.'

Kath's pale skin flushed. 'He is rather wonderful. I never thought I had a chance at love. My dad was a brute. After what he did to me and Bernie I was left with a fear of men. But then I found a passion in the dancing. That saved me. And through dancing, I met Clem. And I found love again.'

Ruby knew Kath deserved love. But did she? She was beginning to wonder lately if love had passed her by. 'You are amazing, Kath. You've been through so much and come out on top.'

'So will you.'

'I hope so.'

Ruby was thinking of Pete. She hadn't told anyone, not even Kath, about her meeting with Johnnie Dyer. She would keep Pete's secret for him, although, perhaps one day in the future, she might be able to unburden herself in the knowledge that society would no longer condemn Pete as a criminal. Until that day dawned, she would honour the pact she kept with her dead brother and know that, wherever he was, he would at last be at peace. 'I want to move on, Kath. I truly do. But I haven't a clue how.'

'You'll think of something. One thing is certain, your Pete would want you to be happy. And your mum too. Isn't that the important thing?'

Ruby nodded. She still had her dad and it was the living who counted, after all.

Kath stood up and opened her arms. 'Happy Christmas, Ruby.'

Ruby returned the embrace, sharing a silent but deeply intimate moment with her dearest friend.

'Enjoying yourself, doll?' Bernie called as they entered the hot and steamy kitchen.

'Don't call me that,' Ruby returned, though with a smile.

While the others were talking, drinking and laughing, Bernie made his way to her side. As she gazed into his dark eyes, she saw how their expression had changed over the years. How rock-steady they were, how honest and genuine. And how the curve of his smile held a warmth that spoke of the bond they had shared through thick and thin. This tall, impressively handsome young man dressed in a dark suit and white shirt had grown into maturity before her very eyes. And the odd thing was, she hadn't really noticed before.

'It's hot in here. Do you fancy a breath of fresh air?' Before she could answer he slipped firm fingers over hers and led her outside into the cold winter air. He saw her shivering and took off his jacket to slide around her shoulders. 'Kath told me what happened with your bloke,' he said abruptly. 'Sorry it worked out that way.'

'You're not sorry at all, Bernie Rigler,' she dismissed. 'You never liked Nick or Anna, did you?'

'Can't say as I did, no.'

Ruby gazed down at the hard winter earth and sighed. 'Why don't you say "I told you so"?'

'Because . . .' He lifted her chin and said huskily, 'I want to say something else instead. But I might get me face slapped.'

Ruby nodded slowly. 'Yes, you might at that.'

'Well, all the same, here goes.' He pushed a hand in his pocket and brought out a wilted green leaf, holding it up between two fingers.

'What's that?'

'Mistletoe. Or it was before I sat on it.' He threw it aside and took her gently in his arms. 'Think I'll just go for it and hope for the best. Happy Christmas, doll.' With tender lips he bent to kiss her, and instinctively she knew he was waiting; waiting for her to pull away and their old pattern of behaviour to resume as the insults flew far and wide. But to her own great surprise, she found her lips remaining, seeking and enjoying, wanting a firmer pressure.

Very slowly her arms went around his neck and his jacket fell to the ground. She barely noticed the cold air on her skin. Or the Christmas breeze that blew her hair around her face, causing Bernie to slide his fingers through its softness. But she did notice the warm rush of desire inside her growing steadily into something very different to anything she had ever known – or wanted – before.